"Are you all right? Is anything broken?"

His warm hand slid over her cheeks, and the awkward disaster turned into something else entirely.

This time when she opened her eyes, she saw clearly. What she saw took her breath away.

Garrett was gazing into her eyes with compassion. The fall had dislodged his cap and ruffled his auburn hair. His cheeks burned bright from the cold, but his concern was only for her. His thumb whispered over her lips, and she trembled at the gentleness of his touch.

"Do they hurt?" His low voice rumbled through her like none other.

"No," she managed to breathe out.

"Do you hurt anywhere?"

Oh, to be able to say yes and feel that touch again. Instead, she had to shake her head.

He breathed out in relief, but he did not draw away.

She could not stop looking into those soft gray-blue eyes. His mouth was so close. She could feel his breath on her lips. Oh, my.

Was he going to kiss her?

A small-town girl, **Christine Johnson** has lived in every corner of Michigan's Lower Peninsula. She enjoys creating stories that bring history to life while exploring the characters' spiritual journeys. Though Michigan is still her home base, she and her seafaring husband also spend time exploring the Florida Keys and other fascinating locations. You can contact her through her website at christineelizabethjohnson.com.

Books by Christine Johnson

Love Inspired Historical

Boom Town Brides

Mail Order Mix-Up
Mail Order Mommy

The Dressmaker's Daughters

Groom by Design
Suitor by Design
Love by Design

Visit the Author Profile page
at Harlequin.com for more titles.

CHRISTINE JOHNSON

Mail Order Mommy

⟨H⟩ **HARLEQUIN**® LOVE INSPIRED® HISTORICAL

Recycling programs
for this product may
not exist in your area.

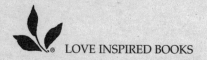

LOVE INSPIRED BOOKS

ISBN-13: 978-0-373-28384-2

Mail Order Mommy

Copyright © 2016 by Christine Elizabeth Johnson

www.Harlequin.com

Printed in U.S.A.

And their sins and iniquities will I remember no more.
—*Hebrews* 10:17

For my SewTogether quilting friends past and present.
Our time together with needle and thread
brings this writer much joy.

Chapter One

December 2, 1870

Amanda Porter had made her decision, and there was no going back on it now.

She had sent the letter off on the mail boat at first light. Before she'd left the dock the crew had cast off lines, and the boat now steamed out the river on its way to Chicago.

The early morning breeze off Lake Michigan stung her cheeks on the walk back to the boardinghouse and made her pull her coat a little tighter. A dusting of snow had fallen overnight. The boardwalks across the soft sand shimmered in the first gleams of sunlight, but she could think only of the painful future that awaited her.

It would take at least two weeks for that letter to travel to New York City and a response to return to this Michigan lumber town. Singapore. The name had sounded exotic when she'd agreed to join her friend Pearl four months ago. Truthfully, she would have done anything to leave the Chatsworths' house and the scene of her humiliation.

She had banked everything on that advertisement for a wife that Pearl had found: "Widower with handsome inheritance seeks wife in booming town soon to rival Chicago. Well-furnished, comfortable house. Inquire at mercantile for Mr. Garrett Decker. Singapore, Michigan."

In Singapore, Amanda had expected to begin anew with someone to love and care for. The past could be forgotten in a bright new future, but it had all proved to be a trick. Garrett Decker did not want to marry. He claimed he'd never placed the advertisement. His children had sent it to the newspaper, because they wanted a new mother. That ought to have changed his mind, but he refused to consider marrying Amanda or one of the other two ladies who'd answered the advertisement. That wasn't the only discrepancy. Located near the mouth of the Kalamazoo River, Singapore was tiny and in no way rivaled bustling Chicago. It boasted just one hotel, one boardinghouse and no church building. Sand constantly drifted off the dunes and onto the streets and boardwalks. Garrett Decker had no inheritance, handsome or not. Once again she'd been misled by a man.

That's why she had to return to the only place that would accept her, albeit as a maid rather than a daughter. That, and Pearl's upcoming wedding. Three and a half weeks were just enough time to finish the wedding dress planned for the special event. Amanda would see her friend married and settled. Then she would depart.

Pearl would not be pleased with the decision, but it couldn't be helped. Since Garrett refused to marry and no other prospects loomed, Amanda must take charge of her life.

She pulled open the back door of the boardinghouse and stomped the snow and sand off her shoes before venturing into the steamy kitchen. The heat made her yank off her mittens and unbutton her coat in a hurry. She unpinned her plum-colored hat, which did nothing to shield her from the cold, and shoved the outerwear onto a hook in the butler's pantry.

Platters of ham and poached eggs waited on the stove's warming shelf, while the teakettle whistled. Since no one was around, she took the kettle off the heat before it boiled dry.

"Miss Amanda, what are you doing out so early on a Saturday morning?" Mrs. Calloway, the boardinghouse owner, breezed into the kitchen and grabbed a tray of cinnamon rolls out of the oven.

"I saw the mail boat was in and wanted to post a letter."

"Oh, my, I should have had you take the boardinghouse mail."

"I took it."

"You're such a fine girl. I don't know what I'd do without you." The boardinghouse proprietress whirled out of the kitchen just as quickly as she'd come in.

Amanda donned one of the aprons that Mrs. Calloway kept in a cupboard and lifted the tray of ham off the stove. Meals were served in a specific order. This time of year, those items that could be eaten cold were served before those that must remain hot. Even with the stoves blazing hot, many of the public rooms remained cool. The bedrooms were icy.

Upon entering the dining room, she found four seated at the table: Pearl, Fiona O'Keefe and two sawmill workers, whose presence reminded her that she'd missed a chance last month to locate her lost brother. Fiona was one of the other ladies who had answered Garrett Decker's advertisement, and was from all appearances his current favorite. She sat with him at church, and he had attended some of her music recitals on Saturdays. Fiona's smile grated on Amanda, so she concentrated on her friend, who looked ready to lecture the men for shoving the warm rolls into their mouths without the slightest regard for manners.

"Good morning." Amanda set the ham on the table, and the men dug into that next.

Pearl shifted her attention to Amanda. "There you are. I wondered where you went so early. Mrs. Calloway said the mail boat is in."

Naturally, Mrs. Calloway had passed along that bit of information. For all her lovely, good-hearted qualities, the boardinghouse proprietress couldn't keep the tiniest scrap of information to herself.

"They've left already," Amanda said. "The captain fears a storm is on its way."

"A storm?" Fiona sipped tea from a porcelain teacup, three fingers daintily extended. "There's not a cloud in the sky."

"I suppose we will know in time." Amanda found it easier to agree with Fiona than to get into a debate. The redhead refused to budge from a single opinion. "Anyway, the mail has arrived. Roland said it'll be sorted by midmorning."

Pearl smiled at the mention of her fiancé, who also happened to be Garrett Decker's brother. When they'd first met Roland aboard the ship from Chicago, there'd been a terrible mix-up about the brothers. All three women answering the advertisement thought Roland was the man seeking a wife. Once they arrived in Singapore, the misunderstanding got sorted out. Pearl fell in love with Roland, and Amanda had managed to catch Garrett's attention through his adorable children. But after last month's fire, everything changed.

Fiona slid the pastry server under one of the cinnamon rolls that the men hadn't gobbled up. "I'm expecting my manager to send word of a role in a new production at Niblo's Garden."

"I hope you get the part." Amanda clapped her mouth shut. Though a booking at the popular theater would be a huge step in Fiona's career, Amanda had said that a bit too eagerly.

Fiona noticed. "Want me gone, do you? Well, I'll have you know that I'm this close to coming to an understanding with Garrett." She held her thumb and index finger a fraction of an inch apart.

Amanda's spirits sank. She had no idea Garrett was that close to proposing to Fiona. She swallowed tears of frustration. Everything had gone wrong here. Everything. It was best she'd decided to leave.

Pearl, on the other hand, set into Fiona with the tenacity of a guard dog. "Then why hasn't Roland heard anything about this? As his brother, he should know."

"Since when do brothers discuss romance?" Fiona brushed back a red curl that had slipped over her shoulder. "Garrett is a quiet, brooding sort. He requires a lively, vivacious woman to counter his natural disposition."

Amanda edged toward the doorway. She would rather fetch the eggs than listen to one more confirmation that she'd lost all opportunity to win over Garrett Decker. Before she could slip away, Pearl's teacher's glare froze her in place.

Pearl returned her attention to the elegant redhead. "I hope you won't be disappointed."

Fiona's brow furrowed. "Disappointed? Why should I be disappointed?"

"A star of the New York stage could never be happy in a lumber town. She must return to the theater at the beckoning of her adoring fans. Garrett doesn't strike me as a man who cares for the big city."

That brought to mind the one thing about Fiona O'Keefe that had perplexed Amanda since they first met. If Fiona was such a star, why would she leave New York to answer a mail-order bride advertisement? It made no sense.

Fiona smiled coyly. "A man will do almost anything for the woman he loves."

Then Fiona is certain. Amanda pressed a hand to her midsection. Her last shreds of hope were rapidly disappearing.

"He will not go against his nature," Pearl insisted.

Amanda could not picture Garrett in evening attire and top hat. Roland, yes. Garrett, never. Not for the first time she marveled at how different the two brothers were. Roland was tall and suave, always dressed in style. The shorter and more powerful Garrett preferred workingman's clothes. His auburn hair was in direct contrast to Roland's dark locks. They barely looked like brothers, though they certainly acted that way, often in playful competition.

Mrs. Calloway entered with the eggs. "Sit, Miss Amanda. Breakfast is served."

Amanda did not feel like a guest, especially given the uncomfortable reality that she had a room here only by the charity of Pearl, who paid the cost of the room from her wages as a teacher, and the Calloways, who gave Amanda board in exchange for housekeeping. She could not ask the Calloways to let her stay free of charge once Pearl wed and moved on. Since Amanda had but one dime left to her name and no paying employment, she'd written her foster family asking for a service position in their household.

Under those circumstances, she should eat in the kitchen, but she'd learned from experience that Mrs. Calloway wouldn't tolerate it. Even when Amanda explained that she'd always eaten in the kitchen at her foster family's house, the boardinghouse proprietress shooed her from the room.

Mrs. Calloway set the eggs in front of the ladies and disappeared.

Amanda had barely taken her seat, prayed over the meal with Pearl and Fiona, and dished up one poached egg and the smallest slice of ham when a forceful knock sounded on the front door. Everyone stopped eating and looked up.

"Who could that be at this hour?" Pearl mused.

The women looked to the men, who both shook their heads.

"Perhaps a visitor came in on the mail boat," Amanda suggested. If only it could be her long-lost brother, but the lumberjack who fit his description had reportedly left the area for work further north.

"More likely it's your fiancé," Fiona said to Pearl.

Amanda noticed a burst of color infuse her friend's cheeks and a sparkle light her eyes. She dearly hoped Fiona was right, but fear niggled at the back of her mind. What if Garrett had come to propose to Fiona? What if it was an unwelcome caller like Hugh Bellchamp? Surely he would not follow her here from New York. She had told no one where she was going, just that she had left to marry someone on the "frontier."

She set down her fork, unable to eat.

"It wouldn't be Roland," Pearl noted. "He would be busy with the mail and any merchandise for the store that came in on the mail boat."

A knock sounded again.

"I don't think Mrs. Calloway heard it." Pearl began to rise.

Amanda set aside her napkin. "I'll get it."

"Sit down, girls." Mrs. Calloway bustled past. "I'm on my way."

That left the five of them in silence. The men shoveled food into their mouths. The ladies ate quietly, listening for a clue as to who had paid a call. Amanda picked at the food, unable to stomach one bite.

The dining room was situated fairly close to the front door. Given the force of the knock, Amanda expected to hear the caller's voice. For the longest time, she heard nothing. She looked to Pearl, who shook her head. Even Fiona hadn't heard a thing, and her hearing was more attuned to the softest nuances than theirs. For long minutes, only the clink of forks on china serenaded them. Then Mrs. Calloway's booming voice broke the quiet.

"Are you sure?"

"Of course I'm sure." The man's irritated voice was unmistakable. *Garrett.*

Amanda stared at the poached egg, its yolk spilling onto the plate. Who had he come to see? Her or Fiona? Or was he here about something that had happened at the mill? She looked to the men, who didn't appear to care that their supervisor was at the door.

"Well, then, take a seat in the parlor," Mrs. Calloway said. "I'll ask her to join you."

Her?

Amanda's nerves tensed as the ladies looked at each other. Amanda held her breath, hoping against hope. *Let it be for me. Please, let Garrett be here for me.*

Mrs. Calloway's footsteps drew near. A second later she poked her head into the dining room. "Miss Fiona, you have a caller."

Amanda's hand trembled so much that she had to set down her fork. Her ears began to ring. She drew another deep breath and pressed a cool hand to her throat. Pearl shook her head, as if to say it couldn't possibly be what she feared, but Fiona had just said that Garrett was ready to propose.

Fiona smiled triumphantly. "Tell Garrett that I will join him in a moment."

Dread wove around Amanda's heart. She raised the teacup to her lips, but the tea tasted like wash water. With a trembling hand, she set the cup down.

Fiona checked her hair to make sure it was in place, while Mrs. Calloway headed back in the direction of the parlor.

Amanda choked out, "You're not going to meet him at once?"

"A gentleman ought not call at this hour. He can wait a moment or two." Fiona inclined her head toward Amanda. "It's best to let them know that you are in control."

Amanda was far from in control. At any moment she might faint dead away.

At last Fiona dabbed at her mouth with the napkin. The moment she made a move to get out of her chair, the man seated closest to her hopped up to help her from the table. Amanda's heart sank even further. Fiona had a way of attracting every man's attention, while she only attracted the wrong sort.

Fiona swept from the room, and the men followed, a cinnamon roll in each hand. That left Amanda alone with Pearl.

"It's over then," Amanda whispered. "He's chosen her."

Pearl slipped a piece of paper from between the covers of her record book and slid it across the table. "You have one advantage that she will never have."

In a glance Amanda could tell that it was one of the student papers that Pearl had collected yesterday. The children were to write about what they most wanted for Christmas. Pearl had supplied her own stationery for the assignment, so each paper looked more like a letter. The signature on this one made Amanda catch her breath. Sadie. Garrett's daughter.

The words drove a knife through her heart.

Can Jesus bring a nu mama? Mis Mana pleez.

This time she could not stop the tears from gathering in her eyes. That poor little girl had lost her mother in a tragic accident nearly two years ago. That she wanted a new mama was understandable. That she wanted Amanda made her heart ache. Amanda wanted that, too. How she wanted to be Sadie and Isaac's mother, but wishing didn't make things true.

"It's too late." Amanda pushed the assignment back across the table to Pearl.

Pearl placed it inside the record book again. "I showed it to Roland last night. He said he would tell his brother after the children fell asleep."

"He did?" Hope blossomed. Could Garrett have called on Fiona this morning to break off their attachment? "Do you think it's possible that—"

"Hire me?" Fiona's screech carried into the dining room and cut off Amanda's thought. "I am not hired help."

Footsteps raced down the hallway and stomped up the staircase. A door slammed.

Pearl's eyebrows lifted even as a grin teased her lips. "Well, isn't that interesting."

Interesting was not the word Amanda would have used. Shocking. Startling. Completely unexpected. Hire Fiona? What on earth for?

Amanda looked to Pearl for answers. "Why would they need a woman at the sawmill?" Not to mention that Fiona would never ever work in a sawmill.

Pearl pressed a napkin to her face, clearly trying to hide the fact that she was laughing.

"What is it? What do you know that I don't?"

Pearl shook her head, but she didn't pull the napkin from her face. A giggle sneaked out.

Amanda heard the front door open, and she instinctively rose. Garrett had come here this morning needing help, and Fiona had outright refused. He must be devastated. Amanda glided to the hallway.

Garrett stared back at her, his gaze stormy. He whipped the cap off his head and crushed it in one hand. With his hair sticking up at a boyish angle and his expression anguished, he looked as uncomfortable as she felt.

She tried to take it all in. Garrett wanted to *hire* Fiona? Not marry her? What had changed? Whatever it was, Amanda felt the tension slip from her shoulders. He looked so uncomfortable standing there, like a boy whose dreams had been crushed. Her heart went out to him, and she took a step in his direction.

He backed up.

She tried to speak, but only a croak came out.

"Miss Porter." He shoved the cap on his head, flung open the door and left, slamming the door behind him.

Garrett stood on the boardinghouse porch and drew in a deep breath of the icy December air. Stockton wanted an answer by nine o'clock, when they were to meet in the hotel dining room. The night before, the mill owner had asked Garrett to head up the building of a new ship, a schooner, that would bear Stockton's name. Instead of slicing logs for other men to use, Garrett would build a sailing ship. The chance to create sparked something inside him. It didn't hurt that the new position also came with a substantial increase in wages.

It also meant much longer hours.

With Roland marrying Pearl the day after Christmas, Garrett and the children had to move out of the quarters they'd shared with Roland since Eva's death a year ago April. His brother and new wife needed a place of their own, and since the lodgings were located above the mercantile that Roland managed, it made sense for Garrett to move.

In the wee hours of the night, he'd come to a decision. He would ask Stockton for the empty house on Cherry Street as part of his compensation as chief shipwright. It was the right thing to do. It also meant he needed a housekeeper to take care of the place and watch over the children when they weren't in school. Together, he and Roland had managed. Barely. Though Sadie helped as best she could, she had just turned seven. He didn't want her near a hot stove. He couldn't ask Roland's new wife to take over. Pearl had enough to do already, teaching school and setting up housekeeping. No, he needed to hire someone.

Not marry. Despite Sadie's school paper. Roland had shoved that tidbit at him last night, no doubt thinking it would change his mind. It didn't. His brother didn't understand that a bad wife was worse than no wife at all. Sadie just missed her mama. In time, those feelings would wane. Moreover, with Pearl joining the family, Sadie would have someone to turn to with questions.

Hiring help, on the other hand, didn't carry the same risk. A bad housekeeper could be fired. A good one would ease the transition to a new house. He'd considered every married woman in town, but that numbered only three: Mrs. Calloway, Mrs. VanderLeuven and Mrs. Elder. None of them would do. Mrs. Calloway had her hands full running the boardinghouse. Mrs. VanderLeuven ran the hotel, and Mrs. Elder was ailing and abed most of the time.

That brought him to the three ladies hoping to gain his hand: Amanda, Fiona and Louise Smythe. The latter already worked for Mrs. Elder, narrowing the field to two. After careful consideration, he'd selected the best baker, but Fiona had jumped away from his offer like a dull saw hitting a hard knot.

He tugged off his cap and raked a hand through his hair. What was he going to do?

The answer was both obvious and gut-wrenching.

He looked to the pale blue sky. *Lord, are You forcing me into this?*

He wasn't ready to spend any time with a woman who reminded him too much of his late wife. It sure didn't help that the children adored her, in spite of the fact that she'd lost track of Sadie in the fire last month that burned down the schoolhouse. Amanda's inattention had nearly caused his daughter's death. No, he was not ready to face Amanda Porter, but he didn't have much choice. Taking a deep breath, he turned around and grasped the knob.

Lord, help me.

He would need it.

Amanda didn't need any more proof that Garrett Decker felt nothing for her. At the mere sight of her, he ran.

She touched a hand to her hair. It seemed perfectly in place. She moved closer to the door, where a small mirror hung on the wall. No stray curl stuck out at an odd angle. No crumbs or irksome blemishes dotted her face. Her dress was the same modest plum gown he'd seen countless times. It had been recently laundered and pressed. In every respect she looked the same as always.

Yet he found her presence distasteful ever since the schoolhouse fire. Pearl assured her time and again that she'd explained to Garrett what had happened that day, how Amanda had struggled to keep the children together. They'd been so frightened when she hurried them out of the schoolhouse and marched them up the hill away from the blaze. She'd been so busy with the little ones entrusted to her care that she hadn't noticed Sadie was missing. How had she missed that?

She swayed and put a hand against the wall to steady herself.

On that terrible day, she had nearly lost her dearest friend and the little girl she loved. From that moment forward, Garrett had stopped talking to her. He no longer asked her to watch the children. Fiona claimed that role.

Amanda glanced toward the staircase. What had happened between Garrett and Fiona? Instead of the proposal she had expected, Fiona had loudly refused to be *hired*. Why would Garrett need to hire a woman? Not for the sawmill. Pearl's laughter had made that clear. Maybe Roland needed help at the store and had sent Garrett on the errand. Then why not offer the position to Amanda? Pearl knew how badly she needed work. Moreover, she had worked at the store once last summer. Fiona had not. Did Garrett mistrust her so much that he wouldn't even recommend her for a job at the mercantile?

Amanda nibbled her lip.

Pearl joined her. "What did Garrett say?"

"Nothing. He left."

"That's curious."

"Does Roland need help at the store?"

"Not that I know of. Why would you ask?"

"Because Fiona refused whatever job Garrett offered her. You heard her."

The front door burst open. Amanda leaped back at the cold rush of air. Garrett paused in the doorway, looking alternately at her and Pearl.

"Come in or leave," Pearl scolded, "but don't stand there with the door open. Mrs. Calloway will wring your neck for letting out the warmth."

Garrett stepped inside, closed the door and removed his cap. His ruggedly handsome face glowed red, though Amanda couldn't tell if it was from embarrassment or the cold.

"I'm sorry, Miss Pearl." He turned the cap around and around in his hands.

Amanda stepped back, ready to bolt for her room, but Pearl caught her arm and would not let her retreat.

"Did you wish to speak with someone?" Pearl asked. "Fiona, perhaps?"

He shook his head, gaze averted, and cleared his throat. "I wondered…" Again he cleared his throat.

"What did you wonder?" Pearl prompted.

He peeked at Amanda before lowering his gaze again. "Might I speak with Miss Porter?" He crushed the cap in his hands.

"Of course. Amanda would be glad to speak with you. Why don't you two go into the parlor?" Pearl pushed her toward the parlor door.

Amanda's heart pounded. Garrett wanted to speak to her? And he was having difficulty speaking? Why? He shouldn't be nervous about offering her employment. Unless his return had nothing to do with that. Maybe he was going to tell Amanda never to see his children again. Her throat constricted.

She looked back at Pearl, who tipped her head, encouraging her to go into the parlor. Amanda couldn't seem to move.

She finally found her voice, squeaky though it was. "I'm sure it's all right with Garrett if you join us."

Pearl waved off that idea. "I have to get to school."

"Me, too," Amanda squeaked. "The little ones will need help with their coats and boots. Then I'm supposed to read to them."

The school operated out of the building that served as a church on Sundays, until a new schoolhouse could be built.

"I'll be fine until you arrive." Pearl turned to Garrett, who was still just inside the front door. "I wondered if you might build us something for Christmas."

He hesitated, clearly wary. "What?"

"We can talk after you get done with work, or you can ask your brother. Roland knows exactly what I have in mind."

"I, uh, I suppose I could, as long as it's not too difficult. It's only three weeks until Christmas Eve."

Pearl's mischievous smile meant she had something up her sleeve. "Oh, it's nothing too terribly fancy. Besides, you'll have help, and I know just the person." She then glided off.

Amanda didn't want to be alone with Garrett in the parlor. Well, that wasn't quite true. She wanted to be alone with him, but only if he was able to look at her and speak with her. Since he'd gone silent again, that didn't appear likely. Nevertheless, the parlor was more private than the front hall. She entered and sat down in her favorite chair, a lovely stuffed one with dainty legs and a flowered tapestry seat. Judging from the toppled pillow, Fiona had chosen the sofa. Amanda would not make that mistake.

Garrett followed her in but didn't sit. He stood across the room, staring out the window. Amanda waited for what seemed like ten minutes, but he said nothing. At last she could stand it no longer.

"I wonder what that was about," she mused. "Pearl didn't say anything to me about building something for Christmas."

"She didn't?" He turned toward her, brow furrowed.

In spite of his burly build and ruddy cheeks, Garrett had an endearing boyish quality that tugged at her heart. The poor man had suffered terribly, losing his wife in a tragic accident, yet he endured, his faith unshakable. That more than anything terrified Amanda. Garrett Decker was a man of God. Could he see the shame hidden deep inside her?

She forced a smile. "She didn't. I have no idea what she wants you to build."

He scowled and turned back to the window.

Amanda waited for him to say something. The silence was beginning to unnerve her. After ignoring her the last few weeks, he certainly wasn't going to ask for her hand. If only he realized how much his children needed a mother, but apparently even Sadie's letter hadn't changed his mind. If he offered Amanda a marriage of convenience, she would accept, but that appeared unlikely.

He sat in the chair opposite her on the other side of the room and continued to twirl his cap between his hands. Even now he said nothing. Her head spun with possibilities. As seconds dragged into minutes, she could no longer bear the suspense.

"You wanted to speak with me?" she prompted.

He nodded and finally looked up, a pained expression on his face. "I, uh, haven't been fair to you lately."

He wanted to apologize?

She gathered her wits. "A lot happened." The fire.

"Don't make excuses for me." He looked up, but not at her. "You see, I'm still grieving my late wife."

Amanda nodded and fixed her gaze on her clasped hands, the knuckles white. She flexed her fingers, but it didn't relieve the tension.

He cleared his throat. "But that's not why I'm here. The fact is that circumstances have put me in a difficult situation." His gaze wandered to the samplers on the wall. "I—that is, we—plan to move to a house. The children and I."

"I see." Though she didn't. Why did this involve her, unless he was going to propose a marriage of convenience?

"Roland and I have managed the cooking and cleaning since, well…you know."

She drew in a sharp breath and captured his attention. Heat flooded her face. Was he going to ask the impossible? Her mouth grew dry, and she wished for one swallow of that unpalatable tea.

He looked down at his cap again. "Yes, well, once my brother marries, he'll be, uh, preoccupied. So I thought it best that the children and I move. I'll ask for a house when I accept the position as chief shipwright for the schooner Mr. Stockton is having built."

"Congratulations."

He nodded. "It's not all settled yet. I have to meet Mr. Stockton in a few minutes. So that's why I, uh…"

Amanda waited.

His lips began to form words before backing off. He twirled the cap again and heaved a tortured sigh. "There's no way around it. I—that is, we—will need a housekeeper."

A housekeeper! No wonder Fiona had stormed out of the parlor.

Though disappointed, Amanda couldn't afford to pick and choose. She needed an income. Garrett was offering a position, doubtless one that paid enough for her to afford a room. Moreover, keeping house meant she could take care of Sadie and Isaac. It wasn't marriage, but it would keep her in Singapore.

"Do the children know they will be moving?" she asked.

He shook his head. "I didn't want to tell them until everything is set. I need to speak to Mr. Stockton in—" he glanced at the clock "—in ten minutes. I'd be much obliged if you would consider the position. I will pay you, of course."

God did answer prayer, though certainly not in the way Amanda had hoped. She needed a paying job, and Garrett was offering just that.

"I accept."

"You do?"

Was that hope she saw in his eyes?

"We should go over the details. For instance, when would you expect me to work? I can't live at the house, naturally." Her cheeks must be as red as a summer sunset.

"Of course not." His expression confirmed that had never been his intent. "I assume you'd stay here and, uh, keep house and whatnot during the day."

"I help out at the school."

"That's right. I forgot." He scrubbed his auburn locks. "On weekdays, you can clean after the school day ends, but I'll need you every day to take care of my son and daughter. Make supper."

Make supper? Amanda gulped. She had no idea how to cook. Maybe Mrs. Calloway or Pearl could give her lessons before she began. "When would you need me to start?"

"Monday, if all goes as planned."

That gave her the weekend to learn how to cook. "So soon?"

His mouth ticked. "I want to move out early to give Pearl time to set up the upstairs lodging the way she prefers."

"That's very considerate." That took away her idea of asking Pearl to teach her to cook. She'd have to ask Mrs. Calloway. "You will have the house ready by then?"

"We'll move the furniture this weekend. I was hoping you could help with the cleaning."

"Now?"

"Next week would be fine." Finally, his gaze landed on her, filled with such gratitude that her heart nearly stopped. "Thank you. This is a big help."

It wasn't marriage or even courting, but it would give her more time with Sadie and Isaac. Perhaps time would change their father's mind.

Amanda stood. "I love spending time with Sadie and Isaac."

This time Garrett gazed right into her eyes.

Her breath caught. Did she see a flicker of affection or was it simply gratitude?

He backed away and nodded curtly. "Thank you, again, Miss Porter. I must be on my way to the hotel for my meeting."

"I hope it goes as you anticipate."

He shoved the cap on his head. "I'm sure it will."

They walked to the front door, where she saw him out. This time the frosty morning air didn't bother her. She would not have to say farewell to Isaac and Sadie, after all. She would see them each and every day. Who knew where this might lead? Perhaps straight to Garrett Decker's heart.

Garrett paused on the porch to don his cap. "I see Mr. Elder's at the mercantile. Probably heard that the mail came in."

The mail!

Oh, no. Her letter begging a position with the Chatsworths was on its way to New York, and she could do nothing to stop it.

Chapter Two

$\backsim\!\!\!\bullet$

Garrett surveyed the Cherry Street house the following morning. It didn't take long to see why Stockton had readily agreed to include use of the house as part of Garrett's compensation for taking the lead building the new ship. His excitement over putting to use skills he'd honed years ago in a Chicago shipyard waned in light of all the work that needed to be done on the house.

"The roof leaks in at least four places." He pointed each one out to his brother. "Right next to the kitchen stove and over the table. Look how warped the tabletop is."

"If anyone can fix it, you can."

"I wanted to move in today."

Roland shrugged. "You don't need to move for a couple weeks. Why not fix what needs fixing first? It's a lot warmer today. We could tackle the roof."

"You?" Garrett had a tough time imagining his brother picking up a hammer, much less using it. "You couldn't fix a crooked picture."

He moved into the first bedroom before his brother could reply. Naturally, Roland followed.

"Another leak, over the bed," Garrett pointed out.

"We'll get the men from the mill to lend a hand and have it fixed by the end of the day."

Roland was right, but Garrett hated to admit that he'd made this deal without checking out the house first. Thankfully, Roland didn't point out that error.

"What about that project that Pearl wanted me to do?" Garrett prodded.

Roland's future wife wanted a stable built for a nativity play she had planned for the children.

"That can wait until you move in." Roland grinned. "Or you could stay put for another week."

Garrett couldn't. "I hired Miss Porter starting Monday."

"Don't you mean Amanda?"

Garrett scowled. "This is a business arrangement, not personal. 'Miss Porter' will do."

If anything, Roland's grin grew wider. "Good decision. She loves Sadie and Isaac and will be perfect for the job."

Garrett bristled, the memory of nearly losing Sadie still raw. "There wasn't anyone else."

"Then God made sure it worked out for Amanda to get the job."

Garrett still couldn't wrap his mind around Roland's newfound faith. "Maybe God didn't have anything to do with it. Maybe it was just circumstances."

"Maybe." Roland's grin said otherwise. "Either way, it ended up the best way possible."

Garrett didn't quite see it that way. "How can I can trust her?"

"She's as trustworthy as Pearl."

They'd had this argument before, but Garrett couldn't forget what happened during the fire. "Thanks to her inattention, Sadie almost died."

"She didn't die." Roland's jaw set. "And you're forgetting that Amanda led eleven children to safety, including Isaac."

Garrett knew he was being unfair. After all, Pearl was the schoolteacher in charge of the children. Amanda had volunteered to help. He shouldn't hold her to a higher standard, but Sadie's brush with death had shaken him. It hadn't been that long since his wife, Eva, died. Less than two years. He couldn't bear losing anyone else.

Since this argument was leading nowhere, he put an end to the inspection. "Guess I'll head back to the mill and round up some help."

"Can you wait a minute? Pearl's on her way here."

"Why?" Garrett asked warily.

"You'll need a woman's opinion on what needs to be done to get the place ready."

"I don't need anyone else's opinion. A woman will want to change everything." Garrett thought back to his late wife's demands. Nothing was ever good enough for Eva. Garrett had bought her everything he could afford, but it was never enough.

Roland walked back into the main room, which combined the kitchen and sitting area with a table for meals, study and anything else the children needed to do.

"The sideboard can go there, and the sofa would fit in that corner." Roland pointed to various spots as he listed off the pieces of furniture that Garrett had put into storage after Eva's death. "The china cabinet would fit in the corner."

"Stop!" Garrett couldn't bear another word. "None of that furniture is coming here. You use it, and I'll haul over the things we're using now."

"Not a chance. Pearl would never stand for it."

"Why? Eva's things are a lot nicer than what we're using now."

"That doesn't matter to someone like Pearl."

That's what bothered Garrett about Amanda. Pearl might not care about worldly things, but Amanda obviously did. Her gowns were stunning. Her hair was always fixed just so. Nothing was ever out of place. She was the very picture of the delicate female. Too much like Eva. No, his late wife's furniture would never do.

"I can't look at that furniture each day," Garrett insisted.

"Pearl feels the children need to be around their mother's things, that they won't get past her death until they can see and touch what's left behind. I happen to agree."

"Stop it. First Miss Porter and now this. Stop pushing me."

"It'll be two years come April. You need to let go."

"Don't tell me what to do until you're in my shoes." Garrett didn't point out that Pearl had nearly died rescuing Sadie in last month's fire.

Judging from Roland's expression, he didn't need to.

"First help me out," Pearl told Amanda as she donned her cloak in the front hallway of the boardinghouse, "and then I'll show you how to cook some basic things, like eggs and biscuits."

"That won't help me for supper. He said I'd need to cook supper."

"All right, then I'll teach you how to make hash and stew and that sort of thing."

"But…"

Amanda had hoped to get started early. Mrs. Calloway had approved, as long as whatever they made could be served to the boardinghouse guests. Given Amanda's current lack of knowledge, the guests were going to suffer. The very thought of cooking something terrified her.

Aside from boiling water and collecting serving platters, she steered clear of the big cookstove.

Pearl held out Amanda's coat. "It will only take a few minutes."

"Then you will teach me to cook?"

Pearl nodded.

Amanda conceded defeat and threw on her coat. The hat took longer, since the pins refused to hold it in the proper place. Every time she thought she had it just right, she'd take a step, and the hat would slide to the side.

"You don't need to look perfect," Pearl complained. "At this rate we will never get there. Here." Pearl tied the ribbons under Amanda's chin.

"You know I hate to have anything tied under my chin." Amanda tugged on the ribbons, but Pearl had knotted them.

"If we don't go now and get this taken care of, there won't be any time left to cook."

"Then we can forget this little errand that you refuse to divulge and go straight into cooking lessons."

Pearl laughed. "You can't wriggle out of this that easily." She opened the front door. "Come along."

Amanda gave up and followed her friend. Instead of heading to the store, Pearl took off in the opposite direction, toward the dunes. Amanda hurried and caught up.

"Where are you going?" Her words came out in gasps.

"It's a surprise. Don't you love surprises?"

"It depends. Some of your surprises didn't turn out all that well. Like the excursions you proposed back at the orphanage."

"They would have been highly educational if Miss Hornswoggle could have overlooked that one little problem at the cathedral."

"The boys claimed we locked them in that room with all

the robes, when they should never have gone in there in the first place. And you made me go tell Miss Hornswoggle, so she could fetch someone to unlock the door."

Pearl shrugged. "She always forgave you anything. I would have had to clean the floors for two months."

Amanda laughed at the memory. "She did have a soft spot for me."

"And no wonder. You are the sweetest, prettiest girl on earth."

Pearl's words sent a shiver down Amanda's spine. Hugh had said the very same thing, but he hadn't meant it. "No surprises, please."

Pearl laughed. "This isn't bad. I promise. And I won't make you do anything you don't want to do."

Amanda wasn't certain she believed her. "Then tell me where we're going and what we're going to do there."

"You'll find out soon enough."

Amanda sighed. She would have to guess. "Does it have something to do with that project you asked me to work on?"

"Perhaps. In a roundabout way."

Amanda hated when Pearl acted like this. It meant she had come up with some grand idea that involved her. When Pearl had approached her about coming to Singapore, she'd held back all the details until Amanda agreed to consider it. By then Pearl had purchased the train ticket to Chicago for her. If Amanda hadn't suffered such humiliation at Hugh's hands, she might have asked more questions, but she was eager to leave. Only after they were settled on the train, carpetbags safely stowed, had Pearl shown her the advertisement. At first Amanda had rejected the idea of marrying a stranger. The memory of Hugh's cruel treatment of her still stung. She couldn't imagine allowing another man to touch her, but as the train ride wore on she began to realize the advantages. A man advertising for a wife would not expect a great deal. He wouldn't care about her past. He must be desperate and could not possibly reject her.

How wrong she'd been.

Again she had to hurry her step to catch up to Pearl, who was heading in the wrong direction. "If we're working on that project, why aren't we going to the school or the store?"

"Oh, I doubt you'll work on it at either place, at least not until just before Christmas." Pearl stopped in front of a weathered house that could use a good whitewashing. Even the shake shingles looked a bit threadbare. "Here we are."

"At a stranger's house? Who lives here?"

Pearl smiled coyly. "Let's find out."

Amanda gasped. "You're going to barge in on strangers?"

Pearl only laughed as the opened the door. "Come in with me." She grasped Amanda's hand. "There's nothing to be afraid of."

Pearl dragged, and Amanda reluctantly followed, but the tug up the single step made her stumble. She looked down to catch her footing, and her hat slipped to one side. She frantically tried to straighten it before entering the house.

"Here we are," Pearl called out as she tugged Amanda through the doorway.

It took a few seconds for Amanda's eyes to adjust to the lower light. When they did, she found herself face-to-face with Garrett Decker.

Garrett should have known that Pearl would drag her friend along. Since the day the ladies arrived on the *Milwaukee*, Pearl had been promoting Amanda. None of that matchmaking had been subtle, but for good measure Roland constantly pointed it out.

"Oh!" Amanda gasped, quickly straightening the hat that had slipped slightly to the side. "I didn't know." Pink suffused her cheeks, not from the cold. "I would never have intruded."

"Nonsense," Pearl said, her gaze sweeping around the room. "You'll need furnishings, of course, but first a good scrubbing is in order." She crossed to the kitchen stove and examined the firebox. "Full of ashes. No doubt one of the workers left it this way. No matter, a little elbow grease will take care of that. Speaking of grease, this stove needs to be scraped. It smells rancid. When was the last time someone lived here? You can't bring children into this house until it's clean from top to bottom."

Garrett's head spun as Pearl continued her instructions. It didn't help that Roland was snickering the whole time. As for Amanda, she looked even more confused and embarrassed than he was. For the first time since the fire, he felt for her. Clearly, Pearl had roped her into this without saying a word. Roland's chortles meant he'd known exactly what his fiancée had been up to, yet he'd failed to mention that Pearl was bringing Amanda along. There was no doubt about it. He and Amanda had been thoroughly set up.

"Of course you will need curtains. With ruffles, don't you think?" Pearl addressed that last to her friend, who stared dumbfounded.

"No ruffles," Garrett snapped. A man had his limits.

Pearl ignored him. "Roland says you can have any of the scraps and discarded fabrics from the store. I saw some pretty lace in the bin."

"No lace, either," Garrett added.

Again Pearl charged ahead without seeming to hear him. "With Mrs. Calloway's sewing machine, it won't take any time at all to make curtains for all the windows." She looked around. "There aren't that many. Two in front and this one in the kitchen. I assume those are bedrooms." She headed to each, poked her head in and came back with the report that each bedroom contained one window. "That's only five windows, and these front ones are the largest. What color would go best?"

Considering the walls were a dingy, unplastered gray, the color didn't much matter. Unless it was too bright.

"No bright colors," Garrett stated.

Amanda finally found her voice. "I think that Mr. Decker and the children must approve the colors and design."

Garrett was warming more to Amanda Porter by the minute.

Pearl blazed right ahead. "Of course. Perhaps you and Garrett should go through the available fabrics now."

Garrett coughed. This was getting out of hand. "I have repairs to make on the house before we move in tomorrow. I don't have time for curtains. That can wait."

"You'll think differently when the cold wind off the lake blows through those loose panes," Pearl pointed out.

Garrett had already noted the gaps between the glass panes and the frame, not to mention the windows and the siding. He'd have to caulk those before the snow began in earnest, or they'd wake up to drifts across the floor.

"That's why I have to get working on this place now," Garrett stated firmly. "There's a lot to do."

"Like cleaning out the firebox," Pearl pointed out.

Roland didn't even attempt to hide his snicker.

That drew Pearl's attention toward her fiancé. "We will make a work bee of this. Roland, you round up as many of the men as you can. I'll get together the ladies. Garrett and Amanda can get the supplies and materials they need from the mercantile."

"Yes, ma'am," Roland answered crisply.

To Garrett's surprise, Pearl's take-charge attitude melted into laughter.

"But Pearl," Amanda said, so softly that Garrett figured her friend wouldn't hear her, especially since Pearl's attention was fixed entirely on Roland. "You promised to help me…at the boardinghouse." Every bit of rosiness had drained from her cheeks.

"Later," Pearl assured her. "I won't forget."

Amanda nibbled on her lip, a girlish gesture that made her even more endearing. "But…"

"I promise." Pearl linked her arm around Roland's. "All right, we'll get everyone together and meet back here in thirty minutes. We can turn this house into the perfect home for Isaac and Sadie."

Garrett caught Amanda blinking back tears. Roland was right. She did care about his children. That made him feel a bit better about leaving them in her care for a few hours each day, but an instant later, those warm sentiments turned to annoyance. Pearl and Roland left, leaving him alone with Amanda.

She gave him an apologetic look. "I'm sorry. Sometimes Pearl gets caught up in an idea, and nothing can make her change course."

Amanda looked as uncomfortable as he felt. They'd both gotten caught in the web of Pearl's plans.

He cleared his throat and shoved his hands into his coat pockets. For some reason he got tongue-tied around Amanda. He had to get out of here and into a public place. "I suppose we'd better get what we need before everyone shows up."

Her face bloomed pink. "I suppose." She glanced up

at him. "I won't make anything for the house that you wouldn't approve."

The tremble in her voice undid him. Amanda was nothing like Eva. His late wife would have begged and demanded until she got her way. Amanda only sought to please. Perhaps Roland was right, and Garrett had badly misjudged her.

He drew in a deep breath. "As long as there's no ruffles or lace, I don't care." An idea crossed his mind. "Have Sadie pick out what she likes."

Amanda visibly brightened, the hesitancy gone. "What a wonderful idea! She has an artist's eye for color."

Garrett couldn't help it. Amanda's obvious affection for his daughter melted the coldness in his heart.

He smiled.

Chapter Three

Since cleaning the Cherry Street house took all day, Amanda never got her cooking lesson. She'd counted on helping Mrs. Calloway prepare Sunday dinner, until Louise Smythe invited Pearl, Fiona and her to join the Elders. Fiona had other plans, but Pearl accepted for herself and Amanda.

"But I'm needed to help with dinner," Amanda had protested.

Unfortunately, Mrs. Calloway overheard and put an end to that thought. "Go. It's only brisket and cabbage. Simple as can be."

Nothing was simple when it came to cooking, but with Pearl and Mrs. Calloway insisting she accept the invitation, once again the opportunity to learn slipped away.

Louise expressed such gratitude that Amanda felt badly for wishing she could be elsewhere. "Captain and Mrs. Elder are desperate for company. She is too frail to go out-of-doors anymore, and he won't leave her side." Her friend blinked back a tear. "He's so devoted to her. I wish…well, I can only hope to find someone like that."

Poor Louise had lost her first husband in the War Between the States. Widowed and poverty-stricken, she had spent everything she had hoping that Garrett Decker would marry her. So had Amanda. As for Fiona, no one quite knew if the concerts were given from financial necessity or to hone her talents.

When Louise learned Garrett did not want to marry, she took the position caring for Mrs. Elder in their home and found a perfect match for her love of books in Mr. Elder's extensive library.

That afternoon they gathered around the Elders' dinner table and listened to Captain Elder's tales from when he'd captained a ship on the Great Lakes. Mrs. Elder smiled at each story, though she must have heard them a thousand times, and encouraged her husband to continue.

He said with a twinkle in his eye, "Adeline indulges me." He leaned over and pecked her on the temple, drawing a playful scolding. "That's why I married her, that and her walnut tarts."

Mrs. Elder giggled like a young girl, her adoration wiping away the years for a moment. "Billy is such a tease."

Amanda's heart ached for such a close relationship, one that weathered the trials of time. Once she had dreamed of it with Hugh. He had been so attentive. Compliments flowed from his lips each time they met, and she began to believe his professions of love in spite of the vast difference between them. He was a man of society, and she an orphan who was little better than a maid in her foster family's home. He told her she was more beautiful than her foster sister, Lena, whom the Chatsworths believed he would soon court. When Hugh said that he would rather marry Amanda, she took it as a proposal, only to discover that his real purpose was to ruin her so she would become his mistress.

She shuddered at the memory of that day and the liber-

ties he had taken in spite of her protests, tears and strug-
gles. If not for Mrs. Brighton's timely intervention...

"Are you warm enough, dear?" Mrs. Elder asked. "I
have plenty of shawls if you need one."

Amanda pulled her thoughts from the terrible past. "Oh!
No, thank you. I am quite warm."

By the time she and Pearl left, daylight was slipping
away. Soon darkness would shroud the landscape, just as
memory had darkened Amanda's spirits.

"What's wrong?" Pearl asked. "You've been quiet since
dessert was served."

Amanda sighed. She could not reveal to anyone the
depth of humiliation and shame she'd endured at Hugh's
hands, so she focused on the other disappointment of the
day. "It's too late to learn to cook."

"Nonsense. I can still show you the basics."

"But Mrs. Calloway said anything we make had to be
available for the guests at the boardinghouse. There aren't
any more meals today. You know that."

"We could make rolls for tomorrow morning."

Amanda shook her head. "Garrett asked me to make
supper, not breakfast. No one eats sweet rolls for supper."

Pearl hugged her around the shoulders as they approached the boardinghouse, with its cheery pine wreath
on the front door and glowing windows. "Then I will help
you fix supper tomorrow. A stew will be simple enough."

"Will there be enough time after school?"

"Of course. Do you know what food he has on hand?"

"How would I know that?" Amanda's mouth went dry.
"Oh, dear, I'm going to fail on the very first day."

Pearl laughed. "No, you won't. I'll be right there helping
you. Besides, there's more to keeping house than cooking.
As soon as you finish the curtains, he'll see how talented
you are with a needle."

"He already knows I can sew. I made the dress and matching doll dress for Sadie's birthday."

"That's right. I forgot." Pearl slowed her step for just a moment. "I'm sure he hasn't forgotten, though. Sadie wouldn't let him. She's so excited that you're going to take care of their new house. Trust me. Her approval will go a long way toward winning over Garrett's heart."

Amanda wasn't so sure. Garrett Decker was a practical man. Like Captain Elder, he would appreciate a woman who could cook, especially since he'd listed that as one of her duties.

Pearl climbed the boardinghouse steps.

Amanda followed her friend. "Don't let me down."

Pearl smiled. "Don't worry."

Amanda couldn't help but worry. Her whole future depended on satisfying Garrett's expectations.

With all that help, Garrett got the house ready one day and moved into it the next. On Monday, he set to work preparing to build the ship. Stockton had left plans with him. Garrett called the best millwrights to his side and laid out the plans on the worktable that he used to repair broken saws and machinery.

"Mr. Stockton wants a new schooner." Garrett explained each element of the plans, especially the length, breadth and draft of the vessel.

Sawyer Evans squinted at the drawings. Even near the window, the light wasn't good, thanks to the thick coating of sawdust on the panes. "He thinks we can build that? I've never built a ship before."

"I have."

That brought Garrett the men's respect. After answering a dozen questions about how and when and where, he outlined his plan to build the launching ways and cradle near the dock that had been built for the glassworks that Roland had planned. First Garrett had to secure his brother's permission. That shouldn't be a problem. November's fire had destroyed the stockpiled building materials and chased away the investors for the glassworks, setting the project back indefinitely.

"The river is deep there," Garrett explained. "There's plenty of room for a broadside launch. We'll build the hull on a launching cradle that can be pulled away with the steam tractor when the schooner is ready."

He sketched his ideas on a blank sheet of paper. The men had a lot more questions and a bit of skepticism. Garrett answered them all, and soon the group seemed less apprehensive.

"With decent weather, we can launch it by early summer, after the first logging rush of the spring."

Sawyer whistled and shook his head. "That'll be a stretch. How many of us is Stockton planning to employ?"

Garrett eyed the men. Many workers had left already, now that the fall rush was tailing off. These would soon follow, returning in late winter for the spring rush. "Any who will stay."

That livened up the discussion and the desire to get started. By nightfall, they'd selected the timbers for the ways and keel blocks. There were enough stout posts on hand to begin driving them into the ground for the ways the next day.

"The ground's at about the right slope," Garrett said at the workday's end, "but we'll need to clear away the brush and do a little leveling at the water's edge. We can take the tractor up there tomorrow."

On the walk home, he mentally went through the checklist of what needed to be done next. He tromped up the inner staircase behind the store, barely noticing that the cookstove was cool. The apartment upstairs was dark as night and dead quiet.

"What's going on? Sadie? Isaac?"

The echo in the room sent a chill down his spine until Garrett recalled that he and his children didn't live here anymore. He growled with frustration at himself as he walked back outside. At least Roland hadn't caught him going to the wrong house. He'd never hear the end of it.

That's what he got for thinking about work when he should be directing his energies toward his children. It was time to forget work and find out how Amanda had fared in her first day on the job.

Garrett heard the giggling before he got to the front door. It felt strange walking here, and it had been even stranger using his old furniture last night when they'd moved in. Pearl had instructed the men from the mill to drag the stuff in Saturday. Even though Garrett was their supervisor, they wouldn't go against Miss Pearl. Roland was going to have his hands full with that woman.

Garrett had stared at the sofa and chairs last night, unwilling to sit on them. Sadie and Isaac had no trouble. They'd run around the house, exploring every nook and cranny. Sadie's cat, Cocoa, had clawed its way into the beds and the chests of clothing that still needed to be unpacked. The wind picked up overnight, and it didn't take long to find the holes he'd missed when trying to shore up the gaps Saturday. Tonight he'd attempt to caulk those he could find in the dark, if he could get the children to settle down.

Judging from the shrieks and giggles coming from indoors, that wouldn't be easy.

He climbed the single step to the stoop and sniffed the air. He should smell supper. Hmm. The wind must be blowing from the wrong direction.

Another giggle gave him an idea. Through the window he could see Sadie and Isaac bent over something in the middle of the table. He waited until all was quiet and then sprang through the door.

"Surprise!"

Sadie shrieked before realizing it was her pa. Cocoa scooted off the table and disappeared into the children's bedroom. Sadie then ran to him, arms outstretched. Garrett scooped her up and she clung to his neck, laughing. "You scared me, Papa."

Though Isaac had yelped, he soon put on the stoic expression of a little boy trying to be a man. "Not me. I knew it was you all along."

"Sure you did." Garrett ruffled his son's hair. "You're always in control."

He glanced down at the table, where a big, black beetle was crawling around. That's what they'd been so entranced by? Or maybe Cocoa had been curious, and they were watching to see what the kitten would do next.

"You brought a bug in the house?" he asked.

"We found it crawling on the boardwalk," Sadie said.

"It came out 'cause of the sun," Isaac informed him as he scooped up the bug. "Beetles and flies like it warm."

Garrett couldn't deny that, but this biological experiment was bound to upset a grown woman. "You'll have to put it back outside, son."

Isaac grudgingly obeyed, setting it just off the stoop before coming back inside.

"You could have taken it farther from the house," Garrett said.

Isaac stuck out his chin. "Maybe he wants to be warm, too."

Garrett could only sigh. His son was growing an independent streak. At least his daughter still depended on him. Speaking of which, one housekeeper should have appeared by now. He looked around the room. Nothing was on the stove, though it was clearly lit. He sniffed. No smell of food. "Where is Miss Amanda?"

"Miss Mana went to get supper," Sadie informed him.

"Shh! You weren't supposed to tell." Isaac's frown etched deep lines in his young forehead. "It's supposed to be a secret."

Sadie started to cry and pressed her face against Garrett's shoulder.

"There now," he managed to say, though he was steaming mad. Amanda had left the children alone? The only reason he'd hired a housekeeper was so someone would be at home to watch Sadie and Isaac. First, Amanda had lost track of Sadie during the fire last month that had destroyed the school building. Now, she'd left both of them alone in a house with a lit stove and a black beetle.

The door cracked open, and Amanda backed into the room, carrying a large basket in both hands. "I'm back. I hope I'm not too late."

Garrett unclenched his jaw and set down Sadie. "It's time we had a talk, Miss Porter."

Amanda nearly lost her grip on the basket. Her knees wobbled as she recalled what Pearl had told her to say if Garrett reached the house before she returned.

She hefted the basket onto the table, the delicious smells of beef stew and fresh-baked rolls emanating from inside. "I brought supper."

She did feel a bit guilty about not making the meal. Thankfully, Mrs. Calloway had enough left from supper there to send this pot of stew with her.

"Sadie, could you set the table? Isaac, please wash up."

Garrett cleared his throat. "Wipe the tabletop, too."

"Why?" Amanda eyed her employer, trying to figure out if his anger had diminished.

Instead of answering her, Garrett turned to his son.

Isaac shrugged. "We found a huge beetle."

"A beetle?" she gasped. "Where is it?"

"Outdoors," Garrett informed her.

She pressed a hand to her midsection. "What a relief."

"Don't you like bugs, Miss Amanda?" Isaac asked.

She shuddered. "Not so much." The outbreaks of fleas and chiggers at the orphanage had kept her itching and scratching. "They belong outside."

Isaac fetched a rag from the dry sink and ran it quickly over the center of the table, while Sadie set the cups and plates in place.

"Are you eating with us, Miss Mana?" the little girl asked.

"No," Garrett answered for her.

Amanda held her breath. The stew the family shared tonight was her portion, plus the little bit left after the boardinghouse guests finished.

Garrett looked her in the eye. "Miss Amanda needs to return home." He motioned toward the door.

Her stomach rumbled. She hoped no one heard. No matter how strong Pearl said she must be, Amanda could not seem to stop the trembling that began deep inside and ended up in her hands. She clenched them tightly so Garrett wouldn't notice. "Let me at least serve supper."

"That's not necessary." Garrett's gaze, darker than his brother's, never left her face.

She could not breathe, could not think, could not move.

"I would like a word with you outside, Miss Porter. Children, you can begin."

"But we haven't blessed the food," Amanda cried out.

He stiffened. After getting the children in their chairs, he said a quick blessing and then ushered her out into the cold.

Amanda's heart pounded so hard it felt like it would leap out of her chest.

"I asked you to look after the children," he said.

"I was only gone a few minutes, and they were quite safe. I told them to stay in the house."

Even before she finished, she could tell he wasn't hearing a word she said. Garrett Decker had already made up his mind.

"I'm not interested in excuses."

That eliminated telling him about the lack of food in the house. He would probably insist she ought to have taken the children with her to the mercantile while she purchased what was needed. The truth wouldn't help. Even if the larder had been full, she couldn't have cooked anything. Pearl had failed to gain Mrs. Calloway's permission to give lessons last night, and the boardinghouse proprietress's brief instructions this morning had left Amanda even more mystified.

She swallowed the last shreds of pride she had left. "I'm sorry. It won't happen again."

"No, it won't." He went back into the house and shut the door in her face.

Chapter Four

"Did Garrett say you were dismissed?" Pearl asked Amanda as they dressed the following morning.

"Not in so many words." Amanda glanced in the mirror. Her color was pale after a night of hunger and tearful prayer, and the plum coloring of the dress did little to hide that fact. "But he did say I wouldn't have a chance to make the same mistake again. Was it really so awful leaving Isaac and Sadie alone for ten minutes? Isaac said his papa and uncle leave him in charge all the time."

"Mmm-hmm. There can be different standards for relatives."

Amanda thought of the Chatsworths. The lines of distinction were clearly marked. Their daughter stood at the top. Amanda ranked a distant second or even third. At times the housekeeper and butler seemed to carry more weight than she did. That's why she'd begged Mrs. Brighton never to divulge what had happened that night with Hugh. The kindly housekeeper promised to hold it in confidence, but watching Hugh announce his engagement to Lena still hurt. He had never seen Amanda as an equal. None of them had.

"I suppose you're right," she admitted, pulling her

thoughts back to last night's painful events, "but what was I to do? The children were hungry, and there was only oatmeal and crackers in the house."

"Did you tell Garrett that?"

"He didn't give me a chance." His refusal to listen still churned her stomach. "He said he didn't want to hear any excuses."

"Completely unreasonable." Pearl tied a length of ribbon into a bow around the high collar of her dress. "And not like Garrett. He's generally quite practical and slow to speak. He must have been upset about something else and took it out on you."

Amanda sank to the bed. She could never win him over, least of all get the job back, if he was disposed to dislike her. "Then what do I do?"

"You march right back to the house after school and carry on as if nothing happened."

"I do?" Even after all these years, Amanda was stunned by her friend's audacity. "But he dismissed me."

"No, he didn't. You said yourself that he simply told you that you wouldn't make the same mistake, which of course you won't, since you're going to stock the larder and learn to cook something simple."

Pearl made it sound so simple, but she wasn't taking into account Garrett's animosity toward Amanda.

"What if he shouts at me? What if he tells me to leave and never come back?"

"Then you'll have your answer." Pearl jabbed a hairpin into her topknot. "His loss, if you ask me. He'll have a difficult time finding anyone else for the job, and there's no one in all of Singapore who can compare to you when it comes to keeping house."

"But I still don't know how to cook."

"That's why you are going to stay here through the

midday meal so you can learn from Mrs. Calloway. She's promised to take more time showing you how to do everything."

"Don't you need me at school?"

Pearl laughed. "I think I can manage for half a day."

"I'm sorry." Amanda blanched. "I didn't mean to imply that I'm indispensable."

"But you are." Pearl gently tugged her to her feet. "I couldn't manage more than a few hours without your help." She grinned. "Don't tell the school committee members, though, or they'll hire you instead of me next year."

Pearl always managed to lift her spirits. "Don't be silly. You're the one doing the teaching. I just help keep everyone occupied."

"So they can learn." Pearl opened the door to their room. "Let's go down to breakfast. It smells like Mrs. Calloway fried bacon this morning."

That morning Garrett's men made great progress cutting the timbers for the launching ways and cradle. Before they could put them in place, the land by the river would have to be cleared. Since Roland owned that land, it meant getting his brother's permission.

With the weather holding fair, Garrett decided they'd best get the location ready before a storm rolled in and blanketed the ground with snow or the temperatures dropped and froze the ground.

During the lunch break, he stopped in the mercantile. His brother stood at the counter, writing in one of the ledgers.

"Roland, I need to talk to you about something."

Roland looked up. "You don't have to use the front door like a customer just because you're living down the street now."

The grin told Garrett that his brother was teasing. That's the way they communicated. Each tried to best the other. Roland won most battles of wit, while Garrett could take his brother in a physical challenge any day. That didn't mean he couldn't throw back a decent retort.

"Last I checked, I am a customer here. And I expect to be treated like one."

Roland's grin broadened. "Then you arrived at just the right time. You can sign for the purchases Amanda is making."

"The what?" Garrett had left early this morning without quite figuring out what he was going to do about that situation. After the way he'd reacted last night, he figured she would never return to work for him.

"Purchases." Roland motioned toward a large basket beside the ledger. Garrett recognized that basket. It was the one Amanda had used to bring the delicious beef stew last night. Every bite had stuck in his throat. He owed her an apology, but...

"Purchases? What kind of purchases?"

"Food, Mr. Decker." The formerly gentle and quiet Amanda Porter placed some tins in the basket. "Your children need more than crackers and porridge to eat." She looked him in the eye, more like Pearl than the shy beauty he was used to seeing.

He opened his mouth and then clapped it shut. What could he say to that? His children did need to eat, and he had neglected to fully stock the kitchen, a fact that he'd noticed at breakfast this morning. He cleared his throat and hoped Amanda didn't see the heat creeping up his neck. "Of course. Well done, Miss Porter."

The faintest smile graced her lips and sent his spirits catapulting upward just as quickly as they'd gone down.

Her attention returned to the basket of food. "I can only cook plain food. I hope that will be good enough."

But the stew hadn't been plain, it had been delicious. With a start, he realized she must not have cooked it. She must have gotten it from someone else, most likely the boardinghouse.

"The stew." He halted, unsure what to say.

She did not look up at him. "Mrs. Calloway's efforts."

"I owe her then."

Amanda shook her head. "It was left over."

"But how, when there are a half dozen guests and the Calloways?" Before he finished saying the words, he knew.

The portion he and his children had eaten was hers. She had gone hungry last night while he dined. Moreover, he'd accused her of neglect, when he was the one who had neglected his family. He owed her more than an apology, but at the moment he couldn't think of what to say.

He walked to her side. Roland scooted out from behind the counter on the pretense of checking for some cornmeal in the back. Anyone could see that the bin was half-full.

Garrett waited until his brother was gone.

Amanda fidgeted with the handle of the basket. "I hope I didn't overstep my bounds."

"No." He cleared his throat again. "Not at all. I did. I'm sorry. For last night. I shouldn't have jumped to conclusions. The wrong ones."

Her head bobbed, as if she was gathering her composure, and the ribbons caught in her dark curls. He had to fight the impulse to lift them free.

"It's all right," she whispered. "I should go. I promised to help Pearl at school this afternoon. If you can sign..."

He turned the ledger and scrawled his signature on the line. But that didn't get rid of the aching guilt. "I'm sorry. I hope we can start over again."

She lifted her tremulous gaze to him, and he was struck again by the similarity of her eyes to those of Eva. If Eva had ever given him such a look, it had been an act so she could get her way. Not Amanda.

"I hope so, too." Her faint smile wavered.

"I can help you carry that basket to the house."

"Thank you, but I can manage. It sounded like you wanted to speak to your brother."

Garrett was ashamed of himself. Amanda thought only of everyone else's needs. He could kick himself for being such a fool yesterday. His children were hungry, and she'd responded the only way she knew how. Instead of thanking her, he'd accused and blamed her. He would change. Next time he would give her the benefit of doubt. He owed her that much.

Making hash looked easy when Mrs. Calloway demonstrated it. First Amanda needed to chop up everything. Then she needed to cook it in a big, heavy skillet. It took a bit of searching with Sadie and Isaac before she found the knives, a big wooden spoon and the skillet.

Peeling the potatoes had proved challenging, but she managed to get most of the skin off without cutting herself. The onion made her eyes water. The salt pork proved easiest of all.

It took a while for the stove to get hot enough. Apparently Garrett banked the fire before sending the children off to school and going to work. That meant an icy cold house and stove, but by the time she'd stowed all the purchases and chopped the ingredients for the hash, perspiration rolled off her forehead.

Now which went in the pan first? Amanda searched her memory but couldn't remember. She took a guess. The potatoes were hardest. She seemed to remember Mrs. Calloway saying they'd take the longest to cook. She dumped them into the hot skillet first.

"It's my turn," Sadie cried out from the bearskin rug, where they were sitting to play jacks.

"No, it's not," Isaac retorted. "My turn isn't over yet."

"Yes, it is. Miss Mana, tell Isaac to let me play."

"Everyone needs to have a turn," Amanda said.

"She just had a turn," Isaac insisted. "And now she wants my turn, too."

At school, Pearl would send one student to one corner and the other to the opposite corner to think about how they ought to behave. At the Chatsworths' house, a dispute had been settled with a few whacks of the strap on her behind. Amanda could not use either method. She wasn't their teacher or their mother.

Instead she joined them and knelt so she could look each child in the eye. "Is this the way your father would want you to behave?"

"He doesn't care about anything but work," Isaac said, his little jaw stiff but his lip quivering.

Amanda's heart about broke. She would have to speak to Garrett about spending more time with his children.

"Papa loves us," Sadie cried out. She grabbed her old rag doll, the one Amanda had repaired soon after arriving, and hugged it tight.

"Of course he does," Amanda said. "He's a busy man. All fathers are." At least Mr. Chatsworth had always seemed busy. He was gone long hours, sometimes until midnight. She couldn't remember much about her real father. He and her mother had died when she was five, but the tiny fragments she could recall always teemed with their love for her and for her brother, Jacob. Jake. A pang shot through her at the thought of her missing brother. They were separated after their parents' deaths. She went to their grandmother, while he was sent to their uncle's farm. For reasons unknown, Jacob ran away and was never found. Someday she would find him. She must find him. No tragedy could break family bonds. That applied in her case and for Isaac and Sadie. "Your papa loves you both dearly. I know he does."

"Then why doesn't he listen to us?" Isaac demanded.

"I'm sure he does," Amanda said.

"If he listened to us, he'd at least try to get married again."

Oh, dear. Amanda had no idea how to answer that statement, especially since Sadie had named her as the preferred new mama.

She began carefully. "Marriage isn't something to be rushed into."

Isaac's eyes widened, and his lips formed an O.

Amanda frowned. Her statement wasn't that difficult to understand. "Your papa wants to find the right woman to, uh, be your mother." Surely her cheeks were bright red.

Instead of agreeing or disagreeing, Isaac pointed toward the kitchen.

Amanda turned to see smoke pouring from the skillet.

Oh no! She scrambled to her feet, grabbed a towel and quickly pulled the skillet from the stove before the whole thing started on fire. She carried the smoking pan to the worktable and poked at the potatoes. Burned. And stuck to the pan.

Oh, dear. Her first attempt at cooking had come to ruin. She swallowed hard, trying to think of what to do. Did she have enough time to start over?

The door flew open.

"I'm home!" Garrett stepped inside and sniffed. "What's on fire?"

Oh, dear. There was no hiding this fiasco.

Chapter Five

"Supper," Isaac declared in answer to Garrett's question.

It didn't take long for him to confirm his son's explanation. Amanda stood at the worktable with a smoking skillet of something burned. The contents were too charred to identify.

"Supper?" he echoed. "You mean the food you just…"

Amanda cringed, and he let the thought trail off. He had vowed earlier this afternoon to give her the benefit of doubt.

"Is it salvageable?" he asked instead.

She poked a wooden spoon at the incinerated contents. "I don't think so." She looked stricken yet determined. "I'm sorry, Mr. Decker. You can deduct the cost of the potatoes from my wages."

"Potatoes." He breathed out in relief. It was only potatoes, one of the least expensive items she could have burned.

"Is there a fire, Miss Mana?" Poor Sadie looked terrified.

The lady dropped to her knees, the burned potatoes forgotten. "No, there isn't. I just scorched the potatoes, like holding an iron too long on a piece of fabric."

Garrett wouldn't call those quite the same, but his daughter accepted the explanation.

"You can hold Baby." Sadie offered Amanda the doll.

"Thank you, Sadie, but she needs you more than I need her. A little hug will take care of everything."

His daughter obliged, hugging Amanda an extra long time.

Amanda finally patted her back. "You did such a lovely job setting the table. Why don't you tell your father what you learned in school while I take care of the mess and cook up some supper?"

Garrett had to admire the way Amanda directed Sadie's attention away from the smoke and onto other topics. Nevertheless, while Sadie described her school day in minute detail, he watched Amanda carry the skillet outdoors to dump the ashes and then return and set the pan on the hot stove. She hesitated over two piles of chopped food. One looked like bacon or salt pork. The other appeared to be onions. She finally put one bit of onion in the skillet. It popped and hopped out.

The fire must have disconcerted her. He was about to suggest cooking the pork first when she began to add it to the skillet. While it cooked, she chopped a couple more potatoes and added them to the pork, finishing off with the onions.

Other than the smoke, which hadn't yet cleared the room, it smelled good. When she placed the hot skillet on the table without a trivet or rag underneath, he grabbed a towel from the cupboard.

"Let's put this under the pan," he suggested. "To protect the tabletop." He could imagine what a mark that pan had put in the varnish.

She blinked and then blushed while lifting the skillet. "I'm sorry. I got a bit discombobulated."

"A little smoke can do that." He glanced in the skillet and his stomach stopped rumbling. She hadn't gotten all the burned potatoes out of the pan.

He took a deep breath. *Give her a chance. Give her the benefit of the doubt.* After all, Amanda was the only woman in town both available and willing to take the job, and she was good with the children.

"Shall we say grace?" He bowed his head.

Isaac followed, but Sadie stared at Amanda. "Aren't you going to eat, too?"

Garrett didn't realize she was still standing halfway between the kitchen and the table. He hadn't considered how awkward it might be to have her watch them eat just so she could clean up afterward.

"Yes, please join us." It was the least he could do after making her go hungry the night before.

She hesitated. "Are you certain?"

"Yes." He had to speak firmly so she wouldn't back out of this. "Please sit before the food gets cold."

She dropped into the fourth chair. "Let's hold hands while praying."

"Hold hands?" Garrett didn't like that. He didn't like that at all. "We're asking blessing on the food, not playing a child's game."

Her color heightened. "I, well, it's something Pearl and I liked to do back in the..." Her voice trailed off.

"Back where?" Isaac demanded.

Judging from the way she'd blanched, Garrett suspected she'd been about to say the orphanage. Roland had told him about Pearl, how she'd been raised in an orphanage. It made sense that her childhood friend had also grown up there.

"Back when we were your age," she said.

Before his son could point out that she hadn't exactly

answered the question, Garrett told them to fold their hands and bow their heads for the blessing. By the time he finished the overly long list of things for which they were grateful, Isaac had forgotten to point out Amanda's misdirected answer.

Amanda stood. "Allow me to dish up the food."

"No, I can do it." Garrett's hand met hers on the spoon, and a peculiar sensation made him look up at her. The jolt reminded him of the stingers he sometimes got from the machinery. Except this wasn't unpleasant. Judging from the way her eyes widened, she'd felt it, too.

She yanked back her hand. "Thank you." It came out in a whisper.

Garrett cleared his throat. "Hand me your plate, Sadie. Ladies first."

Sadie giggled. "I'm a girl, not a lady."

"Of course you are," Amanda said. "You don't have to be as old as me to be a lady. Ladyship is more about one's manners and grace."

She proceeded to explain table manners to Sadie, though Garrett noticed that his son was listening, too. "Hold your fork like this." She demonstrated.

Sadie attempted and dropped the fork. "I can't."

"It takes practice, like learning sums. Keep trying, and soon you'll have it."

"That's not the way men eat," Isaac insisted. "A real man holds on to his fork so no one can take it away from him. Right, Pa?"

Garrett quickly shifted the way he held the fork. Eva had always complained that he acted uncivilized at the table. He'd stubbornly refused to change, even saying that nonsense about needing to hold on to his fork. True, Roland had snatched a fork from him once when they were children and refused to give it back, but that had been roundly reprimanded by their mother. Garrett never dreamed his resistance to Eva's attempts to change him would influence their son.

He cleared his throat. "A gentleman holds his fork like Miss Amanda is showing you."

"I don't want to be a gentleman. I want to be like you."

Amanda's eyebrows shot up.

Garrett felt both pleasure that his son wanted to emulate him and distress that he had set such a poor example. "Well, from now on, I'm going to eat like a gentleman."

Amanda smiled, and warmth spread through him. She approved. That was amazing enough, but even more startling was how much he enjoyed that approval. What was happening to him?

He took a bite of the hash and choked.

"What is it?" She looked horrified.

He swallowed without chewing more than necessary and washed down the rest with half of the cup of water in front of him.

"It's...different."

She took a small taste, and the expression of horror intensified.

"It's salty," Isaac pointed out.

"Thank you, son." Garrett motioned for him to say nothing further while Amanda guzzled water.

Sadie, always a dainty eater, picked out little pieces of onion and ate them as if there was nothing wrong with the hash.

Amanda recovered. "Oh, dear. I added too much salt, but Mrs. Calloway said everything needs salt."

"Except perhaps salt pork," Garrett said.

She looked mortified. "I'm sorry. I—I don't know how to fix it."

Garrett had learned a few tricks from those days when

Roland was busy and he had to cook something for the children, mostly because he made a lot of mistakes. He grabbed the skillet and stood. "We'll dilute it."

We? Amanda rose and set her napkin on the table. Garrett Decker was helping her?

She followed him the few steps to the kitchen. Her face must be flaming red. It certainly felt that way. How could she have made such a blunder? Mrs. Calloway had suggested she taste before serving. With the fiasco over the burned potatoes and Sadie's distress, Amanda had forgotten that all important tip.

Now she stood beside Garrett at the kitchen worktable. It was such a small surface that their arms nearly touched.

"Get a bowl from the cupboard," he commanded.

When she picked out a soup bowl, he sent her back for a serving bowl. Then he scraped the salty hash into it.

"Chop two more potatoes," he said. "Did you get any other vegetables, like carrots?"

"Yes, of course."

"Good. We'll add four of those, too. Chop them fine so they cook quickly."

She could figure out that much, but considering her record tonight, she didn't think it wise to mention.

Meanwhile, the children watched every move with wide eyes. Isaac crawled onto his chair and leaned across the table to whisper something to Sadie. She giggled. Dear me, even the children found her efforts humorous.

"Isaac, bring your plates here. Then bring ours." Garrett then added the contents to the bowl on the worktable.

Amanda finished peeling and chopping the potatoes and carrots. Garrett added a little of the hash to the skillet and then had her add the raw vegetables. When they had gotten tender, he added a bit more of the hash and stirred it all together. After it heated, he had her taste the mixture.

"A little bland," she reported.

He added more of the salty hash and then a little more until it tasted just right.

"How did you learn to do that?" she marveled.

"From experience. The best teacher." He smiled at her. "The same thing happened to me once."

His words were intended to comfort, but his smile went a lot further. She had hardly ever seen Garrett Decker smile. He was the sorrowing widower, never pleased with anyone or anything. Even in church or when escorting Fiona to the hotel dining room, he hadn't smiled. Only with his children did he smile. It changed him so much, from a rigid, dour perfectionist to a compassionate man.

Amanda breathed out. "You have a beautiful smile."

It instantly vanished. "Everyone's hungry. Let's eat."

Amanda reveled in what had happened long after she returned to the boardinghouse and settled into bed. Her mind whirled round and round, going over the events in minute detail. Garrett hadn't yelled at her. He'd worked with her. He'd shown her consideration and compassion. He'd granted her leniency. He'd smiled at her.

The sheets being cold, she blew on her icy fingers and wiggled her toes, trying to warm them.

"Could you be still?" Pearl grumbled. "I'm trying to get some sleep."

For a second Amanda tried to imagine not having to share a room and a bed with her friend, who was every bit as dear as a sister. No one to complain when she moved around in bed. No one who knew every little thing about her. Just like it had been at the Chatsworths. She shuddered. Pearl meant everything to her. With her married and gone, Amanda would no longer have someone at the ready to hear about every moment of her day and give her advice and consolation.

"I will miss you," she whispered.

"Me, too. Now go to sleep." Pearl's muffled tones came from beneath the pillow that she'd jammed over her head.

"I'm sure Roland will want to talk at night, too."

Pearl rolled over and emerged from beneath the pillow. "What's bothering you?"

"Nothing."

"Then why are you pestering me?"

"I can't sleep after what happened today."

"Oh?" Now she'd caught Pearl's attention. "What happened today?"

Amanda hedged, not quite ready to explain everything. "Did you know that Garrett has a lovely smile?"

"Hmm. I suppose so."

"He should smile more often."

"Why don't you tell him, and let me get some sleep?" Pearl plunked the pillow over her head again.

Amanda quieted, but she couldn't imagine going up to Garrett and telling him to smile more. Just mentioning the smile had turned it to a frown, as if that smile had been in error. "He doesn't want to hear it."

Pearl said nothing.

Amanda glanced in her direction, but in the darkness couldn't tell if her friend was sleeping. Her thoughts drifted back to the hours with Garrett. He'd been kind today, so different from the day before.

"I made a mess of supper tonight," she whispered. "I burned it terribly and then added too much salt. It tasted awful, but he didn't yell, like he did yesterday. He told me he'd done the very same thing."

"He did?" Pearl slid out from under the pillow, definitely more interested.

"He did. Like all was forgiven. He's never been like that with me before. Oh, he liked to talk about Sadie and Isaac, ask about school and all that, but never take my feelings into consideration. It was almost like he wouldn't look at me. Not today." Amanda sighed. "Did you ever notice that his eyes are more gray than blue?"

"What does that have to do with anything? Roland's eyes are blue, too. They're brothers."

"Yes, but Garrett's eyes are grayer. And his hair is much lighter, with that bit of red in it. He and Roland don't look much alike."

Pearl groaned. "This is what's keeping you awake?"

Amanda ignored her friend. "And his hair has this way of sticking out like a little boy's. It takes all my self-control not to smooth down the cowlicks."

"I can imagine how he would react if you did that."

"Definitely not with a smile." Amanda giggled. "I think this new job will turn out well, as long as I don't let the children distract me too much."

"Then it's hopeless."

"Hopeless?"

"I've never known you *not* to be distracted by children."

Amanda heaved a sigh. "It's a fault of mine."

Pearl squeezed her shoulder. "It's a testament to your caring nature. I'm glad Garrett finally noticed that. Maybe he's finally coming around to see the treasure you are. Fiona will regret turning down the position."

"Does she still have her cap set on Garrett?"

"You can be sure of it. She asked if she could help with the stable that I asked Garrett to build for the children's nativity play."

"The what?"

"Garrett didn't tell you about it?"

"No," Amanda said hesitantly. "Was he supposed to?"

"I asked Roland to make sure Garrett talked to you so you two could figure out what needed to be done."

At first Amanda wondered why Pearl didn't just tell her herself, but the answer was obvious. Pearl was trying to get her and Garrett together as much as possible. But having her help build a stable made no sense. "Talk to me? Why? I can't use a hammer."

"No, but you can decorate the stable and make costumes for the children."

"Decorate it? I don't think the stable that Joseph and Mary used was decorated."

"I'm thinking more along the lines of toy animals. You know, the lambs and the sheep and so forth."

Amanda gasped. "That's a lot of fabric and a lot of something or other to stuff them."

"It's been so warm and dry of late that I'm thinking we could make a day of it and gather dried grasses. Maybe invite Roland, Garrett and the children. Roland already told me that he will donate some old flour sacks and muslin. It'll be wonderful."

Amanda wasn't so certain, but the idea of working anywhere near Garrett overcame her hesitation. Perhaps he was beginning to forgive her for losing track of Sadie during the fire. Perhaps he could begin to trust her. A Christmas nativity would be lovely, especially with the children involved.

"What are the children going to do?"

"Play the roles of the shepherds, angels and Mary and Joseph."

Amanda could guess who Pearl had pegged for the parents of Jesus, but she had to ask, anyway. "Who's playing Mary and Joseph?"

Pearl murmured, "Sadie and Isaac. It will help convince Garrett to build the stable. Now go to sleep. I have a busy day of school tomorrow, and I'm expecting you to help out."

Amanda couldn't begin to think of sleeping. Her mind whirled with everything that had happened today and would happen over the coming weeks. Pearl's wedding. Pearl moving to the rooms above the store. Amanda's new job. Garrett warming to her. So much joy.

The only thing missing was her brother. When she'd learned this autumn that a lumberjack named Jake was working upriver, she'd thought at once of her lost brother. The man fit Jacob's description. She'd waited day after day for this lumberjack to arrive in Singapore with the last logs rafted down the river, but he'd headed for the camps up north instead. That opportunity had slipped away.

Perhaps this one with Garrett wouldn't. Now they would work together on the nativity play.

No doubt Pearl and Roland had arranged this "project" in order to get Amanda and Garrett together. After today, that didn't seem like such a hopeless prospect. Garrett was beginning to treat her with compassion and respect, something she enjoyed but was having trouble accepting. If she did a great job with not only the curtains for his house but also the costumes for the nativity play, maybe he'd forget about Fiona and begin considering her for a wife. Maybe. Just maybe. As long as he never learned about her past.

Chapter Six

Saturdays gave Amanda more time to work on her sewing projects. For the last week, she'd cut and basted and sewed Pearl's wedding dress in every spare moment. By this afternoon, she switched to making Garrett's curtains, in case Pearl returned to the boardinghouse early.

Curtains should take no time at all, but the treadle sewing machine was finicky to operate. The bobbin kept snarling, and she would have to stop and take apart what she'd just done and start over. She'd run into the same problems when making the dress and doll dress for Sadie this past August, but it was still faster than sewing every seam by hand. For the trickier parts, she still preferred hand-stitching, but she kept the curtains simple.

"No ruffles or lace," Garrett had said.

So that's what she did. She would not risk the progress she'd made with him over something as unimportant as curtains. Though he hadn't smiled at her again the rest of the week, he had been most cordial. Her supper offerings had improved, thanks to Mrs. Calloway's coaching, and he had complimented Amanda on them.

She dearly hoped these curtains would continue to elevate her in his esteem.

With Sadie's prompting, Amanda had chosen a service-able muslin fabric in a pretty yellow color with tiny flow-ers. The fact that Sadie picked it out would go a long way toward winning Garrett's approval if he thought the color or pattern too dainty. It would also brighten the rooms, which were terribly dark, between the ponderous walnut furniture and the unpainted walls. It was a leased cottage, she had to remind herself, nothing like the Chatsworths' home or even the three-story orphanage.

"A tablecloth would help brighten things, too," she said aloud to no one but herself. If she cut the cloth precisely, she might have enough left over to make one.

"Brighten things where?"

The masculine voice made her pause the treadle and look up. Garrett stood in the entrance to the writing room where Mrs. Calloway housed the sewing machine. Amanda had not expected to see him this Saturday afternoon, since he had given her the day off until suppertime.

"You're not with the children?"

"They're spending the afternoon with Roland and Pearl," he pointed out. "What are you making?"

Amanda turned back to her sewing. "These are the cur-tains for your house."

She heard him step into the room until he stood just a few steps behind her. "They are bright."

"Sadie and I thought they looked like sunshine."

He didn't respond right away.

She glanced back.

He looked down at the hat in his hands. "I suppose you're right, but they're...bright."

"Cheerful. They make me smile, especially knowing how much Sadie liked the fabric."

As expected, that wore away the last of his resistance. "You really did ask Sadie to help you pick out the cloth."

"Of course. She has excellent taste, especially when it comes to color. You must have noticed that she's quite the little artist."

He didn't answer.

Again Amanda paused long enough to glance back. He was frowning. Why? "Do you disapprove of artists?"

"It's not very useful."

"Sometimes the most important things in life are not useful. Beauty lifts our spirits."

If anything, he looked more uncomfortable.

"A tablecloth would only get stained," he said gruffly.

"It could also teach the children to take care when eating." She didn't mention Garrett's tendency to shovel food in his mouth as fast as possible. She'd seen starving children do the same thing in the orphanage. Perhaps he'd had to battle Roland for enough to eat. "Were you poor when you were growing up?" The moment she said the words, she regretted them.

Garrett's complexion darkened, and she steeled herself for a rebuke.

Instead he denied it. "No. Not at all."

"I'm sorry. I didn't mean to pry."

He walked over to the window. Already the light was low. Soon darkness would settle over the land. "Forget it."

She searched for another subject. "You must have come here today for a reason."

He cleared his throat. "Roland and Pearl insisted I speak to you about the project they have for me. Us."

She had forgotten. "The stable?"

"I don't need help. I'll cut the sheep from wood."

"That would work, but they won't be very nice for the children to cuddle." When Pearl had first broached the idea, Amanda had imagined the children holding the lambs and perhaps even taking them home.

"Cuddle? I thought this was a depiction of the nativity."

Amanda bit her tongue. Garrett was right. This was a holy, solemn moment. "I'm sorry. I wasn't thinking. But how will we make them look like the animals? I don't know anyone with paints."

"I do." Fiona swept into the room. "The moment Garrett told me about the project I sent for my painting supplies. They should be on the next mail boat from Chicago."

"You paint pictures?" Amanda had to shut her gaping mouth.

Fiona smiled indulgently. "Singing is not my only talent. In the theater, one becomes accomplished in many arts."

Amanda wondered why she'd never mentioned this before, especially when watching Sadie, who loved to draw.

Fiona had turned her attention away from Amanda and lavished it on Garrett. "You look quite handsome tonight."

For the first time, Amanda noticed that Garrett was wearing his Sunday suit and good coat. He carried a felt bowler rather than the cap he wore when working in cold weather. His hair was combed into place, and he'd shaved.

He extended an arm to Fiona. "Shall we?"

"Of course," she purred, casting a triumphant glance at Amanda. "We wouldn't want to be late."

Amanda turned back to her sewing and pretended to work. Almost immediately the bobbin thread snarled. Still, she worked the treadle, making the knot worse and worse. Only when she was certain Garrett and Fiona had left did she stop. The mass of knotted thread would take forever to untangle, but not as long as her foolish hopes.

Garrett felt awful from the moment he stepped into the boardinghouse and Mrs. Calloway sent him to the writing room. The woman clearly thought he was there for

Amanda. The fact that she was working on curtains for his house only made things worse.

He should have explained that he'd agreed weeks ago to escort Fiona to her Saturday concert, when Sawyer Evans, her accompanist who usually walked her to the hotel, asked him for the favor. Sawyer had left this morning for Chicago to meet up with family ahead of the holidays.

"I don't trust anyone else," Sawyer had told him when Garrett hesitated.

The man must not have realized Fiona's ambitions toward Garrett, or he would never have asked the favor.

At the time, Garrett couldn't find a single reason to object, so he'd agreed. It wasn't that he felt anything for Fiona. True, they'd dined together on occasion at the hotel, but they were just good friends. At least that's what he told himself.

Fiona's actions revealed just how wrong he was. She'd made a point of besting Amanda over the animals for the nativity play. Maybe he should have agreed with Pearl's idea to make stuffed animals, but it had seemed like far too much work for Amanda, who was already helping at the school, working for him and making the costumes for the play. He'd wanted to ease her burden, but instead he'd paved the way for Fiona to triumph over Amanda.

The walk to the hotel dining room was uncomfortable. Fiona chattered on. He heard little of it, since he couldn't get the image of Amanda's disappointment out of his mind. She deserved better treatment. She at least deserved an explanation, but would she listen? He could kick himself for not warning her before Fiona swooped in.

"…and coffee, won't you, Garrett, dear?" Fiona asked.

Garrett caught only those last few words. Embarrassed, he stumbled over a reply. "Can't say. The children will want to go home."

"But Garrett, they are home. You told me yourself that you lived above the store for a year and a half. That must seem more like home than the new house."

Garrett thought back to the last few evenings. Isaac and Sadie seemed to have adjusted admirably, especially when Amanda was there. They hung on her every word, even if they didn't always obey.

"They like the new house."

"I'm sure they do, but a few minutes for a wee slice of pie and cup of coffee won't upset them too much. They are going to have supper with their uncle and soon-to-be aunt, aren't they?"

He nodded glumly. Pearl had insisted on that much. That meant no pleasant evening playing marbles or jack-straws with the children after supper. Amanda had suggested he participate in the activity, and yesterday he'd convinced her to join them. Amanda!

He halted. "I forgot to tell Amanda that she wouldn't need to cook." He looked back at the boardinghouse. "I should tell her. I'll run back after we reach the hotel."

Fiona pouted. Though the light was low, he could see that much. "You're not going to listen to my concert?"

"Of course I will. Once I return." A brilliant thought popped into his head, one that would put the perfect buffer between Fiona and him. "Hopefully, Amanda will join us."

"You want me to go where?" Amanda stopped working the treadle long enough to stare at Garrett. Surely he had not said what she thought he'd said.

"Join me at the concert. Miss O'Keefe is singing."

Fiona always sang at the Saturday concerts.

Amanda turned back to her sewing. "I don't know. There's so much to do."

"The curtains can wait."

She glanced at him again. He'd sounded like he was pleading. "But you escorted Fiona. What happened?" No small part of her hoped he'd say that they'd had an argument or that Fiona had switched her affections to a different man.

"Oh, that." His laugh sounded forced. "Sawyer Evans asked me to make sure she got safely to the hotel and back, since he wasn't going to be here."

That sounded reasonable, except for Garrett's formal attire and Fiona's obvious attempts to link herself to him. Perhaps they felt sorry for her, or maybe Fiona wanted to rub in her victory just a little more. Either way, Amanda did not care to become the butt of whatever was going on between the two of them.

"I believe I will continue working."

Garrett put a hand on the fabric, stopping her sewing. "Please join me. Join us."

"I don't care to be the third wheel on a cart."

"There is no relationship between Miss O'Keefe and myself. At least not the kind you're thinking."

He did sound and look sincere, but Amanda had been fooled by seeming sincerity before. Hadn't Hugh professed undying love? Hadn't he promised a lifetime together? She would not tread that path again.

"I am not dressed for the occasion." She glanced at the mantel clock. "The concert will soon begin."

"You're beautiful." The sucking in of his breath told her that he hadn't meant such a bald declaration. "That is, your gown is perfect. Quite acceptable."

"Not as beautiful as Fiona's."

"I'm not fond of bright colors."

She couldn't help taking a jab. "Are you talking about curtains or clothing?"

"Both, I suppose." Passion hid behind those words.

She averted her face. "The answer is still no."

"It will only be a short while, and then we can pick up the children at the store before heading back to the house."

She nibbled on her lip. "I do need to prepare their supper."

"No, you don't. That's what I should have told you earlier. Roland and Pearl are making supper for the children. We can eat at the hotel."

Her stomach churned. "Fiona will join us?"

"Perhaps. Perhaps not. But I do owe you a decent meal after neglecting to inform you of the change of plans."

Her resistance was slowly eroding. It would be lovely to dine with Garrett in front of everyone. Perhaps that would put to rest the niggling doubt that he and Fiona truly weren't courting. And then she and Garrett would fetch the children. Together. Like a couple. The enticement was almost enough. Almost. The hovering threat of Fiona could spoil everything.

Amanda drew in a deep breath. "Since Roland and Pearl are watching the children, you don't need me at all tonight."

He stiffened, and his hand came off the fabric. She straightened it into the sewing machine's feed.

He cleared his throat. "Actually, I do."

The ragged declaration shivered down her spine. He needed her.

"You do?" she whispered.

"Yes." His gaze did not flinch, even when she met it.

She wanted to believe him, truly she did, but to appear in public as if courting might spark speculation and gossip. It would certainly inflame the animosity between Fiona and herself.

"I—I shouldn't." But it would take only one more bit of persuasion to convince her.

Garrett supplied it. "I've changed my mind about the animals in the pageant. If you think you can make them, we will use stuffed animals."

"Oh! The children will be so pleased."

"You'll need all the time you can get, though. We could get the fabrics you need when we fetch Isaac and Sadie."

"We could." She dropped the curtain fabric and rose to her feet, the ideas swirling in her head. "Some sheep's wool or cotton will make them look even more like lambs. Oh, they'll be perfect, just perfect."

"Yes, they will."

Only then did she realize that she stood mere inches from Garrett. She drew in her breath sharply, suddenly aware of the scents of soap and freshly hewn timber that were uniquely Garrett's. She was several inches shorter than him, yet his lips were all too close. Her pulse raced. Would he?

She held her breath.

"Amanda!" Mrs. Calloway's voice pierced the moment.

Garrett backed away, his complexion red, and stared out the window. Amanda smoothed her skirts and attempted to regain her composure before Mrs. Calloway stormed into the room.

"Oh, there you are," the boardinghouse proprietress said as she entered. "We've all decided to attend the concert, so supper will be held until afterward." She looked from Garrett to Amanda and back again. Then a grin curved her lips. "You're welcome to join us, Mr. Garrett."

He bowed slightly, the dour expression back. "I thank you, but I have other plans, providing Miss Amanda will agree to join me for the evening."

Amanda felt her own cheeks blaze. "I should help you, Mrs. Calloway."

The woman waved off her concern. "Nonsense, there

are only the four of us, rather like family. Go and enjoy yourselves." She bustled from the room.

That left Amanda alone with Garrett. She touched her hair. It all seemed in place. "Let me get my hat and gloves from upstairs."

"Of course." Garrett smiled, sending warmth clear to her toes.

He'd chosen her. Over Fiona. Over everyone.

Chapter Seven

If not for Fiona's presence at the dining table and her obvious attempts to divert Garrett's attention from Amanda, the evening would have been perfect. Amanda took comfort and even delight in the fact that Garrett looked to her with a shrug whenever Fiona attempted to take charge of the conversation. It felt like they shared a secret pact to humor the redhead because they were sure of their own position with each other. That made Amanda's heart soar.

The concert was lovely, and she regretted missing so many simply to avoid her fiery competitor. She had heard Fiona sing in church services, but with the variety of songs and performers, the evening brought laughter and smiles to everyone. Amanda had never imagined there were that many musicians in Singapore.

"Your voice is so beautiful," she told Fiona. "I could listen to it all day."

The compliment smoothed the redhead's competitive edge. Fiona might not be a friend, but she no longer acted like an enemy. Amanda must remember that. Perhaps inviting Fiona to join them more often would end the hostilities. She and Pearl had too often excluded and avoided her.

"I like the banjo," Garrett said between bites of squash pie.

Amanda found that instrument a bit strident for her taste, but when mingled with the harmonica, violin and even the odd sounds made on a washboard, she found the whole effect oddly pleasing.

"I wish I could play an instrument," she sighed.

"I play piano," Fiona stated. "Every child should learn."

Amanda couldn't forget the disastrous attempts Fiona had made to teach Sadie to sing. Piano would fare no better if the children were not interested, and she had seen no interest in music from either child.

"I used to play harmonica," Garrett said.

"You did?" Amanda could not hide her surprise. "I had no idea."

He shook his head. "I haven't played in years."

"Perhaps it's time to start again." Fiona leaned a bit closer to him. "I could accompany you on the piano."

Playing music with Garrett would create a bond that Amanda could never share. "I wish I could play."

Garrett smiled at her. "Maybe I'll teach you harmonica one day."

Again her heart soared.

"I have to warn you," he added, "that I'm not very good."

"Your playing would sound wonderful to me."

"You're being too modest," Fiona interjected. She actually slid her chair a bit closer to Garrett. "You could teach me, too."

He did not lean away. In fact, he listened intently to her ideas.

Amanda swallowed an unconscionable wave of envy. What right had she to be envious of Garrett's choices? He could choose whomever he wished. She was, after all, only his housekeeper, a fact that she'd best remember. Hugh's attentions had led her to think she might rise above her station. His cruel actions and subsequent dismissal put her squarely in her place. Better to lavish her attention on the children, who could not hurt her.

"I love to learn new things," Fiona was saying, her hand now resting on Garrett's arm.

He had turned dark red, tugging at the collar of his shirt and looking like a cornered rabbit. He obviously hated all this attention.

"Perhaps we should get back to the children," Amanda suggested.

Though Garrett cast her a grateful look, Fiona pressed on. "I'm sure they're having a fabulous time with their uncle. Shall we set a time to begin lessons?"

This time Garrett didn't meet Fiona's eye. "I'm too busy right now to give lessons. The new ship. The nativity play. And spending time with my son and daughter."

"Of course." Fiona smiled. "As you should. We can talk again after Christmas."

That seemed to resolve the situation, at least as far as Garrett was concerned, but Amanda could not shake the idea that Fiona was acting just like Lena. Amanda's foster sister hadn't shown the slightest interest in Hugh Bellchamp until he began paying attention to Amanda. Then he suddenly became the prize in Lena's eyes. She would appear at the most inopportune times and drag Hugh away on the most ridiculous pretenses.

Amanda should have paid attention to what was happening, but she'd told herself that Lena was only jealous and it would pass. It hadn't. The day after that horrible night that changed her forever, Hugh had publicly declared his affection for Lena, completing her triumph over Amanda. Even so, Lena began complaining that Amanda was trying to steal her beau's affections.

Was Fiona the same type of woman? Or should Amanda extend the benefit of the doubt?

Fiona was smiling at Garrett, who stared straight ahead as if the empty stage was the most fascinating thing he'd ever seen.

"We will spend a lot of time together making the animals for the pageant," Fiona said.

Amanda glanced at Garrett. He must not have told Fiona that plans had changed. When he said nothing in response, she began to wonder if they had at all. Or had Garrett merely promised she could make stuffed animals to get her to come to the concert with him? A flicker of anger grew. Hugh had used her for his own purposes. Was Garrett the same?

She rose. "I must return home."

Garrett snapped out of that stoic trance. "I'll escort you."

"But you're escorting me," Fiona protested.

"We can all walk back to the boardinghouse together." Garrett sounded apologetic, and he didn't say one word about the change in plans.

The flicker of anger grew to a flame. "You did say we could have Roland show us fabrics for the play."

Fiona looked from her to Garrett. "Fabrics? Oh, for the costumes." Her smile grated on Amanda. "You're the perfect person to make them. In your hands, they will look wonderful."

Amanda waited for Garrett to explain the real reason they needed to look at fabric. He tugged at his collar again and made a show of donning his coat, but he didn't say one word about the change in plans.

She could not bear it any longer. This time she would not wait until she was humiliated before questioning a man's intentions. She blazed ahead.

"We need to pick out material for the animals."

* * *

Garrett cringed. What was wrong with Amanda? She must know how this would upset Fiona. He'd planned to gently break the news to the redhead, offering her a substitute role in order to keep the peace. He sure didn't want all-out war. Judging from Fiona's high color, that's exactly what was about to happen.

"You don't need fabric for the animals," Fiona said slowly, each word nailed down with the effort to control her temper. "I'm painting them."

Instead of replying, Amanda turned her focus on him. That drew Fiona's ire his way also.

"What is she saying, Garrett?" the redhead asked.

He couldn't help but notice that the remaining patrons in the dining room were listening to every word the trio uttered. Since they were standing in the middle of the room, appearing ready to leave, this argument would provide endless fodder for gossip.

"Let's discuss this on the walk home." He motioned for the ladies to precede him to the door, while he paid the amount due to Mrs. VanderLeuven.

Neither lady budged.

He extended an arm toward Amanda, who instead of accepting it crossed her own arms and glared at him. When he turned to Fiona, she snatched his elbow.

"Tell her that she's mistaken," Fiona said as they swept out of the hotel.

Garrett waited for Amanda to step onto the wooden porch before closing the door behind them. For an establishment with such an elegant name, Astor House, it could at least refresh the paint on the front door. Instead, it was chipped and peeling, just like the whitewash on the porch railings.

"I'm waiting," Fiona stated once they'd descended the few steps. "You promised I could paint the stable animals for the pageant."

He searched for another duty for her. "You will be singing."

"Of course I will. That has nothing to do with helping you create the setting for the show."

Garrett had to bite his tongue at that last word. He didn't consider reenacting the story of Jesus's birth as a "show." There was something sacred about it, reverent, even though children would be playing the roles.

"The setting," Amanda cried. "Of course. Wouldn't it be wonderful to show the whole setting? Fiona, do you think you would be able to paint a starry night sky with the star of Bethlehem over the stable?"

"Of course, but it's so simple," the redhead replied.

Garrett just wished they would move away from the front of the hotel. The dining room guests were now filing out, their steps slower than normal as they no doubt listened in on the conversation.

He took each woman by the elbow. "Perhaps we should discuss the particulars with Pearl. She is in charge."

Though the women came with him on the boardwalk, they didn't stop their discussion.

"You could add the sort of trees and plants that grow in the area," Amanda suggested.

"Palms and tall grasses, like the ones where Pharaoh's daughter found the baby Moses."

Garrett didn't point out that those were rushes. Tall grasses on land looked pretty much the same as tall grasses in the water.

Amanda continued, oblivious to his discomfort. "And I will need the animals' features painted onto the cloth. Their noses and eyes and so forth."

"Of course! Otherwise no one will know what sort of animal they are."

By the time they reached the boardinghouse, the war had been averted. Fiona retired with a promise to sketch out her ideas for a backdrop.

That left Garrett alone with Amanda.

He scrubbed his chin, deeply aware of how she had calmed a volatile situation. "That, uh, ended up better than expected, thanks to some quick thinking on your part."

Instead of accepting the compliment like any man would, she turned on him. "How dare you." The words were thick with tears.

Garrett stepped back, surprised. "You're upset."

"Yes, I'm upset. Anyone would be. How can you promise me one thing and promise Fiona another?"

Garrett tried to make sense of this sudden fury. What had he promised? "I, uh, don't understand."

"Don't understand? Haven't you any sense at all? You cannot promise two different things to two different women."

"What did I promise?"

That just threw kerosene on the fire.

"You don't even know?" Her indignation could have scorched the paint off the boardinghouse porch. "How can you stand there and say you don't know what you've done?" Amanda shook her head. "What were you thinking?"

He had no idea.

Thankfully, the light was too low to see the expression on her face. No doubt tears streamed down. Eva had always shed tears when she accused him of some wrong or other. He would capitulate to her demands, the tears would stop and she would curl in his arms, professing undying love. Amanda Porter wasn't likely to do more than make demands. He steeled himself.

"Men," she huffed. "It's a good thing Pearl is in charge of the nativity play. She'll make sure everything turns out all right."

He couldn't deny that, and since Amanda was calming down, he figured it was time to put an end to the evening.

"I'll just build the stable." He cleared his throat. "Thank you for joining me tonight. I enjoyed it."

He heard her draw in her breath sharply. What had he done wrong now? Naturally, she didn't tell him.

After an awkward, silent pause, he said, "I should fetch Isaac and Sadie."

"Of course." Though her words said she understood, her tone did not. "They would be too tired by now to do anything but go to bed."

"Um. Right." He had no idea what she was getting at, but she clearly wasn't pleased. Why couldn't women speak their minds? He'd struggled with Eva, and he had no inclination to struggle with another woman, whether she was pleasant to look at or not. "Good night, then."

He backed away, hands in the pockets of his coat.

She stood absolutely still. Only when he turned did he hear a faint goodbye.

Garrett had forgotten. Either that or he'd never wanted to look at cloth with her. Amanda blinked back tears as he disappeared into the night. Garrett Decker changed as often as the wind. First escorting Fiona to the concert and then returning to ask her to attend. Then that whole bit with the nativity play animals. She'd smoothed it over as best she could with Fiona, but damage had been done. Through it all Garrett did not support her.

He should have told Fiona that he'd changed his mind.

He should have said something.

Amanda had been left to flounder in the wake of Fiona's indignation. If she were Fiona, she would be angry, too, but his silence had hurt her more.

It reminded her of the days in the orphanage. Some of the boys or girls would gang up on the weaker or smaller children. Since Amanda was delicate and was given the prettiest gowns, she'd often ended up the brunt of their attacks. Pearl stuck up for her. Pearl would chase those bullies back to their beds and often get punished for it. Miss Hornswoggle was oblivious to the trouble those dresses caused.

Oblivious. That's how Garrett looked during the argument, as if he had no idea that he'd wronged both of them.

Amanda heaved a sigh. She would rather believe him ignorant or forgetful than cruel and manipulative like Hugh.

"So he left you, too." Fiona's statement cut through the icy night air.

Amanda turned to see the redhead on the porch. "I didn't hear you come outside."

"When you didn't come in, I had to see if you'd left with him."

Amanda looked away. She'd planned to do just that, fetching the children with him and picking out cloth for the pageant animals.

"I work for him."

Fiona's mouth twitched. "Of course."

"There's nothing more between us than that." Yet her blazing cheeks betrayed her—if they were visible in the dim light.

"Naturally."

"We should go inside before we catch a chill from the cold."

Fiona opened the door and held it for her. Amanda scooted inside and unbuttoned her coat.

Fiona touched her lightly on the shoulder. "It's not your fault, honey. Some men don't know how to treat a woman."

Memories of Hugh rose to the surface. Was Garrett really like him? He looked so devout at Sunday services. He read the Bible to the children after supper. His help in the kitchen had seemed so artless and filled with genuine caring. Until tonight, he had appeared to be the very opposite of Hugh. Surely that had not changed.

"He's a kind man," she said.

"He's a man who needs a strong woman for a wife." Fiona's statement left no doubt that she didn't consider Amanda strong enough for the task.

"He needs compassion."

"Naturally." Fiona draped her cloak on one of the pegs. Its fur collar looked so warm and soft that Amanda longed to touch it. Perhaps she could find something like that for some of the animals.

"I'm sorry he didn't tell you about the change in plans for the nativity play."

Fiona shrugged. "My talents will be put to better use on the backdrop." She headed down the hallway, but then paused and turned back. "Thank you for thinking of that."

Amanda nodded. The truce had been drawn and signed. Unfortunately, that left her no closer to Garrett than before the evening began.

Chapter Eight

The keel was the singularly most important part of the ship. The ribs of the hull, the sheathing, stem, transom—really, every single bit of the vessel—relied on it. A weak or misshapen keel could doom a ship and its crew.

Garrett tackled the project with the serious attention it required. Men's lives and livelihoods depended on his work at this critical stage. While his men readied the building berth and launch ways, he sought the finest straight-grained timber for the keel. It had to have the correct strength and give. A fir or pine would work best, but he didn't have one in the warehouse that was long enough.

So he sent word upriver to the mills and camp foremen to keep an eye out for the right timber and send it downriver. If they sent a log, he'd have to fashion it and let the wood season until it was the correct dryness, delaying shipbuilding as much as a year. If a seasoned beam arrived by barge, they could begin at once, and Stockton would have his schooner much sooner.

In the meantime, Garrett and Sawyer Evans, who had returned from Chicago that morning, selected oak and chestnut for framing and good clear white pine for the planking.

Garrett mopped the sweat off his brow. Though it was cool in the warehouse, the month had remained abnormally warm.

"Think that's enough?" Sawyer asked as he stretched his back after hefting a stack of pine to the area Garrett had set aside for shipbuilding materials.

"Maybe, but I'd rather have too much. Let's check that pile over there." He arched his aching back also. "In a minute." Again he mopped his brow.

Sawyer eyed the window. "No snow yet."

"Nope. Warm December. Reminds me of spring."

Spring reminded Garrett of death. Eva's death. While others reveled in the first signs of plants and flowers, he remembered the icy river and his wife slipping beneath the surface.

"This boat will not sink." Perhaps he'd said that too forcefully, for Sawyer gave him a funny look.

The truth was that most boats foundered at one time or another, but an alert captain could beach her and save the crew. Garrett shuddered.

"Cold?" Sawyer asked.

"No." Garrett decided to turn the conversation. "Next time you need someone to escort Fiona O'Keefe anywhere, ask my brother."

Sawyer roared. "She's a handful. I pity the man that takes her on."

"You're not interested?" Garrett had assumed they were courting, or at least considering it.

"Look at me. I'm a lumberman. They don't call me Sawyer for nothing. A rough man like me got no business around a cultured woman like her."

"But you spend so much time together."

"She lets me play piano and fiddle for her, and I make sure none of the others get their hands on her. That's all."

Garrett couldn't let it rest at that. "You share a love of music. That means a lot."

"I ain't got enough coin in my pockets, boss."

"Maybe this ship'll put it there."

"Only if I'm a captain and a boss like you."

"I'm no captain," Garrett protested. "I'm not even a sailor." He had set foot on a ship only once, when he came to Singapore. He'd been sick the whole trip and didn't plan to ever travel in one again. Ironic, considering he'd built ships back in Chicago and was now building a schooner. Other men could sail them. "Definitely not a captain."

"You're still in charge."

Again Garrett's gaze drifted to the window. This time he spotted Amanda and Pearl walking toward the store, with his children running ahead.

His gut clenched out of habit. Eva had spent everything he earned and then some. Though Amanda didn't appear to be a spendthrift, she had purchased a pantryful of supplies without his authorization. Coupled with Pearl, she might do anything.

He eyed the stacks of lumber and came to a quick decision. "Sawyer, you're in charge. Get one of the men to help you move all the white pine into a pile over there. I'll be right back."

Instead of hurrying off, Sawyer grinned.

"What's holding you back?" Garrett barked. "Didn't you hear my orders?"

"I heard." Sawyer nodded toward the window. "Trouble with the missus?"

Garrett stiffened. He meant Amanda. Was that what everyone in town thought? "I'm not married, and you know it." He jabbed a finger into Sawyer's chest. "I hired Miss Porter to take care of the children when I'm at work. That's all. Understand?"

Sawyer backed away, clearly remorseful. "Sorry. I didn't mean anything by it. That's just what I heard people say."

"People? What people?" Garrett retracted his hand. "Never mind. I don't want to know. Just tell them the truth—that she is hired help. Period."

"Yes, sir. Yes, boss." Sawyer scooted away to direct the men.

Garrett couldn't help replaying the conversation on his walk to the mercantile. Someone was spreading rumors about Amanda and him. His first instinct was to blame Fiona. After all, she and Sawyer practiced their music nearly every evening. But Garrett couldn't bring himself to blame a woman, especially when she and Amanda had appeared to mend their differences. More likely some of the men were speculating.

He blew out his breath and pulled his coat tighter. Regardless of the source, the fact was that Amanda's reputation could suffer. Yet he needed a housekeeper and someone to watch the children. And she was so good with Isaac and Sadie. He couldn't fire her when she'd done nothing wrong. He would have to watch his step and maintain the strictest propriety.

"This cotton will do admirably," Amanda said as she plucked at the fluffy fibers. "I don't suppose you have any scraps of fur."

"Fur?" Pearl and Roland asked at the same time.

Pearl's lifted eyebrows warned her that there was no way they could afford to add fur to any of the stuffed animals. "We gathered plenty of dried grass yesterday to fill the animals."

"Not for the stuffing. A little bit of fur would feel so soft against a child's cheek."

"Then you're looking for enough to cover a cow or donkey." Roland grinned.

"I'm not. And you know it."

"Oh," Pearl exclaimed, "you meant for one of the robes. A little bit would do."

"Well, no." Except Amanda wasn't sure where she would use it. She'd just envisioned the children hugging the animals. The soft cotton and some fur would make them even more touchable. "Forget I said anything."

Pearl and Roland looked at each other, and then Roland headed for the back storeroom. Amanda caught her breath at their silent communication. She certainly didn't have that with Garrett. She didn't share that with anyone.

"Are you sure you can find anything in that mess?" Pearl called out after her fiancé.

He cast her a grin before disappearing into the back. "Faster than you could."

A faint memory poked at Amanda, of her brother teasing her when she was very little. The way Pearl and Roland had just teased each other. Dear Jacob. How she missed him. She didn't even know for certain if he was alive. After he ran away from Uncle Griffin's farm in Missouri, he was never seen again. Tears rose to her eyes.

"Oh, dear," Pearl said. "I didn't intend to make you cry. I was talking to Roland."

"I know. That's not what brought the tears. The way you and Roland tease each other reminded me of how my brother used to tease me."

Pearl glanced at Roland, who had just returned, before speaking to Amanda. "I'm sorry that the lumberjack you thought might be Jacob didn't return to town."

Amanda's spirits dropped. "Me, too."

Now that this man had left the area, she might never know if he was her Jacob.

"Perhaps this will cheer you up." Roland laid a beautiful rabbit pelt on the counter. "No one wanted to buy it because it's too torn up by shot to be worth much." He flipped over the pelt to show her the tears and holes. "If you can use it for a costume, it's yours."

Amanda ran a hand over the soft fur. How could one brother be so generous while the other frustrated her? "Are you sure?"

"Absolutely. I've had that on my shelves for years."

Ideas flitted through Amanda's head. "I could trim one of the magi's robe, but I didn't think we were going to include their visit, since it happened so much later."

"I wasn't," Pearl admitted, "but we could add it."

Amanda shook her head. "It would be nice on one of the animals."

"A very small animal," Roland said. "I'm not sure there's enough to even make a rabbit, and a rat doesn't set the right tone."

Pearl swatted him, and Amanda's heart ached for that kind of relationship. Why couldn't a good and decent man truly love her? Were her flaws that obvious? She bit her lip to stem more tears.

"I don't know why Garrett didn't tell us about the change in plans," Pearl said. "We all assumed the animals would be cut from wood."

"Because I forgot." Garrett strode into the store from the back. "If you three are here, where are Isaac and Sadie?"

Amanda jumped, terror knifing through her. The water. The slippery docks. Anything might happen if the children had sneaked outside while the adults were busy. "They were looking at the toys."

Yet they'd been awfully quiet, come to think of it.

She hurried over to the shelves, to find the area empty.

"Oh, dear. Oh, dear." Now Garrett truly would dismiss her. "Where could they be?"

Pearl grabbed her hand. "You and I are going to search upstairs. Garrett, you check outside. Roland, comb the store."

Amanda gladly followed Pearl, but her heart was beating so hard she had to struggle to climb the steps.

Pearl hugged her. "It'll be all right. You must believe that God is watching over them."

Amanda wanted to believe, but God hadn't watched over her parents when the train crashed. He hadn't kept Jacob and her together. He had separated her from Pearl by sending Amanda to the Chatsworths, and hadn't protected her from Hugh. He hadn't spared Isaac and Sadie's mother. How could she believe in God's goodness and protection when all that had happened?

The inside staircase led directly to the dining table where Amanda and Pearl had eaten when they first arrived in Singapore.

Pearl halted when she opened the door. "Isaac Decker. Sadie Decker. You scared us half to death."

Amanda squeezed past Pearl to see the two children sitting at the table as if it was any ordinary day. Sadie's eyes were round, while Isaac stared down at the pile of jackstraws in front of him.

"I'm sorry, Miss Lawson." Sadie slipped down from the chair and ran not to Pearl but to Amanda. She threw her thin arms around Amanda's waist, and Amanda couldn't help but hug her. Seconds later, the sobs began.

"Hush, now," Amanda whispered as she smoothed Sadie's dark hair. "Just tell us where you're going next time."

"I told Isaac we shoulda said something," Sadie sobbed.

Isaac had folded his arms, a scowl digging into his brow.

Pearl addressed him. "You're older and know better. Why didn't you say something to one of us?"

"You don't care," he cried in a voice filled with little-boy hurt. "No one cares what I do."

"That's not true," Pearl said. "We all do."

"Not my pa."

Amanda's heart broke. That little boy needed so much love. Though Garrett gave him some attention, it wasn't enough.

"He's searching all over for you," Pearl pointed out.

"Not here." Isaac's tough expression began to crack, and his lip quivered ever so slightly.

"That's because I asked him to search outside," Pearl said.

It all made sense to adults, but not to little boys.

"He should have known I'd bring Sadie here. I was taking care of her. I'm in charge."

Amanda left the little girl after drying her tears, and knelt beside Isaac. "You were very smart to bring your sister somewhere safe. Just tell an adult next time, all right? We don't always see everything that happens." Such as when Sadie slipped out of the schoolhouse during the fire last month. Amanda would never forgive herself for that.

Pearl indicated she was going to pass on the news to Garrett that the children had been found, and headed down the staircase. Isaac watched her leave, still with that scowl furrowing his eight-year-old brow.

Now alone with his sister and Amanda, he gave one last complaint. "You're too busy to pay attention to us."

Amanda caught her breath. Had she been too concerned with costumes and curtains and winning Garrett's respect to notice what was happening with Isaac and Sadie?

Amanda put an arm around each child. "You're right,

Isaac. I haven't paid attention to the right things. I promise that both of you will come first from now on."

"No more silly play?" Isaac asked hopefully.

"You don't want to be part of portraying the Christmas story? It's the most important story ever told. It could change people's hearts."

"Will it make Papa get us a new mama?" Sadie asked.

Now Amanda's eyes were brimming. "I don't know, dear one." She hugged them both close. "I don't know, but if anyone can do that, Jesus can."

As she kissed the children and held them tight, she knew exactly where in the nativity play that soft rabbit pelt belonged.

Once again Amanda Porter had lost track of his children. Garrett stormed up the stairs, determined to tell her that she was dismissed. Then he opened the door to find his two children clinging to her as she knelt on the floor.

"Papa! Papa!" Sadie cried out, running to him.

He scooped up the little girl. Isaac immediately pulled away from Amanda and stiffened, his expression taut, as if he was struggling to look like he hadn't been upset enough to need a hug a moment ago. Garrett's little boy was growing up.

Amanda stood and touched Isaac lightly on his head. Seeing her comforting his children only made Garrett realize how much they were gravitating toward her and away from him. But what could he do? He had to spend all those hours at work in order to provide for them. Until Amanda Porter arrived in Singapore, they'd understood, but lately Isaac fought everything Garrett asked the boy to do.

"What were you thinking, running off like that?" he demanded.

Amanda flinched. She was too soft-hearted. A child

needed to know when he'd done something wrong so he didn't repeat the mistake and cause injury to himself or others.

Isaac scowled. "I didn't do anything wrong."

"You left without telling any adults where you were going."

Isaac's little jaw stuck out. "I brought Sadie someplace safe."

"Yes, you did," Amanda said, again placing her hand on the boy. "Remember what we talked about. Next time you'll do better."

Garrett tensed. She was undermining his authority. If he didn't regain control, his children would have no respect for his rules and would end up injured—or worse. Garrett's chest tightened at the thought of losing either one of them.

He held his emotions in check. Barely. "Miss Porter is going to go home now. Say good-night to her."

Amanda looked surprised, but made no protest. She hugged Isaac, who squirmed out of her grasp, and accepted Sadie's open arms, giving her a kiss.

"Good night, Garrett." Her violet eyes lifted to him, and he was struck again by their resemblance to Eva's eye color. "Perhaps we can talk tomorrow about the play."

He didn't want to talk about the nativity play or anything else with her. He needed time to think things through. The speculation pairing them in courtship, coupled with yet another of her inattentive moments, pointed to a single conclusion, but he knew better than to make a decision in the heat of the moment. By morning he would know if he must dismiss Amanda.

Chapter Nine

"I finished the curtains last night," Amanda said to Pearl as they dressed the following morning. "After I get back from Garrett's house tonight, I'll start on the costumes." She ran a hand over the soft rabbit fur. "I had an idea for the fur."

"Oh?" Pearl braided her hair in a single long plait, which she would then coil on top of her head.

"Wouldn't it make a beautiful blanket for the baby Jesus?"

"I thought he was swaddled."

Amanda waited until Pearl finished pinning the coils atop her head. "But we won't have a real baby, only Beth Wardman's doll, and I thought the story might mean more to the children if we make the setting look more like right here."

Pearl's hands dropped. "That's a brilliant idea."

Amanda could practically see Pearl's thoughts whirling as she paced around the small room.

"Instead of palm trees, we could use branches or saplings." Pearl's words sped up with every statement. "Maybe some of that cotton could be snow. The stable could look like one of our stables, not something we imagine was in

Bethlehem at the time. I think you're right. That could make a big impact on people."

"Then you don't need costumes?"

Pearl stared off into space a moment before coming to a quick decision. "We'll keep the robes. The children are looking forward to dressing up. But the setting can be like here. Maybe an animal or two like those around here."

"A seagull?"

Pearl laughed. "I was thinking more of a squirrel and a bunny."

"Then you don't want me to save the rabbit pelt for the baby Jesus?"

Pearl's eyes twinkled. "Why don't you ask Garrett's opinion? Sadie will be the one holding him, after all."

"I was going to ask him yesterday, but he told me to go home."

"Not that bluntly, I hope."

Amanda bowed her head. The look on his face had troubled her until late into the night. The morning's snowfall had only echoed those icy thoughts. "He wasn't happy. He could barely contain his anger." Her hand trembled. "I failed again."

"You did nothing of the sort, and if Garrett sees it that way, then he does not deserve you."

That was easy for Pearl to say. She had found the man of her dreams in Roland. He doted on her and listened to every word she said. Garrett wouldn't even let Amanda speak. Perhaps it wasn't just her losing track of the children. Maybe it had begun with that disastrous evening at the concert. Garrett hadn't said much to her on Sunday after services. The children had chattered away, but he'd stood behind them looking out the window of the church.

"I'm afraid he's going to dismiss me," she whispered.

"What would he do then? There's not another soul in

Singapore who can take care of those children and clean the house."

"There's Fiona," Amanda pointed out.

"Who already refused the job."

"Who might have reconsidered by now."

Even Pearl must see it. Amanda's days in Garrett's employment were numbered.

"Then you have to fight," Pearl stated emphatically. "Make Garrett see that no one else can do the job the way you can."

"But how?" With dread holding her in its icy grip, she couldn't think, least of all imagine something so wonderful that Garrett would change his mind.

Pearl glanced at the small watch Roland had given her, before pinning it to her dress. "We have time to come up with a plan." She crossed the room and looked out the frosty window. Her eyes twinkled. "I have an idea."

Garrett paced the length of the room, waiting for Amanda to arrive after school. Leaving work early had stung, but he'd make it up tomorrow. This was too important to leave until suppertime. So he'd left Sawyer in charge and headed home when school ended. Soon Amanda would appear, and he'd have to give her the news. The children wouldn't like it, especially if she broke down in tears.

He would send Isaac and Sadie outside for a few minutes. Once Amanda left, he'd tell them his new plan.

Roland had not been pleased but had finally agreed.

First, he'd scolded Garrett like a mother hen. "You'll never find anyone who loves those children more."

"Except you and me."

"I can watch them for now," Roland had pointed out, "but that's not a lasting solution."

"I'll get someone from Saugatuck if I have to. Mrs.

Wardman is capable *and* respected." He couldn't help thinking of the rumors pairing him with Amanda. "It's better for everyone if a married woman takes the job."

"How?"

"I'm protecting Miss Porter's reputation."

"By being bullheaded? Any lout who spreads gossip has to answer to me. And to you." Roland pointed at him. "You would defend her, wouldn't you?"

Two days ago, Garrett would have, but the events of yesterday had changed everything.

"She lost track of Sadie and Isaac. For the second time. Make that the third time. She left them alone the very first day. If she truly loved them, she would never leave their side."

Roland had grunted in disgust. "You're forgetting that Amanda wasn't the only adult there. I didn't notice them leave and neither did Pearl, yet you're not blaming either one of us."

"You weren't in charge of them."

"In a manner of speaking, we were. Sadie and Isaac were in my store. That makes me responsible. So if I lost track of them then, what's to say I wouldn't lose track of them again?"

"You wouldn't."

Roland had refused to back down, and Garrett had stormed off rather than continue the argument. His brother had a way of confusing things. When Garrett was alone, he could think more clearly.

Now, he was alone, and the decision was clear. Amanda Porter could not be entrusted with his children.

Something hit the window, making Garrett jump. He glanced toward the open yellow curtains—Amanda's curtains—and saw only snow plastered against the window. That was peculiar. The sun had been shining when he walked home. The weather must have picked up all of a sudden.

Then another clump of snow hit the window, followed by giggling and laughter. Someone was throwing snow at his windows. Who had the nerve? Garrett flung open the door, ready to box the ears of the troublemakers, only to find his two children hopping around and laughing.

"Not the window," Amanda said, as she bent over to scoop up a handful of snow in her woolen mittens, "the door."

She tossed the snowball. It struck him on the shoulder and sprayed all over his face.

He heard her gasp as he wiped the melting snow from his eyes.

"Oh, Garrett. Mr. Decker. I'm so sorry. I didn't know you were inside the house. I didn't see the door open. Oh, dear." She attempted to brush the snow off his flannel shirt. "I never would have thrown it if I'd seen you."

He shrugged off her attentions and was about to rebuke her, but her frantic pleas were drowned out by his children's squeals of laughter. First Sadie and then Isaac ran up to him, their faces red from the cold air and the excitement.

"Papa. Papa. Miss Mana says…" They talked over each other in their rush to tell him something.

He hadn't seen them this excited since before Eva died. Even Cocoa the kitten's arrival hadn't generated this much enthusiasm.

Bits and pieces of their excited chatter dropped into his consciousness: afternoon, dunes, sled, together. *What?*

"Whoa now," he said, attempting to hold his son in place, "slow down. One of you tell me what's going on."

Naturally, the children began to speak at the same time again. Isaac was louder, but Sadie tugged on his shirt with surprising strength.

"One at a time," Amanda said, bringing the chatter to a stop. "Isaac, why don't you tell your father our plan?"

Plan? Garrett didn't like the sound of that.

Isaac stood straight and proper, as if addressing the classroom, but his eyes danced with excitement. "Miss Porter suggested we go sledding this afternoon, since the snow from last night is still on the ground."

"I'm sorry, son, but we don't own a sled," Garrett pointed out.

Isaac had an answer. "Roger Bailey said they take their mama's skillet up to the top of the dunes and slide down all the time. Can we, Papa?"

"We only have one skillet," Garrett stated.

Amanda's eyes sparkled. "If everyone will wait right here one moment, I have a surprise."

She hurried off with a lilt in her step. If Garrett wasn't mistaken, she was just as excited as the children. Funny. He'd never figured Amanda Porter as someone who would want to ride downhill in a skillet. She seemed delicate and fancy, like Eva. His late wife would never have done such an undignified thing.

"Did you go sledding when you were little, Papa?" Sadie asked.

"I did." Garrett stomped his feet. He hadn't worn his coat or hat when he stepped outside. Though the late afternoon sun had a little warmth to it, he was cold.

"In a skillet?" asked Isaac.

"On a sled."

"A real sled?" Isaac's eyes were wide. "Did you go fast?"

"The fastest in the neighborhood."

"Faster than Uncle Roland?"

"Much faster. Let me fetch my coat and hat." Garrett

opened the door and reached inside for the garments. Before he'd shut the door again, his son cried out.

"Wow!"

Garrett followed the direction of the boy's rapt gaze and saw Amanda pulling a wooden sled big enough for two or three to ride together.

"A sled! A sled!" Isaac raced off to meet Amanda.

He and his sister danced around the sled while she drew near.

"Where did you get that?" Garrett asked Amanda.

"Mr. Calloway had it in the garden shed. He said it was about time someone used it."

Garrett looked down at those fancy boots of hers, covered in snow and sand. Likewise, the hem of her dress was coated in sandy snow and ice. Yet her cheeks were rosy, and her eyes sparkled with such delight that he couldn't help but agree to the outing.

"Only until the sun reaches the horizon," he conceded. "We'll climb the first dune. It has good snow on this side of it."

"Me first," Isaac cried out, already running down the street in that direction.

Sadie was a little more cautious, extending her hands for him to pick her up. As Garrett stood up with his precious daughter in his arms, his heart swelled with gratitude. Somehow Amanda had managed to turn everything upside down. His son, who had shot defiance at him yesterday, now called out for him to hurry. Sadie clung to his side, begging for a ride on the sled.

It was all Amanda's doing.

Amanda watched Garrett take the children down the hill on the sled and then pull it back up with both of them aboard. He was a strong man, a loving father. And he was laughing with his children.

"Thank you, Pearl," she whispered.

Her friend's suggestion had been a perfect way to bring the family together. Even if Garrett dismissed her at the end of the day, Amanda could rest in the knowledge that the children had their father back.

She bit her half-numb lip and fought back tears. If only she could be part of that family, too. But Garrett's anger yesterday had made it clear that he could never trust her.

"Someone needs to get off the sled," Garrett huffed as he neared the top of the dune.

The children rolled off, giggling.

Garrett pulled the empty sled to Amanda's side and stretched his back. "Whew, they're getting heavy."

"They're growing up."

"That they are." A wistful expression crossed his face. "So quickly."

Until meeting Garrett and his children, Amanda hadn't understood why parents sometimes wanted to slow down time. In the orphanage, every thought was directed toward getting a family or growing old enough not to be bullied anymore. Mrs. Chatsworth had doted on her daughter, Lena, but had treated Amanda like an adult from the moment she'd arrived. Amanda was always old enough to scrub floors or polish silver, while Lena could never do such things, even though she was a year older than Amanda. Perhaps Mrs. Chatsworth had been clinging to her only daughter the way Garrett tried to hold on to Isaac and Sadie.

"Time marches on, no matter how much we want to still it," Amanda murmured.

Garrett looked surprised that she understood what he

was feeling, but then just as quickly turned to the children, who were racing toward him.

"My turn," Isaac called out. "Can I take the sled down the hill by myself, Papa?"

"Not quite yet, son."

"I want to go with you, Papa," little Sadie insisted.

Amanda smiled at the girl, who hung so desperately on her papa. Sadie wasn't shy about demanding attention, but Isaac needed it just as much, even if he tried too hard to act grown-up.

"I can handle the sled without help," Isaac insisted, his little shoulders squared exactly the way his father's were when confronting a challenge.

Again Garrett denied the request, but this time for a reason. "First Miss Amanda needs a ride."

She gulped. That was the part of the plan that she'd hoped to avoid. She had never been on a sled. There was no opportunity in the city, and when the Chatsworths went on a sledding party in the country, she was left behind with the servants.

"Poor Amanda," Mrs. Brighton, the housekeeper, would cluck. "You and me'll make something pretty for you to wear."

In those long, lonely hours, the sewing lessons gave Amanda purpose. She could create something beautiful and practical. Perhaps one day she might have a pretty gown like Lena. Over the years she'd practiced until she could sew almost anything. But she never learned to sled or to enjoy any rapid conveyance. The train ride to Chicago had nearly paralyzed her with fear. She had lost more than one meal before Pearl managed to calm her nerves.

"Sit right here with your feet braced on this bar," Garrett instructed.

The same nausea she'd experienced on the train returned. Amanda pressed a hand to her midsection. "I don't need a ride. Take Isaac and Sadie down again."

Garrett grinned. "Afraid?"

She couldn't admit fear. "There isn't a lot of daylight left. It's unfair for me to use any of it when this is for the children. Let them enjoy an extra slide down the hill."

Instead of agreeing with her, Garrett turned to his son and daughter. "What do you say? Shall we send Miss Amanda downhill?"

"Yes!" the two screamed out together.

"By myself?" she squeaked. Visions of crashing and breaking an arm or a leg danced in her head. "I don't know how."

She began to back away but ran into Garrett's solid form. He placed his hands on her shoulders while the children positioned the sled.

"I'll be right behind you," he assured her.

Amanda craned her neck to look back at him, and the smile on his face made her catch her breath. He would be right behind her, ready to catch her if anything should go wrong.

"You'll go with me?"

He nodded. "Every inch of the way."

Though reassured, she found her heart still hammering in her chest. What if…? No, nothing could go wrong with Garrett in control. He had taken his children down the hill a half dozen times already without a single mishap. She could rely on him.

She swallowed the knot of fear. "All right."

He grinned and gently pushed her toward the sled. "Sit down and tuck your skirts under your legs so they don't drag on the snow and get under the runners."

Her nerves ramped up again. Between the petticoats and large skirt, there was a lot of tucking to be done.

Garrett chuckled, and she glanced up at him. "Did I do it wrong?"

He shook his head. "Just scoot a little forward so there's enough room for me to sit on the sled."

Heat rushed to her cheeks. Even a fool would realize she couldn't take up the whole sled unless she intended to ride it alone. She did not.

Holding her skirts, which threatened to spill out with every movement, she slowly inched forward. "Is that enough?"

"More," he urged.

She scooted farther, but again it wasn't enough. Finally, when her knees were nearly pulled up to her chin, he stopped her.

"Good enough."

She felt his weight on the sled behind her...terribly close behind her. Her skin prickled at the thought of him holding her, and the most delightful sensation teased her senses when his breath whispered against her ear. He placed one hand on her shoulder, and she couldn't breathe. Garrett Decker was practically holding her. Maybe this wasn't such a good idea.

"I'll need both of you to push us," Garrett said to the children. "Get behind me and push on my back."

The children whooped and hollered as they complied. The sled slowly inched forward on the snow. Then Garrett gave the greatest thrust with his booted feet and free hand. Just when she was certain they were far too heavy to ever catapult down the dune, the sled began moving. Slow at first, it soon crested the rounded top, and the precipitous decline loomed ahead.

"Eeek!" Amanda screamed.

Garrett's boots landed beside her feet. The sled picked

up speed, and tufts of dune grass flitted past at alarming speed. Ahead loomed a small shrub.

Amanda shrieked.

Garrett seemed not to notice.

They would hit it!

She pointed.

The sled continued toward it.

She turned to warn him, and her head clunked on his jaw. The whole world tumbled as she hit the snow, back of her head first. Her hat went flying. She tumbled and slid, her eyes and ears and mouth filling with snow. Sandy snow.

Using every means possible, she scooped and wiped and removed the snow from her face, but her eyes were watering and her mouth felt gritty.

"Are you all right? Is anything broken?" Garrett must have landed near her, for he gently raised her to a sitting position. "Your arms? Your legs?"

"Handkerchief."

"What?"

She stuck out her sandy tongue and attempted again to wipe her eyes, but just got more snow and grit in them from her mittens.

"Stop. I've got it." With tender swipes, he cleaned the gritty wetness from her eyes and gave her some fresh snow to melt in her mouth in order to rinse away the sand. "I'm sorry." His warm hand slid over her cheeks, and the awkward disaster turned into something else entirely.

This time when she opened her eyes, she saw clearly. What she saw took her breath away. Garrett was gazing into her eyes with compassion. The fall had dislodged his cap and ruffled his auburn hair. His cheeks burned bright from the cold, but his concern was only for her. His thumb whispered over her lips, and she trembled at the gentleness of his touch.

"Do they hurt?" His low voice rumbled through her.

"No," she managed to breathe out.

"Your arms? Your legs? Do you hurt anywhere?"

Oh, to be able to say yes and feel that touch again. Instead she had to shake her head.

He sighed in relief but did not draw away.

She could not stopping looking into those soft gray-blue eyes. His mouth was so close. She could feel his breath on her lips. Oh my. Was he going to kiss her? A drop of melted snow perched on the bow of his upper lip. Oh, to drink it in, to drink in the love of a good man. Tremors shook her. She closed her eyelids.

"Papa!"

"Miss Mana!"

Garrett shifted away. Amanda opened her eyes to see the children running down the dune toward them. Garrett had removed his coat and wrapped it around her shoulders.

"Don't do that," she protested. "You need it."

"I'm plenty warm, but you're shaking."

She could not tell him that she was shaking from the hope that he might kiss her and might one day come to love her.

He touched a finger to her forehead. It stung.

"You're going to have a bruise there, I'm afraid," he said, that look of compassion still in his eyes.

Small price to pay.

Chapter Ten

Garrett had been tempted. The softness of her lips, the flush of her cheeks and the hopefulness in her eyes had lured him to the brink of a decision he would later regret. A kiss invariably led to expectations, and he was not ready to marry. Thankfully, his children's voices pierced the fog of desire and rescued him from disaster.

"We saw you crash," Isaac said, concern furrowing his little brow.

"Are you hurt?" Sadie's lip quivered.

He hugged them close, drinking in the smell and feel of his children. "I'm fine."

"We're fine," Amanda echoed, though she was still sitting in the snow.

The children relaxed and then squirmed from his grasp.

"Boy! You should have seen it," Isaac said excitedly. "You tumbled end over end in a big cloud of snow."

Amanda winced, and Garrett wondered if she really was hurt. It would be just like a woman to claim she was fine when she wasn't.

"Now, Isaac," Garrett chided, "it's not polite to speak about another person's misfortune."

"But—"

Garrett spied Amanda's embarrassment and cut him off with a single upraised finger. "Apologize to Miss Porter."

Isaac bowed his head and muttered something unintelligible.

Garrett was about to insist he repeat the apology with more oomph when Amanda told Isaac that she was quite all right and accepted his kind words. Garrett frowned. She couldn't possibly have understood a word Isaac said. This was yet another case of her overriding his authority.

Amanda extended a hand toward Isaac. "Will you help me to my feet?"

Garrett frowned. Shouldn't that be his duty? Isaac was too small to pull a grown woman to her feet.

He watched in amazement as his son leaped to assist. When Amanda got upright and thanked Isaac with a little curtsy, the boy beamed.

Sadie sat down. "Help me get up."

Naturally, Isaac ignored that request.

Garrett swooped in to the rescue, snatching up his little girl and swinging her around until she giggled. "That's my princess." He set her down and looked around. "Where's the sled?"

Isaac pointed to the back of the hotel. "All the way down there."

Garrett had to squint in the dimming light of late afternoon. Sure enough, the sled had lodged under the rickety fence behind the hotel. He sure hoped Lyle VanderLeuven didn't see it before they retrieved it. The hotel owner would gripe about the sled damaging the fence, when in truth that fence had been falling down for years.

"Amanda, er, Miss Porter, would you take the children home while I fetch the sled?"

"No!" cried Isaac and Sadie in unison.

"Can't we have one more ride?" Isaac begged. "Please?

You didn't let me go down the hill by myself, and you promised I could after Miss Amanda went."

In this low light, Garrett wasn't at all thrilled at the idea of sending his son down the dune by himself, especially considering the last crash.

"That will have to wait for another day."

"But you promised!" Isaac's face grew red and his little jaw jutted out.

"I promise you will. Just not today." Garrett steeled himself for Amanda to override his decision yet again, but she said nothing. "You can go downhill alone the next time we go sledding."

Judging from Isaac's expression, that was a bitter pill to swallow. "That's not the same."

"No, it's not," Amanda said.

Garrett set his jaw. This habit of hers to interfere was a big problem.

She knelt beside the pouting boy and attempted to lift his face with her finger. Isaac was in full protest, though, and could not be budged. The boy had resorted to this tactic too much of late. After supper, Garrett would have a stern talk with him.

Instead of being dissuaded, Amanda continued. "I realize you're disappointed. We all get disappointed when fun times have to come to an end, but they always do."

If anything, Isaac's stance got stiffer.

"Do you know what the best part is?" she asked, and then waited an incredibly long time for Isaac to respond.

Garrett was about to demand they all head home when his son muttered something that must have satisfied Amanda.

"We can remember the fun times we had and look forward to the next time," she said, brushing a lock of hair from Isaac's eyes. "Imagine how fun it will be with even more snow on the ground. Maybe some of your friends will be able to join in."

Garrett noticed the stiffness easing from his son's shoulders. Had Amanda really gotten through to him? She had made a suggestion that Garrett would have to keep, but at least Isaac wasn't fuming any longer.

"I wouldn't be surprised," she finished, "if your father knows how to make the sled go even faster."

That brought Isaac's attention squarely to him. "Will you do that, Papa?"

Garrett felt a swell of pride that his son trusted in him. "I know a thing or two. But first I'm going to need your help fetching the sled."

The disappointment of ending this day's sledding was forgotten as Isaac beamed at the assignment Garrett had just given him.

Amanda smiled and nodded. "I'll take Sadie home. You two men can handle things from here."

Isaac stood a full inch taller.

Garrett would have to remember that. By giving Isaac responsibility and expressing confidence, the barrier between them had been broken down. As he walked with his son to fetch the sled, letting the boy's excited chatter roll over him like a wave, all felt right with the world.

Thanks to Amanda.

Amanda bubbled with excitement as she stitched the costumes the next evening.

"He even complimented my beans. Mrs. Calloway says a little molasses makes them taste wonderful, and she's right."

Pearl looked up from the lessons she was planning for the following week. "He?"

"Garrett." Amanda sighed at the memory of their near

kiss. He had wanted to kiss her. She was sure of it. If the children hadn't arrived, he would have. Her foot stilled on the treadle, and she closed her eyes to savor the memory. "He is the best father I've ever met." Certainly nothing like Mr. Chatsworth, who would breeze into the house and go straight to his study.

"The best ever? That's a pretty bold statement."

"It's the truth. He even pulled Isaac out of that dreadful sullen mood that he's been exhibiting of late."

"I have noticed that Isaac is much more cooperative in class. I can't imagine how that happened." Pearl shot her a grin. "Perhaps your influence?"

"Maybe a little, but Garrett figured out on his own that a boy just wants his father's love and respect."

"So does a woman who loves that man."

Amanda ducked her face so Pearl couldn't see the sudden heat in her cheeks.

Pearl wouldn't let it rest. "It sounds like that situation might be changing for the better."

"Maybe, but it's only been a day. Your suggestion to go sledding really helped."

"That was only an idea. How you handled it was the real difference-maker."

Amanda touched the scrape on her forehead. It had turned purple overnight. "I have the scars to prove it."

Pearl laughed. "Battle scars, but well worth it, especially if Sadie's Christmas wish comes true."

Now Amanda couldn't possibly hide her blushes. Marrying Garrett and becoming those children's mother was everything she could hope for, but Garrett had proved so changeable. One day he seemed to respect and admire her. The next he glowered and threatened to dismiss her.

"I hope you're right," she sighed.

"Pray on it. God will lead you exactly where He wants you to be."

Amanda couldn't echo Pearl's confidence. Her path through life thus far had been filled with ruts and potholes. Looking back, she couldn't see God's hand in any of it. Though Pearl's dreams had come true, Amanda's dreams always turned to dust. Dare she hope in Garrett?

Pearl had returned to her schoolwork, so Amanda resumed stitching the shepherd's robe. These costumes were so simple that she would finish them well before the rehearsal a week from Saturday. The robes for Mary and Joseph she kept until last. They were especially precious to her, since Sadie and Isaac would wear them.

"Why did you choose Sadie and Isaac to portray Mary and Joseph?"

Pearl looked up. "They are brother and sister."

"The Norstrands and Clapps also have boys and girls in their families."

"That's why I put the family names in a bowl and drew out one."

"You did? I don't remember that." Amanda had missed parts of the school day now and then, but she'd been there just before the parts were announced—or had she?

"Mrs. Calloway supervised the selection." Pearl laughed. "And added her opinion."

Amanda could believe that. "I'm sure she's pleased that Isaac and Sadie won the draw."

"Pleased might be an understatement. Did you realize she donated sheets for the costumes?"

"That explains a great deal except the colors."

"She dyed them. Isn't the fabric for Mary's robe a beautiful blue? A bit like your good dress, with that hint of violet, only a little darker. That gown favors your eyes,"

Pearl added. "I'm sure Garrett has noticed. He can't drag his gaze from you Sunday mornings."

"While he scowls," Amanda said with a laugh. She finished another seam and snipped off the threads.

"Roland says Garrett's late wife had the same color eyes as yours."

"She did?" Amanda's hands stilled on the fabric. It explained his occasional pained expression. "My eyes must be a daily reminder of his loss."

"Roland is sure Garrett's getting past his grief and now sees you for who you really are."

"Who I really am?" Amanda wasn't sure of that herself.

Pearl didn't have a chance to answer, for Fiona swept into the room with the usual rustle of silk skirts.

"Good evening, ladies. I just heard news that may be of great interest to you."

Pearl gave Amanda a pointed glance and would probably have rolled her eyes if Fiona hadn't been standing near enough to notice. The redhead loved to bring news, especially if it elevated her status.

"I'm sure it can't be that important if we haven't heard already," Pearl said drily.

"Actually, this particular bit of news pertains to Amanda." Fiona crossed the room and stood beside her. "The nativity play costumes?"

"Yes." Amanda finished the next seam before looking up. Despite her intent to treat Fiona better, the woman's constant butting into matters that didn't concern her set Amanda on edge. Whatever gossip Fiona had to share, it wouldn't be good. It never was. Amanda simply hoped that nothing had happened to any of the Deckers.

"Don't you want to know?" Fiona asked from over her shoulder.

Amanda snipped the threads. "I suppose I must."

"Don't sound so worried. It's good news."

Amanda warily met Fiona's gaze. Sure enough, the woman looked pleased, as if she did indeed have good news to impart.

Fiona pulled a ladder-back chair to Amanda's side and settled upon it, her back ramrod straight. She leaned slightly forward, as if sharing a confidence. "I've heard that the lumberjack named Jake, the one you think is your brother, has returned to the area."

Excitement prickled over Amanda. Could it be true? Might she soon find her long-lost brother? Even if this Jake was her brother, would she recognize him? She hadn't seen him since she was five years old. What if Fiona was wrong? She bit back the hope. Last month she'd thought he was coming to Singapore, only to learn he had gone north instead of following the logs downstream.

"Are you certain?" she breathed.

"Sawyer Evans told me he saw one of the foremen on the boat back from Chicago. That's who told him that the Jake you're looking for returned to the crew." Fiona squeezed her hand. "Sawyer just told me. You've been kind to me. I wanted you to know before anyone else."

Amanda swallowed the lump in her throat and thanked Fiona. If all this was true, she might at last find her brother. All prior attempts to find Jacob or Uncle Griffin had come to naught. Her letters had been returned, addressee unknown.

Fiona left for the parlor, where she could entertain herself and the other boarders on the piano.

Only then did Pearl lift her head. "What are you going to do?"

It didn't take a second to decide. "Find him."

"How? Fiona didn't say he planned to come to town.

They've probably just arrived for the winter's logging. He'd be out at one of the camps."

Amanda hadn't thought of that. "I might find passage upriver with someone. There's that ferry that goes to Allegan on occasion."

Pearl looked skeptical. "And then you would need to find the camp. They're not in town. It's rough country."

"I know." But she hadn't really thought that through. "Maybe someone will take me."

Pearl moved to the chair that Fiona had abandoned and clasped Amanda's hands. "Be careful. Some of those men aren't quite the respectable sort."

Amanda shuddered at a flash of memory. Hugh had looked like a fine gentleman but ended up as disreputable as the men Pearl was warning her about. "I'll find someone to make the journey with me."

Garrett. His name came first to mind. She could trust him. With the children along, there could be no rumors of indiscretion. And it would solve the problem of her duties for the family.

Pearl still looked concerned. "Christmas will soon be here. And my wedding. I had hoped you would be my bridesmaid."

Amanda caught her breath. She had selfishly plowed ahead without considering the needs of her dearest friend. As Pearl had gently pointed out, the men would be cutting timber all winter. This lumberjack wouldn't be going anywhere anytime soon.

She squeezed Pearl's hands. "Of course I'm going to be your bridesmaid. This excursion won't take place until after your wedding."

The reassurance eased Pearl's concerns. Amanda would plan ahead. This man—her brother, she hoped—would not escape her again. At the earliest convenience, she would ask Garrett to accompany her. Considering their improved relationship, he would surely agree.

Garrett whistled as he hammered together the planks of the stable for the nativity play. Since the school used the church building during the week, he was assembling each wall separately. Next Friday evening he would put it together in the church.

"Can I hammer in a nail?" Isaac asked.

"Next board. Hold this one steady until I get it nailed on."

Ever since the sledding expedition, Isaac had followed Garrett around, asking questions about everything he did. After school today, he'd left Sadie in Amanda's care and showed Isaac the launch site and building berth for the new schooner. The boy hung on Garrett's every word.

It had been a long time since his son wanted to spend time with him.

Or maybe he'd been the one too sunk in grief and regret to notice his son's needs. At least that's the way Amanda saw it.

Amanda. A smile curved Garrett's lips. She was a fine looking woman, a decent housekeeper and a tolerable cook. He wouldn't grow fat on her offerings, but there were more important traits in a wife than her ability to cook.

Wife! Where had that come from?

The fact was, he'd let his thoughts drift that way this week. After all, the children liked her. Sadie had even written that school paper asking for Miss Mana, as she called her, to be her new mama for Christmas. That was pushing things a bit far, but it wasn't looking quite as impossible as it had seemed at first. Maybe if things progressed on course through the winter, he'd consider marriage—for the sake of the children. Then again, things were fine as they were. Amanda had settled in as housekeeper. The children were happy. Yep, things were just fine.

"How long are you gonna sit there?" Isaac asked a bit petulantly.

"Sorry, son." Garrett roped in his runaway thoughts and hammered the last nail in that board.

He hefted a new board from the stack of slab wood and laid it in place.

"My turn!" Isaac hopped from foot to foot in excitement.

Garrett found a clear spot without a knot or blemish. "Get a nail from the tin."

Isaac examined the nails and chose one.

"Now hold it against the board like this." Garrett demonstrated how to position the nail, point down, with his thumb and index finger. "This is the tricky part. You need to hold it steady and perfectly straight. Then tap on the head with the hammer."

Isaac tapped, but it wasn't strong enough to set the nail in the wood.

"Try again."

This time Isaac tilted the nail and nearly hammered his fingers.

"Want help?"

His son screwed up his face with concentration. "I've got it."

Garrett itched to help him hold the nail. At this rate the boy was going to end up with bruised fingers, and Amanda would scold Garrett to no end. But a boy had to learn by doing, just like Garrett had learned when he was young. Not from his father, who worked at the Board of Trade, but from Mr. Sullivan, the kindly carpenter down the street. He'd gotten a few bruised fingers, but he'd learned.

He held his breath as Isaac swung the hammer down

again. This time it landed square and tapped the nail securely into the wood.

"Well done," Garrett exclaimed. "Better than I could have done at your age."

Isaac beamed.

"Now, finish hammering that nail in. Take your time to make sure the hammer head lands square on the nail."

Every blow was an exercise in patience. Garrett had to fist his hands to stop himself from assisting. It took forever, since each blow of the hammer yielded little force, but eventually, the nail went into the board. The head was folded a bit, and the last blow made it not quite square, but those were small matters.

"Well done, son."

Isaac's grin was so wide that it made the long and painful lesson well worth the effort.

"Can I do another?" the boy asked eagerly.

"Maybe tomorrow. It's getting to be suppertime. Shall we find out what Miss Amanda has cooked up for us tonight?"

Isaac shrugged. He probably could have spent the night without a bite of supper, but Garrett's stomach rumbled at the thought of food. It had been a long day.

"The women will be waiting," Garrett pointed out as he put the hammer back in his toolbox.

Isaac tilted his face up to look at him. "Are you gonna marry Miss Amanda?"

Count on a child to get straight to the point. Garrett didn't have an answer. Not yet.

Chapter Eleven

Since the children were always around Garrett, Amanda delayed asking him to take her upriver to the lumber camps. Pearl was right. She had plenty of time. Moreover, with the nativity play and Pearl's wedding in a little over a week, Amanda spent every spare moment on the sewing machine.

She begged Pearl for time off from school so she could complete the costumes and the animals, but most of that time was spent sewing the wedding dress. Mrs. Calloway, Fiona and Louise had purchased the beautiful taffeta in shimmering white. Amanda was to make the dress.

"White for winter," Mrs. Calloway had insisted the November day they'd picked it out from Roland's supply catalog.

Amanda hadn't been quite as certain. "Pearl is practical, and white has little use beyond the wedding day. She won't be pleased. I can hear her now, calling it a needless extravagance."

They had laughed at that, for over the years Amanda had learned Pearl's speech mannerisms to perfection. But the problem still remained.

"She could dye it," Louise had suggested.

Amanda feared disaster if that wasn't handled correctly. She had no idea how to dye silk. Mrs. Chatsworth had her gowns—and those for her daughter—made by a dressmaker. Amanda had worn little but muslin. Here in Singapore, only Fiona wore silk, and she had never dyed fabric.

"Ivory would be better," Amanda had suggested.

Mrs. Calloway put a stop to such talk. "If ever there was a bride who deserved white, it's Pearl."

Amanda's thoughts drifted from Pearl to the wedding she one day hoped to have. Pearl did deserve white, but not Amanda.

In the end, she was outvoted and the white taffeta was ordered. In the beginning, while Pearl was confined to bed recovering from the burns that she'd gotten during the November fire, Amanda could work on the dress without fear of discovery. Once Pearl healed enough to leave their room, Amanda sneaked in every precious moment while Pearl was with Roland. Then the costumes and animals for the nativity play were added to her load, along with the curtains for Garrett's house. The latter had not taken long, but she was woefully behind on the wedding dress, with the ceremony just ten days away. At this rate Pearl would walk down the aisle in her Sunday best.

So on those afternoons when Pearl gave her leave from school, Amanda sewed and sewed until her fingers stiffened and her head ached from concentrating so hard.

"It's beautiful," Mrs. Calloway said as she passed through the writing room, dust rag in hand.

"I hope it fits. I would feel a lot better about that if I could have her try it on."

"That's impossible, and you know it. If Miss Pearl laid eyes on that gown before her wedding day, she would refuse to wear it."

Amanda sighed. "I'm afraid you're right."

"But once it's done and presented as a gift from all of us, she can't refuse."

That was their hope, but when Amanda thought back to how long it took Pearl to accept the green dress from Roland after the fire, she wasn't so certain. She wouldn't even open the package for the longest time. It took a big nudge and a little guilt to prod her.

"Maybe I'd better have Sadie give it to her. That's the only thing that got her to accept the green dress."

Mrs. Calloway laughed. "Roland was smart to include her in that gift."

"Pearl knew Roland bought the dress, but she thought Sadie was upset that she hadn't opened it."

"If you ask me, it couldn't hurt to bring Sadie in on this." Mrs. Calloway paused. "You could ask her tonight. Can she keep a secret?"

"I'm not sure." Now that Sadie—who four months ago had been too grief-stricken to speak—was talking, she didn't hold back her thoughts. "She might not when Pearl is concerned."

"Hmm." Mrs. Calloway wiped the writing desk and then moved on to the bookshelves, which were painfully bare, since she let anyone borrow a book and few were ever returned. "Perhaps we could include Sadie's gift with ours. Do you know if she picked out anything?"

Amanda didn't. Considering the groom ran the general store, it was unlikely Garrett had ordered anything. More likely Sadie had made something for her teacher and soon-to-be aunt.

"I'll ask tonight." Amanda glanced at the clock. "Oh, my. The time has gotten away from me. The children will be headed home." She clipped the threads and carefully rolled the half-finished gown so it wouldn't crease too badly. "Would you stow this for me?"

Since Pearl and Amanda shared a room, the ladies had agreed early on that Mrs. Calloway would keep the dress in her bedroom. Pearl would never accidentally stumble across it there.

With the gown safely in Mrs. Calloway's hands, Amanda bustled off to meet the children. They were slowly meandering toward the house, stopping every few steps to look at something in the street. Isaac bent over while Sadie squatted in a most unladylike posture.

Amanda drew near, ready to instruct Sadie on the finer points of becoming a lady, when the little girl jumped to her feet.

"Miss Mana! Look what I found. Look!"

All thoughts of correcting Sadie's manners disappeared in the face of that little girl's joy. What had Amanda been thinking? There was plenty of time to learn manners. Let Sadie enjoy the wonder of each moment.

Amanda bent over to peer at the object nestled in Sadie's mitten. The fuzzy brown wool made it difficult to make out at first, since the object was a similar color.

"Look," Sadie urged, lifting her hand a little higher.

Amanda removed her own mitten and fingered the pebble, for that's what it was. A mere stone. "Very nice."

"It's red."

More like reddish-brown, but to a little girl it might indeed appear red. That was Sadie's favorite color, after all. If the little girl had truly picked out Pearl's dress last month, it would have been red, not green.

"It's pretty." Amanda handed it back.

"It's got its own hole and everything."

Amanda hadn't noticed that, but upon closer inspection, she saw Sadie was right.

"Well, look at that. I wonder how a hole got in it."

"From the sand and the waves," Isaac stated with the

authority of a scientist. "It rubs and rubs until it makes a hole in it."

"That's quite an observation," Amanda said, even though she had her doubts. After all, sand would rub the whole thing, not just one hole. "How did it get here, so far from the waves?"

"It's been here all along. The wind just uncovered it," Isaac stated.

"Why, that's a splendid deduction."

He frowned. "A what?"

She laughed. "It means that you're very smart."

Isaac stood a bit taller.

She'd noticed he carried himself with a lot more confidence and less fear ever since Garrett began taking him to the shipbuilding site. Since the planning and sawing took place inside the sawmill, she was a bit nervous that an accident might happen, but he'd assured her that he brought Isaac inside only when the machines were quiet. Still, Amanda wondered how long it would take before after-hours visits turned into daytime visits.

She would never forget how the oldest children at the orphanage would go to Miss Hornswoggle's office and walk away with a gentleman or a lady. Not parents. Parents always came together. These children hadn't been chosen. They'd been sent away because they were too old for anyone to want. They had to work in service or in the factories. Pearl had escaped that destiny. Maybe she'd been too outspoken for even the foremen and housekeepers to accept.

A family chose Amanda, but it had not turned out much better.

"What's wrong, Miss Mana?"

Little Sadie's voice pierced the fog of memory and pulled Amanda back to the present.

Amanda smiled. "I'm fine. Just thinking about something."

"It must be bad."

"A little sad."

"Oh. We won't think about sad things, right?" Sadie stuffed the stone into her coat pocket.

Oh, the simplicity of childhood! Amanda longed to hold these two tight and prevent any more pain from entering their lives. Before the age of eight they'd lost a mother and suffered a terrible fire.

"No, we won't," she agreed. "Only happy thoughts from now on. That's a royal decree."

"What's a royal decree?"

Isaac answered before Amanda could. "It means you have to do what the king tells you to do."

"Or the queen," Amanda pointed out. "Queen Victoria reigns in England right now."

Judging from the look on Isaac's face, he didn't think much of taking orders from a woman, even if she was queen. "We don't have to listen to any old queen. We live in America."

Amanda nudged them back toward home. "True, but you do have to listen to your papa and your teacher. Oh! Speaking of Miss Lawson, do you plan to give her anything on her wedding day?"

Isaac stared at her blankly, but Sadie pumped her head up and down.

"I'll show you." Sadie ran ahead and entered the house.

"Your shoes!" Amanda called out, but it was too late. The girl had tracked sand through the rooms.

"My pa said we're gonna give her something together," Isaac said. "I wouldn't forget to wipe my feet."

He then made exaggerated motions to knock the sand from his shoes.

"Thank you, Isaac." Amanda nudged him inside and smothered a smile.

The house was cool, as it always was by late afternoon. Garrett banked the fire, so the stove didn't put off much heat. Before Amanda pulled off her coat, she grabbed a chunk of wood to stoke the blaze. It was the last piece.

"Isaac, does your father have more wood outside?"

"I'll check." He headed out while she worked to get the fire going again.

It took some effort, but soon flames cast a scorching heat against her skin and the scent of wood smoke filled the air. After last month's fire, that smell sent shivers down her spine. She would never forget the fear when she'd realized Sadie was missing.

"Miss Mana?"

Amanda started. "I did it again, didn't I? Thinking bad thoughts."

Sadie nodded solemnly, and Amanda wondered if the smell of smoke had the same effect on her. After all, Sadie had been surrounded by flames.

"It's all right." Amanda wrapped her arms around the little girl and hugged her close, breathing in the scent of little girl. So precious. So very precious.

"I got my present," Sadie said at last.

Amanda realized she'd been holding on too long and released her. "Let's go to the window where there's better light."

There Sadie unclenched her hand to reveal a stunning silver necklace set with a lavender stone that must be amethyst. How had a little girl gotten something so precious? It made Amanda remember the half locket that she'd had at the orphanage. It was not valuable, but it had come from her parents. Amanda always imagined the other half went to her brother, Jake. That's how she would know if the lumberjack was her brother.

"Do you like it?" Sadie asked.

Amanda pulled her thoughts back to the present. "It's very pretty, but it's a little too dear for you to give away. Did it belong to your mother?"

Sadie nodded. "Mama looked like you."

Amanda drew in her breath. Pearl had told her the same thing, but she hadn't quite believed it.

Sadie held out her hand with the necklace dangling from it. "For you."

Tears bunched in Amanda's eyes. She folded Sadie's fingers over the necklace. "You need to keep this, sweetheart. Your mama would have wanted you to have it."

Sadie frowned. "But I need to give you something."

Amanda hugged the little girl again. "Oh, you have. You already have."

"Then I'll give it to Miss Pearl."

Amanda held Sadie at arm's length. "I think Miss Pearl would like a necklace made from that pretty stone you found. It suits her hair color nicely."

Little Sadie's eyes lit up.

"Do you have a narrow ribbon?" Amanda suggested. "That would make a perfect necklace."

Sadie hurried off to her bedroom.

"Bring them all," Amanda called out as she stood. That way she could select the most appropriate.

Only then did she notice that Isaac hadn't returned. It shouldn't have taken that long. Garrett kept wood stacked alongside the house.

She hurried outside, calling Isaac's name.

The woodpile was gone, and he was nowhere in sight.

They needed solid timbers for the ways upon which the completed schooner would slide broadside into the river when launched. Fortunately, sufficient logs were left outside the warehouse, not well seasoned but not fresh-cut either. Garrett spent the morning with the men loading the logs onto the heavy wagon and hauling them to the mill with the steam tractor.

After lunch, they ripped them to size on the large circular saw. By late afternoon, Garrett was coated with sawdust, and only half a dozen logs remained. Six men loaded one onto the log carriage, while Garrett guided it to exactly the right position before running it through the saw.

The howl of the blade could make a man deaf, but Garrett had learned years ago to stuff his ears with cotton. If he hadn't, he'd be struggling to hear his children or Amanda. The higher tones were already difficult to make out.

Maybe Roland was right, and he needed to get out of the mill and into management. It's just that Garrett couldn't stand to sit at a desk and push around papers. The thought of figures made him nauseous.

He'd told his brother that, but Roland just shook his head.

"You don't seem to have any trouble poring over those schooner plans," Roland had remarked.

"That's different."

"And coming up with how many board feet you need of each type of wood, not to mention the hardware." Roland had proceeded to read off the list of the various fasteners Garrett had ordered.

"Stop! I know what I ordered."

"That must have taken some serious calculations."

Garrett had shrugged. For some reason the math didn't bother him when it involved building. "Maybe if I could manage a shipyard…"

That was as much as he could concede, but it would never happen. Stockton might build a ship or two while the timber held out, but Roland was right that eventually it *would* run out. Stockton was already sniffing around for new stands to exploit in the northern part of the state. At the current rate, it would take a decade or two. By then, Garrett might make a name for himself as a shipwright and get in with a big yard. Unfortunately, those were in larger cities. He liked Singapore, where everyone knew each other.

Newcomers couldn't escape being noticed. Like Amanda.

He smiled.

Sawyer motioned to him.

Garrett jerked out of his thoughts and signaled to the saw operator to release the blade.

Instead of doing so, the man pointed behind Garrett.

What now? He turned around and froze. Not twenty feet away, within reach of a snapped belt or plank that bucked away from the blade, stood Isaac. The boy's eyes were wide as he took in every bit of machinery and the men who were now all staring at him.

Garrett motioned for Sawyer to stop the saw. "Take a break for a minute."

He tugged the cotton out of his ears and went to his son. "Didn't I tell you never to come into the sawmill without me?"

Isaac's wondering expression hardened, and his lip quivered ever so slightly before he got it under control. "You're here."

"That's not what I meant." Garrett checked himself before he said something to undo all the progress he'd made the last few days. He shouldn't scold the boy out of fear. Isaac didn't know about the dangers. Garrett had never explained them to him.

Amanda always crouched or knelt when speaking to the

children, so she could look them in the eye. Though Isaac strained to control his emotions, the disappointment he felt was palpable. Garrett yanked off his cap and raked a hand through his sawdust-filled hair. The men might consider it weakness to get down to a child's level, but Isaac was more important. Garrett would deal with the men's attitudes later.

He crouched. "Now, son, you must have come here for a reason."

The stiff shoulders relaxed. "We need wood, Papa. I went to the woodpile, and there wasn't any. Sadie and Miss Amanda will get cold. They might get sick."

The hysteria in Isaac's explanation drove a spike of guilt into Garrett. Rather than tell the children that their mother had drowned, which would have led to the question why, he'd told them that she fell in the river and got too cold. They'd assumed she got sick and died. He'd never corrected that assumption. One day, when the children were old enough, he would tell them all that had happened. That day hadn't arrived yet, but his stretching of the truth was creating a problem.

"They won't get sick and die from a chilly house," he tried to explain, but Isaac clearly wasn't accepting that assurance.

"We can't take a chance."

Garrett swallowed the lump that had formed in his throat. This was all his fault. He'd been so busy with the ship project that he'd neglected restocking the woodpile. Isaac was merely trying to help. His heart was in a good place—better than Garrett's.

He rose to his feet and grasped his son by the shoulders. "Look at me, Isaac."

The boy lifted hesitant eyes to him.

"You did right to come to me for wood, but you shouldn't have come into the sawmill. Uncle Roland would have helped you."

Isaac made a face. "Uncle Roland is with Miss Lawson." His tone made it clear he found the idea of his uncle and his teacher that close to each other distasteful.

Garrett stifled a smile—and the urge to suggest Isaac could have just taken some wood from the stockpile beside the general store. That pile was for all the Deckers to use as needed, but Isaac didn't know that. Again, Garrett had neglected to inform his son. It was time he remedied these omissions.

"All right. We'll get some wood. Why don't you go outside and wait for me. I need to give the men some instructions so they can continue working while we fetch some wood."

Isaac must have feared a reprimand. When it didn't come, he visibly brightened. "Will you show me how the saw works sometime?"

Garrett would rather his son grow up to become a craftsman or even a business owner, but he supposed it was natural the boy would want to know what his father did every day.

"I will. Sometime when the saws aren't running. How does that sound?"

Isaac's eyes shone. "Splendid!"

"Splendid?" That didn't sound like something his son would say. "Is that one of Miss Pearl's words?"

Isaac shook his head. "Miss Amanda."

That lady was filled with surprises. No doubt she'd be grateful to get an armload of wood, perhaps even splendidly grateful. With an extra bounce in his step, Garrett sent Isaac outside and went to tell the men how to proceed without him.

* * *

Isaac was gone.

Amanda cupped her hands around her mouth and called out his name.

The winds howled off the dunes. The mill belched smoke. Something rattled in the distance, but she couldn't hear a single voice. The hotel was quiet, with no ships in port. Soon even those stragglers would stop, according to Roland. The townsfolk had stocked up their larders. Fresh milk and eggs could be bought from nearby farms if the trails were passable. Meat would come in occasionally, but folks mostly relied on canned, smoked and dried meats over the winter.

She walked to the other side of the house and called again for Isaac.

No answer.

Oh, dear. What should she do? Garrett had been furious at her for leaving the children alone for ten minutes. Now she'd gone and lost one of them again. Though visions of Isaac tumbling down a dune or slipping into the river threatened to destroy her remaining calm, she roped in her emotions.

Pearl would say that success depended on solid planning. Before Amanda went searching for Isaac, she needed to pull her scattered thoughts together. First, she must fetch Sadie and take her to the boardinghouse so Mrs. Calloway could watch over her. With the skies dull and overcast, the day was rapidly growing dark. Amanda would need a lantern. And help. Mr. Calloway would step up. Pearl would get Roland and everyone else to set off on the search.

Amanda hurried into the house. Since coming home from school, she found the wind had picked up. It now threatened to rip the door off its hinges. With effort, she got it closed and latched. Her hair was a mess, and she hadn't wiped her feet, but none of that mattered.

"Sadie, do you know where your brother might have gone?"

The girl looked up from stroking her kitten and shrugged. "I don't know." Unconcerned, she went right back to her kitten.

"I noticed the wood bin is empty. Does your papa keep firewood somewhere else?" Maybe that's where Isaac went. If she knew the direction he'd taken, she could narrow the search and perhaps find him before calling out the rest of the town.

Unfortunately, Sadie shook her head. "That's Isaac's job."

Amanda had a sudden image of Isaac combing the patch of forest just outside town, looking for wood they could burn. "Would he have gone to the old schoolhouse?"

"Why would he go there?"

The schoolhouse had burned nearly to the ground in last month's fire. The foundation was still there, and in this dim light Isaac could easily fall into it. She envisioned him lying amid the charred timbers at the bottom, unable to move because his leg was broken.

Oh, dear.

In the past, frightening circumstances had paralyzed Amanda, but during the fire, she had acted upon Pearl's command. Alas, she didn't have Pearl here to direct her. But her friend was only a couple minutes' walk away.

Amanda grabbed Sadie's coat from the peg. "Let's put on your coat, hat and mittens. We need to go to the boardinghouse."

"Why?"

Amanda wasn't used to resistance.

Yet Sadie didn't look defiant. She simply didn't understand.

Amanda drew in a deep breath. She didn't want to frighten the girl, but they needed to get going before all daylight faded. "I need to find out where your brother went for wood. Mr. Calloway might know. Let's go ask. Mrs. Calloway probably baked some cookies today."

That got Sadie moving. She let Amanda help her into her coat and even fastened the buttons herself. Her hat would never stay on in such a wind, so Amanda tied a bonnet on Sadie while the girl tugged on her mittens.

Amanda reached for the door, eager to get started.

"Aren't you going to wear *your* hat and mittens?" Sadie asked solemnly.

The little girl was already developing a mothering instinct and would not let this rest. So Amanda tugged on her mittens and grabbed the useless hat, which would blow clear to Allegan in this gale. She glanced around for a lantern, but saw only candles. Garrett must not have lanterns, at least not at the ready. She could get one at the boardinghouse.

She stretched out her mittened hand. "Let's go."

Again, the wind nearly snatched the door from her grasp. It took all her weight to shove it back in place.

Night was descending quickly with the dark storm clouds. It wasn't cold enough for snow—not yet—but rain could certainly fall. She needed to get Sadie to the boardinghouse quickly and then start people searching. Isaac would not fare well in a cold downpour unless he could find cover. If he was lying at the bottom of the burned-out schoolhouse foundation...

"Quickly now," she urged Sadie, as they hurried toward the boardinghouse.

"Will Cocoa be all right?"

"Cocoa will be just fine." The kitten was the least of their worries, but that little ball of fur had been the reason Sadie slipped out of the schoolhouse last month and ended up trapped by the fire. "There's no fire. Remember?"

If Sadie nodded, Amanda couldn't see it. If she spoke, the words got snatched away by the wind. Sand off the dunes pelted them, stinging their skin like the pricks of a thousand needles. Sadie averted her face. Her eyes were probably shut. Amanda had to close her own eyes to slits against the sand. In the dim light, she had only the glow of the boardinghouse windows to guide her. Thankfully, it wasn't far.

But how would they ever find Isaac in this gale?

Amanda half dragged and half carried Sadie up the steps. They burst through the front door to find Mrs. Calloway and Pearl standing in the hallway.

"My, oh my," the boardinghouse proprietress said, as she unbuttoned Sadie's coat and shook the sand out. "I saw someone heading this way. Why on earth are you out in such a blow? It'll take the skin off your face."

Amanda didn't have time for chitchat. "Pearl, can you get Roland to put together a search team? Isaac's gone missing."

"What?" Mrs. Calloway asked.

Pearl already had her cloak on. "I'm on my way."

"And I'm joining you." Fiona scooted out of the parlor and grabbed her fur-trimmed coat from one of the hallway pegs. "We must find him."

"Now, slow down," Mrs. Calloway said, "and take a lantern. You'll have to keep it mostly shut against the wind, but it'll give you enough light to get to the store."

Seconds after making that suggestion, Mr. Calloway appeared with two lanterns, his mackinaw already donned.

"What direction did the lad go?"

"I don't know," Amanda admitted. "I asked him to fetch wood from the bin. When he didn't come back in a few minutes, fifteen at most, I went to check, and he was gone. The bin was empty, so I'm guessing he went to fetch wood from somewhere else. Do you know where he would have gone?" she asked Pearl.

Her friend shook her head. "But Roland might."

None of them said what they all were thinking. If Isaac got lost, they would have great trouble finding him before daylight. Instead, they clung to the hope that Roland would indeed know where to look.

Pearl, Fiona and Mr. Calloway stepped outside.

Amanda started to follow. "I should go with them."

Mrs. Calloway held her back. "Someone needs you."

Amanda's gaze dropped to Sadie, whose thumb had found its way into her mouth.

Please, Lord, not again. These children have already been through too much.

Chapter Twelve

By the time Garrett stepped outside, dark clouds had rolled in, blotting the setting sun. Isaac crouched in the shelter of the building, his auburn hair tossing in the winds.

"I'm ready," Garrett said, clapping his son on the back.

The two headed around the mill and caught the full force of the wind. This was a gale, with a storm brewing. Garrett hunched against the blast. He could feel its strength, but Isaac was struggling to walk into it.

"Want me to carry you?" Garrett asked.

"No," the boy replied tersely.

Isaac was too old to be carried. Garrett had to handle this carefully.

"Walk behind me." His bulk would block the worst of the wind.

"I'm all right."

Garrett recognized that stubborn streak. It came from him.

He glanced ahead, but had to narrow his eyes against the pelting sand. Already the grit had gotten into his mouth. The dimness made it difficult to make out buildings except by the lights in their windows. The store lay ahead and to his left. He should see lights in his house from here. Many an evening those lit windows had drawn him home, like a harbor sentinel.

Tonight he saw only darkness in that direction. At first he figured it had gotten too dark or the sand was obscuring the view, but he could make out the hotel lights, and that building was much farther away. Isaac said they were out of wood, but Garrett had plenty of candles in the house. Even if the last ember went out in the stove, he had matches on hand. There was no reason for the windows to be dark.

A chill ran through him.

Had something happened to Sadie and Amanda?

Ignoring his son's protests, he grabbed hold of the boy and picked up his pace. Every instinct told him to head to the house first, but then a thought crossed his mind. Maybe Amanda had taken Sadie to the store or the boardinghouse to keep her warm. He'd check first with Roland.

Rather than heading around back to the woodpile, he tugged Isaac to the front of the mercantile. The wind tried to rip the door right out of his hands. Once inside, with the door secured, Garrett stomped the sand off his boots.

"Well, look who's here." That was Roland.

"Isaac? Garrett?" Pearl swooped in and caught up Isaac in a quick embrace. "I'm so glad you're all right."

"Garrett!" Fiona flung herself at him. "We were so worried."

He extricated himself from her grasp as quickly as Isaac squirmed out of Pearl's. "Why? I was just at work."

"No one knew where Isaac was," Pearl stated.

The pieces started to fit together. Garrett looked down to see his son with head bowed and hands shoved into his coat pockets.

"Isaac? Did you tell Miss Amanda where you were going?"

The boy didn't answer.

Garrett realized he'd been standing, not crouching like Amanda always did. He got down on one knee. "Son, you need to tell me the truth. People are worried about you. We don't want anything to happen to you."

Isaac's lower lip quivered. "I didn't mean to, Papa. I just wanted to help. I can do it. I can take care of things."

A lump formed in Garrett's throat, and he pulled the upset little boy into an embrace. "Of course you can. You had a good thought, son, and a good heart."

As tempted as he was to point out the obvious—that Isaac was supposed to tell an adult where he was going—he couldn't do it in front of the handful of people gathered around them. There would be time to reinforce that point later.

"Where is your sister?"

"At home," Isaac sobbed.

Garrett's heart went cold. The house had been dark. What if something had happened to them?

Fiona placed her hand on his shoulder. "Don't worry. They're both fine. Amanda brought Sadie to the boardinghouse."

Garrett let out his breath with a whoosh. His daughter was fine. Amanda had made certain of it. The warmth of that realization bubbled over into gratitude.

"Thank you." He stood and looked at those gathered around him. Mr. Calloway, Roland, Pearl, Fiona. And Charlie, who helped out at the store. A handful of lanterns stood at the ready on the counter. They'd been prepared to search for Isaac.

Garrett swiped at his mouth. "Thank you."

He couldn't think of anything more profound to say, not while the emotions still threatened to spill over.

* * *

After the joyful reunion, Mrs. Calloway insisted they all eat supper together at the boardinghouse. She had more than enough, especially when Amanda helped her make another batch of biscuits to go with the sausages, potatoes and cabbage. The hearty fare pleased everyone, and Amanda reveled in the full table. It resembled a family holiday, though she had observed those only from the Chatsworths' kitchen. Stories were told, laughter pealed out and Isaac's embarrassment eased.

The poor boy had looked most miserable when Garrett steered him in front of her for an apology.

"Sorry, Miss Amanda," Isaac had mumbled.

"Tell her it won't happen again," Garrett had prompted.

"Won't happen again," Isaac echoed, his face averted so she couldn't see it.

"I'm certain it won't," Amanda had assured him, "now that you see how much everyone cares about you."

He'd looked up then and flushed when he saw the smiles of family and friends, but as the meal progressed, he began to chatter like a normal boy. Since Sadie's thumb left her mouth and never returned, Amanda considered the outcome a success, but she did miss the time she would have spent with just Garrett and the children that evening. Those moments together were precious.

This time Garrett did not hold Isaac's disappearance against her. His laughter and pointed attention to her made that clear enough. Also clear was Fiona's attention to him. When Pearl announced that they could assemble the stable and backdrop tomorrow for the nativity play, Fiona glowed.

"You will help me with the backdrop, won't you?" the redhead asked Garrett. "I'll need someone strong to hang it."

Garrett didn't look one bit like a cornered rabbit. He even smiled at her. "I can do that. I'll ask Roland to help us."

"Of course," Fiona purred. "We'll need more than one man to put it up."

"I kin help out," Mr. Calloway offered.

Amanda had to stifle a laugh at the look on Fiona's face. Clearly, she had not counted on the boardinghouse owner to volunteer for the job.

When the children began yawning soon after supper, Garrett bundled them up to take them home. Roland offered to bring a load of wood in the pushcart and took off into the windy but as yet dry night. Pearl needed to work on the script for the play, which they would rehearse tomorrow. One by one, everyone drifted off, leaving Amanda alone to say good-night to Garrett and the children.

She gave Sadie a hug and a kiss and managed to embrace Isaac before he pulled away.

Then she faced Garrett. "I'm so glad everything turned out all right."

His blue-gray eyes looked black in the low light filtering into the hallway from the parlor. "I'm sorry for alarming you."

"It's not your fault." Yet something in his look made her heart beat a little faster. "These things happen."

"Yes. I guess they do."

She could feel that tension between them, just like when they'd gone sledding and crashed at the bottom of the slope. Her lips tingled, and she was suddenly aware of the tiniest details, like how one side of his mouth ticked up a little when he was embarrassed, and the slight bend to his nose, as if he'd gotten into a scrape when young. Both made him even more handsome.

Silence stretched between them for what seemed like minutes. She could not break his gaze, did not want to.

"Papa." Sadie tugged on her father's coat.

He bent over and picked her up. "Time to go home, sunshine."

She giggled and hugged her papa.

Amanda both regretted the lost moment and longed to be the one that Sadie turned to when she needed love and encouragement. Perhaps that day would come. Patience. Amanda must wait for them to come to her. Tonight Garrett would head home with his family, while she remained at the boardinghouse.

"Good night, then," she said with a wave.

"We'll see you tomorrow." Garrett's smile sent her heart fluttering again.

She stepped toward him, but he herded the children through the door, leaving her alone in the front hallway. She watched them walk away until she couldn't stand the cold any longer. With a sigh, she closed the door.

Tomorrow seemed an eternity away.

Roland had arrived with a cartload of wood by the time Garrett got back to the house. While Isaac and Roland carried firewood into the house, Garrett stacked the rest in the bin. He'd nearly lost his head with Amanda back at the boardinghouse. In front of his children, no less. If Sadie hadn't jerked him out of the moment, he might have kissed Amanda.

What would Isaac and Sadie think of that?

Yes, Sadie had written the school paper asking for Miss Mana to be her new mama, and both children had started the whole mail-order-wife fiasco, but they probably didn't realize that a new mama for them also meant a new wife for him. Including kisses.

Garrett wiped his brow before hefting more logs into the wood bin. The exertion must be making him hot. It couldn't be the thought of kissing Amanda. Other than the foolish stolen kisses of youth, he hadn't truly kissed any woman but Eva.

She was his one and only. He'd thought she felt the same. When she'd admitted to a love affair with a traveling peddler in the last year of their marriage, he'd been crushed. All trust in his wife vanished. How many more had there been? She'd refused to answer. Breaking his vows had never crossed his mind. How could she?

She threw out excuses. That Garrett had taken her from the life she loved in Chicago, that he couldn't give her the luxuries she wanted, that he was dull—the list went on and on. She even went so far as to say that she should have married Roland, whom she'd dated before Garrett courted and married her. At the time, Garrett had seen Eva's attentions as a victory over his younger brother. Now he realized she'd played him against Roland in order to get Garrett to marry her. Why? Because Garrett was the oldest and would inherit, she had boldly proclaimed. When that inheritance came to naught thanks to their father's debts, she'd felt betrayed.

In turn she'd sought revenge through an adulterous liaison.

The knowledge had nearly destroyed Garrett. His fury had driven her to her death.

Bitterness began to creep in, but he shook it off. The past was over and done. Eva was dead. Her lover would never return. Much as he wanted to pound the man to a pulp, the Bible made it perfectly clear that vengeance was the Lord's. Garrett had to forgive and try to forget.

Thus far he'd failed miserably at both.

Amanda helped. A lot. When he was around her, he could momentarily forget Eva's betrayal and imagine a future. He could see Amanda as a mother to his children. She was good with them, and tonight's incident showed she could act appropriately when something went wrong. She would make a good mother—but a wife?

Garrett licked the perspiration off his lips. Could he love her the way a wife deserved to be loved? Could he open his heart to another woman? She seemed perfect on the surface, but then so had Eva. Beneath the pretty exterior, his late wife had proved demanding and self-centered. Amanda did not appear to be either of those, but Garrett could not take a chance. Until he was absolutely certain of Amanda's character, he couldn't contemplate marriage.

There. Decision made.

Then why didn't he feel better?

He tossed the last chunk of wood in the bin and rolled the cart to the front of the house. Roland was still inside with the children, making sure they were all right. That's the sort of instinctive attention Garrett needed in a wife. That's what he would try to determine about Amanda. Tomorrow would give him the perfect chance. They would spend long hours together preparing for the nativity play. He would watch and listen and seek God's counsel.

Soon enough he would have his answer.

Chapter Thirteen

Chaos ruled in the church building and temporary school-house. Amanda stood near Pearl, who was trying desperately and unsuccessfully to teach the speaking parts to the children. Only the littlest ones sat still for more than a minute before racing around the benches that served as seats during school days and pews on Sunday. Even Isaac and Sadie were filled with more than their usual energy. Last night's episode had apparently been forgotten.

"I helped build the stable," Isaac told Amanda with pride. "I hammered in a nail."

"You did? I had no idea you were so skilled."

That response must have met with his approval, for he darted back to the front of the church, where Garrett was assembling the stable. It was shallow, capable of housing just the holy family and a few stuffed animals, but it was tall enough for a shorter adult, like her, to stand in. Even the Bailey brothers, who were playing the magi, would have no difficulty fitting under the eaves.

Near Garrett, Fiona had spread out an old, black canvas tarpaulin that someone had donated for the cause. She added the stars in white and yellow, stopping after each to talk to Garrett. Her obvious attempts to interest him were beginning to get on Amanda's nerves.

The pounding of Garrett's and Roland's hammers, combined with the shrieks and giggles of children, made it nearly impossible to hear anything. When little Evelyn Clapp let out a particularly shrill squeal, Amanda cringed.

Why was she here when she had so much to do? She hadn't even begun the costumes for Mary and Joseph and the magi. And then there was Pearl's wedding dress. With her friend occupied, this would be the perfect opportunity to finish the bodice.

Instead, Pearl waved her over. "I need you to help me teach lines to the children. Could you take Isaac, Sadie and Angela Wardman?"

Angela was playing the angel of the Lord who announced the birth to the shepherds.

Amanda sighed as she accepted the sheets of paper from Pearl. There went her chance to get more sewing done. She would tackle the costumes this evening. The wedding dress would have to wait for another opportunity. Perhaps she could talk Garrett into inviting Pearl and Roland to Sunday dinner. No, that wouldn't work, because then he'd want her to do the cooking. It would have to be the other way around. Roland inviting his brother's family to join Pearl and him, but then Pearl would be stuck cooking.

Amanda gave up and gathered the three children to the back corner, farthest from the construction noise.

"It's snowing," Angela announced.

Amanda looked out the window at the lazy flakes and smiled. "Just in time for Christmas."

"We can't stay if it snows too much. Mama said I have to bring Beth home if it starts snowing."

Amanda sighed. Based on that stipulation, Angela probably should take her little sister home now, but the snowflakes were few. None were sticking on the ground yet. They hadn't had much cold weather this month beyond that fateful snowfall when she went sledding with Garrett. The memory sent heat to her cheeks. She couldn't resist looking in his direction. Once again Fiona had cornered him. Her head nearly touched his as they peered at her sketch for the backdrop. Now *that* was enough to cool any blush.

Amanda drew her attention back to the children, all of whom were watching her intently.

"I'll keep watch," she promised eleven-year-old Angela, "and let you know if it begins to snow any harder."

The girl accepted that without question. The children here were so willing to trust. It hadn't been that way in the orphanage or at the Chatsworths' house. Lena had viewed Amanda with suspicion from the moment she arrived. The brother, Edward Jr., who was enrolled in an elite boarding school, barely noticed her existence when he came home on holiday. She might have been another servant for all he cared. Here, the children relied on the decisions of their elders.

Amanda glanced at the window again. The snow had picked up but still wasn't accumulating. However, if this continued, three-quarters of the children would need to leave.

"I have the most important speech," Angela was telling Isaac and Sadie.

"Well, I'm playing Jesus's father," Isaac responded, his face darkening just the way his father's did when he was upset. "That's the most important part."

"Everyone's role is important." Amanda tried to regain control of the rapidly disintegrating situation. "That's why you need to learn your lines."

"I know mine," Angela stated. "'Fear not, for I bring you good tidings of great joy.'" She then proceeded to recite the entire passage, not quite accurately, ending with, "'He'll be wrapped in swatting clothes and sleeping in a manger.'"

Amanda tried to stifle a smile. "Thank you, Angela. Clearly, you've practiced."

"I can remember anything I read. It's simple."

"Well, we'll still need to practice." And teach her the correct words.

"I can do all the practicing I need at home," Angela informed her. "I don't need this silly rehearsal. I know my part, even though I have the most lines."

Oh, dear. Sadie's thumb was back in her mouth, and Isaac looked ready to smack the older, taller girl.

"It doesn't matter how many lines you have," Amanda tried to explain, but the children weren't listening.

She felt a tug on her skirts. Sadie had grabbed hold.

During that moment of inattention, Isaac exploded. "You're not so smart. My pa says common sense smarts are more important than book smarts."

"Well, your pa ought to know—"

"Stop this at once!" Amanda pushed Angela and Isaac apart, keeping them at arm's length from one another. "You are in church."

"It's only church on Sunday," Angela pointed out.

Amanda was not about to let that technicality get in the way of ending this dispute. "It is a house of God. Do you think He wants you to act like this? Especially when you're going to portray the birth of His Son?"

"But it's a sch—"

This time Amanda cut Angela off with a glare. "Miss Lawson will not tolerate such misbehavior in the classroom. Do you want me to tell your parents about this?" She looked first Angela and then Isaac in the eye.

Both children backed down.

"No," each grudgingly admitted.

"Just no?"

"No, Miss Porter," they said in chorus.

"Very well, then. Let's get back to work. I expect your full attention. Understand?"

The children nodded, and Amanda could relax a little. She had solved the dispute before it escalated into a crisis. Pearl would be grateful. She looked toward her friend, huddled with the rest of the children in the opposite corner, and instead saw Garrett Decker watching her every move. He was not smiling.

Oh, dear. She'd just disciplined his son.

Memories bobbed to the surface of the repercussions when she'd dared to tell Mrs. Chatsworth that Lena had ruined Amanda's best dress by cutting it to pieces with a pair of scissors. Instead of disciplining her daughter, the woman had sent Amanda to her room without lunch and supper. Later, Mrs. Brighton sneaked a few biscuits into the room in her apron pocket, but she also brought the unwelcome news that Amanda was expected to repay the Chatsworths for the ruined gown by cleaning every piece of silver and brass in the house.

Garrett was not Mrs. Chatsworth, but what father would not favor his son over a housekeeper? Amanda turned back to the children and tried to remember what she was supposed to be teaching them.

Garrett had to get away from Fiona. Every time he reached for another nail, she was at his elbow asking his opinion of the latest stroke of paint she'd applied to the canvas backdrop, or if she should change some element of her preliminary sketch.

He'd explained over and over that he wasn't an artist, but she continued to seek his approval. This last consultation had gotten far too close. Out of the corner of his eye he'd noticed Amanda glance in his direction just in time to see Fiona inch so near that she almost touched him. From that distance, it probably appeared that she had. Since he'd been forced by politeness to duck just enough to look at the sketch, Amanda probably thought something else was going on.

It wasn't.

Garrett had no interest in Fiona O'Keefe. True, he'd once considered her. She brought him the most delicious sweet rolls and bread, after all, but that had stopped once Amanda began working for him. He'd figured Fiona had turned her attention elsewhere, such as to Sawyer Evans, her accompanist at the Saturday concerts. Apparently not.

So once he gave his opinion on the type of trees to paint on the backdrop, he made an excuse about needing to stretch his legs and headed for his children, who were huddled with Amanda and one of the Wardman girls in the back of the church.

He'd arrived in time to overhear his son get in an argument with the Wardman girl. It was the sort of foolishness children often fell into—boasting and making prideful statements. Though Isaac was correct, the boy knew better than to argue with a girl. Garrett would have to have a talk with him later.

The moment he was about to step in, Amanda came between the two, holding them physically apart and firmly putting an end to the dispute. Garrett was impressed— no, shocked. He hadn't figured Amanda could discipline. Moreover, she'd done so kindly, without placing blame on one child over the other.

Maybe that was the confirmation he'd been seeking. Amanda would make a fine mother to his children. Maybe even a good wife in a friendship sort of way. Marrying for love was out of the question, but marriage for the sake of the children wouldn't be the worst thing he could do.

If she would agree to it.

Surely she would, seeing as she'd come to Singapore in answer to that advertisement his children had asked Mrs. Calloway to place. What a mess that had been, but maybe something good might come out of it, after all.

When Amanda finished settling down the children, she cast a final glance his way. Instead of the shy smile he'd expected, she looked upset and nervous. She quickly turned away.

What was that about?

"Garrett, Garrett!"

Fiona, paintbrush in hand, had tracked him down.

He slowly turned to face her.

"Should I paint snow or grass?" She waved the paintbrush, wet with the yellow artist's paint that she was using on the backdrop. "It is wintertime."

If she wasn't careful, she'd get paint all over the benches and ruin someone's dress or suit tomorrow morning.

He took her by the elbow and calmly directed her back up the aisle to the front of the church. "Be careful that you don't splatter paint anywhere."

"Oh!" she exclaimed, as if the thought had never crossed her mind.

Perhaps it hadn't, considering her apron and dress were spotless. Perhaps her quest to snare him had pushed all other considerations from her head. But Fiona was much more intelligent than she sometimes led people—especially men—to believe.

They'd just reached the front when the door burst open, and Mr. Wardman entered. He stomped snow off his feet.

"Miss Lawson," the man said in a booming voice. "The snow is getting deep just inland from here. I can take the

Saugatuck children home. I passed Earnest Clapp and Lars Norstrand on the way here."

Pearl set about at once getting the children dressed in their coats and hats and mittens. Amanda joined in. Within ten minutes, most of them had left, and the building quieted considerably. Of the children, only Isaac and Sadie remained.

Garrett looked out the window. The snow was getting thick, and an inch or so coated the ground. "I suppose I should get Sadie and Isaac home." He glanced back at the stable, which wasn't quite finished. "That'll have to wait until next Saturday. Isaac, Sadie, get your coats on."

Amanda hurried down the aisle. "I can take them, so you can finish your work."

He glanced out the window again. "Are you certain?"

"Roland said he has to go back to the store. He can walk with us to the house."

"I sure appreciate that." Garrett couldn't help but think of the thirty-first chapter in Proverbs that outlined the qualities of a good wife. More and more Amanda was meeting those qualifications.

Then he felt Fiona at his back. "That's so considerate of you, Amanda. We have a lot to do here before we're finished."

Amanda blanched, but not nearly as much as he cringed. If Roland left, then Pearl might decide to go with him. That would leave him alone with Fiona without anyone as a buffer.

"On second thought, my brother could take Isaac and Sadie to the store with him," he said to Amanda. "Then you can finish your work here."

She blushed the most lovely shade of pink, and her gaze drifted down. "I thank you, but my work is not here."

He could not tear his gaze from her, the very picture

of virtue with her hands clasped and her gaze lowered in humility. "The virtuous wife puts the needs of her husband ahead of her own."

Amanda gasped softly and clenched her hands.

"Humph," Fiona grumbled.

Had he really said *wife* aloud? He cleared his throat. "Virtuous *woman*."

The women didn't appear to accept that amendment.

Amanda backed away. "I need to go."

A wife. Not only had Garrett called her virtuous, but he'd also called her a wife. Surely he did not mean it. Surely he was not considering her...or was he? Oh, dear. She wrung her hands. If he knew everything about her past, he would never consider her the paragon of virtue.

"I, uh," he stammered, "have been reading Proverbs. I didn't mean...that is, it wasn't what it sounded like."

Fiona smiled. "You were just paraphrasing a Bible verse."

"I guess. More of a summary." He squirmed like a boy caught looking at another child's test paper. "I was just thinking aloud."

"Naturally," Amanda managed to reply through her partially closed throat.

At that moment, the impossibility of her hopes hit her with gale force. He sought a wife who measured up to the perfection delineated in the last chapter of Proverbs. Amanda fell far beneath that standard. Perhaps every woman did, but the secrets she carried were particularly damaging.

"I will take care of Isaac and Sadie."

Without waiting for his response, Amanda hurried to the back of the church, where she had to lean against the wall so she didn't collapse.

Pearl touched her arm. "What's wrong?"

Amanda shook her head. Pearl must have heard the exchange. Without the pounding of hammers and squeals of children, every word could be heard in this small building. On the surface, Garrett had issued a compliment. Then why did she feel her world crashing in?

"Sit down." Pearl guided her to a bench. "I don't want you fainting on the walk back."

Amanda sat heavily and leaned forward to draw a few deep breaths. This was what she wanted—to marry Garrett and become a mother to those precious children. Then why this overpowering fear?

"I don't know what came over me," she whispered, still conscious that everyone could hear what she said.

"You didn't eat much for breakfast and nothing for lunch. No wonder you feel faint."

God bless Pearl. She'd found a way to divert attention from the emotional turmoil to what she assumed was physical distress.

Once Garrett began hammering, Amanda could finally speak the truth—at least all she was willing to share. "Did you hear what he said?"

"Of course." Pearl rubbed her back. "It's about time."

"But…" But what? Amanda couldn't articulate it. "I'm afraid."

Pearl's brow creased in a frown. "Has he hurt you?"

"No! Never! He is the kindest man I know. Aside from Roland, of course," she added, for Pearl's sake. "But I'm not worthy."

There. She'd said it.

Pearl looked her right in the eyes. "I don't want to hear one more word like that from you. You are not only worthy, you love those children."

The children! They had witnessed the whole exchange. Oh, dear.

Amanda frantically looked around. They weren't anywhere.

She stood. "Isaac! Sadie!" She ran for the door and yanked it open.

Snow blew in, temporarily blinding her.

Pearl slammed the door shut. "Roland took them to the store with him. He'll watch over them."

"He did?" Gradually the fear ebbed away. "I didn't even notice." Again the tears rose. "What sort of mother would I be if I don't even notice that the children entrusted to my care leave with their uncle?" The question ended with a pitiful wail, and she buried her face in her hands. "What's wrong with me?"

Pearl slid an arm around her shoulders. "You're tired and overworked. And you've been hoping so much for this that the first sign it might come true has set your nerves on edge. It's completely understandable. Now, will you sit down a moment? I need your opinion on what to do for the nativity play now that we've lost our best chance to rehearse."

Thinking of something practical helped calm Amanda's jangled nerves. Though Garrett and Fiona still worked in the front of the church, she could manage to concentrate without worrying that she'd ruined her chances with Garrett.

Pearl laid out the problem concisely. "Neither the shepherds nor the magi are willing to speak lines, least of all learn them. How did Isaac and Sadie do?"

"We never got that far," Amanda admitted, "but Angela knows her lines fairly well, though she did mix up some of it and got a few words wrong. You will probably need to correct her, though, since she believes she already knows her lines perfectly."

Pearl chuckled. "That sounds like Angela. Do you think Isaac and Sadie can learn the lines?"

Amanda hesitated. "Sadie hasn't been talking that long. I'm not sure if she'll speak in front of a roomful of people."

Pearl nodded. "I think you're right. We need to come up with another plan. Do you have any suggestions?"

Amanda thought back to the plays that Lena forced her to participate in when they were children. Amanda had to play the villain or the one who died, and she never got the lines right, in Lena's estimation, so her foster sister would read both parts.

"You could have a narrator," Amanda suggested.

The worry lines vanished from Pearl's face as a huge smile burst forth. "Exactly!" She hopped to her feet. "It's the perfect solution, and I know precisely who should do it."

Chapter Fourteen

"No." Garrett must have told Pearl that a dozen times. She didn't listen.

He was not going to narrate the nativity play. Garrett did not speak in public. Bad enough he had to stand up with his brother at the wedding the day after Christmas. That at least did not involve speaking. This? There was no way.

"You'll be perfect." She practically danced in front of him. "Your voice is deep and carries well."

"I can help narrate," Fiona offered.

Great. Just what he needed. Not only would he have to humiliate himself in front of a churchful of people, but Fiona, a stage actress, would show him up at the same time.

"No," he said again.

Pearl seemed not to hear him. "Just Garrett. His baritone will ring out, like the teachers of old." She beamed at him. "You will be perfect, and you simply have to read from the Bible. Amanda said you read aloud every evening. Think of all the hearts you could touch with God's word. Perhaps He's calling you to do this."

If that was true, then why was his throat as narrow as a pencil? He glanced at Amanda. All the color had drained from her face, as if she feared his answer. But which one?

Was she hoping he would do it or afraid he would agree? As far as he knew, she didn't have a role in the play beyond making costumes and animals. And helping Pearl rehearse the little actors. Her investment was completely in the children. His children, especially, who could be disappointed to learn they wouldn't have speaking roles.

"I thought Isaac and Sadie were playing Joseph and Mary."

"They are," Pearl assured him, "but without sufficient time to memorize lines, it would be a lot easier on all the children if they could simply concentrate on where they have to be and not worry about remembering lines."

Amanda added softly, "Your presence would give Isaac and Sadie confidence. They're a bit intimidated by having to speak. This would help them so much."

"Plus you could rehearse together each evening," Pearl said. "Amanda, give Garrett the pages for Isaac and Sadie. It describes where they are supposed to be during each part of the play. You can read the passage directly from Luke's gospel."

She then jotted down exactly which verses to read. "Thank you, so much. It will make our only remaining rehearsal go much more smoothly."

Garrett had been cut down right where he stood. He could no more refuse Pearl than if a preacher had asked him.

Fiona leaned close and looked over his shoulder. "I would be glad to help you rehearse. I do have some experience with stage productions."

Garrett stiffened. "No, thank you."

"You'll do it, then?" Pearl asked.

At least she sought confirmation, but Garrett didn't have much choice. If he refused, Fiona would swoop in.

Sadie, in particular, seemed to fear the bold redhead. He couldn't let his children down.

"All right."

Pearl beamed, but it was Amanda's shy smile that warmed his heart. He would do this for his children.

The snow stopped as quickly as it had begun. By midafternoon, the sun appeared, turning the two inches of snow into a glistening white carpet.

"Isn't it lovely," Amanda sighed to herself.

She'd stepped to the window to ease the ache in her back from spending so much time bent over the sewing machine. Three hours of steady work and the costumes were nearly done. She just had to hem Mary's veil.

"They're all beautiful." That was Pearl.

Amanda turned to greet her friend, whose cheeks were flushed from the cold. Pearl had gone straight to the store after they left the rehearsal, and was probably back for supper. Amanda needed to tidy up and head over to Garrett's house to cook for them.

"The children were fine?" she asked Pearl.

"They're going to have supper together at the apartment once Garrett returns. Roland told me to tell you that you might as well take the day off."

Off again. At this rate she would not earn enough to pay for her lodgings after Pearl's wedding.

Pearl crossed the room and wove an arm around her waist. "What's wrong?"

"Nothing."

"I know you. When that little indentation forms between your eyebrows, you're worried about something."

"It's nothing important. Better that we think about your wedding. It's only a little over a week away."

Pearl sighed. "If the preacher gets here."

Singapore didn't have a regular preacher. Instead they relied on Brother John, whose circuit took him this way once a month. Other Sundays they sang hymns, read passages from the Bible, and the men took turns reading from Mr. Calloway's book of sermons. Come to think of it...

"Have you ever seen Garrett read aloud in church?"

Pearl's left eyebrow lifted. "I don't believe I have."

"Yet he reads aloud beautifully at home. Do you think he's afraid of reading in public?"

"Most people are."

"But he knows everyone," Amanda pointed out.

"Even worse. I've heard it's easier to speak in front of strangers than those who know you intimately."

Intimate. That word brought heat to Amanda's cheeks. To distract Pearl, she turned back to the sewing machine and continued the train of thought that had led to that unfortunate word. "I can't see why he would be nervous. None of us would laugh at him. No one would dare!"

"Would you like to read in front of the congregation?"

Amanda gulped. "Oh. I understand what you mean."

Pearl joined her at the sewing machine. "Is this the costume for Mary?" She held up the blue robe. "It looks like it'll fit Sadie perfectly. And I see the other costumes are done, as well. You've been working hard."

"I just need to hem Mary's veil, and then you can hand out the costumes to the children."

"I think I'll wait," Pearl said with a laugh. "You saw how difficult it was to keep their attention. If I hand these out in class, there will be bedlam. We will try them on during rehearsal next Saturday morning. Will that be enough time to make adjustments?"

"I'll bring pins, needle and thread along so I can do it on the spot."

"Perfect." Pearl stood back and surveyed the dozen costumes for shepherds, angels and the holy family. "This play will turn out wonderful."

"All we need is baby Jesus. Did you get Beth Wardman's doll?"

"Oh, dear."

"Oh, dear? You didn't forget, did you?"

Pearl did indeed look chagrined.

"It might have slipped my mind. Does Sadie have a doll we could borrow?"

"Only her rag doll."

"That will do in a pinch. On Monday I'll ask Beth to bring hers to school so you can get it ready. There, that's settled."

Amanda marveled at how Pearl could make decisions so quickly and then dismiss the matter from her mind. Amanda would turn it over and over for hours—all night even—until she unearthed a solution or tied herself in knots fretting over it.

She pinned the hem for the veil and assumed her friend would head off to do whatever needed to be done. Instead, Pearl pulled a chair close and sat down.

Amanda looked up. "Surely you have something to do."

"Trying to get rid of me?" Pearl's grin showed she took the comment in good humor.

"That's not it. Your wedding is coming up quickly. You must have preparations to make."

"Why? Once Brother John arrives, we will set a time. Then we will all gather at the church and say our vows."

"Who are you inviting?"

"This isn't a lavish ceremony," Pearl said. "Just family and friends. Of course you and Garrett will witness our vows."

The thought of standing near Garrett during this most solemn of occasions sent Amanda's insides fluttering

again. Could she have misread him? Was he really showing interest in her? What did it matter, when she could
never measure up to the ideals he held?

She set down the veil and pressed a hand to her tumbling midsection.

"All right," Pearl said, in her matter-of-fact manner.
"It's time you stopped avoiding my question. Something
is wrong. Spill it."

Normally Amanda appreciated her friend's frank ap-
proach. There was no illusion or doubt around Pearl. She
spoke her mind, plain and simple. But Pearl did not harbor
secrets. Her life was lived in the open. She freely admitted that her parents had abandoned her at the orphanage.
Amanda knew the hurt that caused Pearl, but her friend
had never let that stop her from following her dreams.
She'd wanted to teach school, so she'd worked hard to
get the learning she needed to land this job in Singapore.

Amanda wanted to marry and have a family, but that
wasn't something she could decide on her own. A man
must be willing to wed her. She'd thought that being a
mail-order bride was the perfect solution. The man needed
a wife. She needed a husband and wanted children. Love
was not necessary. Perhaps it only complicated things.

"What did Garrett say to you?" Pearl leaned close to
whisper that question.

Amanda started and busied herself lining up the pinned
hem on the sewing machine. "Nothing important."

"Stop." Pearl held the pulley so Amanda couldn't get
the machine working. "You're burying whatever happened
deep inside, and nothing good will come of it. I have eyes.
I know something happened between you two. You'll feel
much better if you tell me."

Amanda stared at the machine, caught between the desire to unburden herself and the need to keep anything heavy-hearted from her friend so close to the wedding day.

"Don't you trust me to keep it to myself?" Pearl asked.

"Of course I do." Amanda couldn't believe she could ask that.

"Then spill it."

"But…"

"Is it because I'm marrying Garrett's brother? I promise not to tell Roland any confidence you share with me."

Amanda sighed. Her head throbbed. She wanted to crawl into bed and hide, but she wasn't a little girl anymore. "I thought maybe Garrett was starting to warm to me."

"I know he is."

"But—" this was the tough part "—he seems to have an impossible standard for his future wife."

"Oh." Pearl sat back heavily. "That." Her brow furrowed. "I suppose it comes from being afraid he'll get hurt again."

Amanda didn't understand. "How? I thought his wife died tragically."

"She did." Pearl sighed. "I suppose Roland wouldn't mind me saying this. He hasn't told me not to, after all. He courted Eva before Garrett did."

That didn't clear up anything. "I don't understand."

"I think there was some jealousy between the brothers over the years. Garrett seems to think he's not as attractive to ladies as Roland is. From what I understand, Eva was very beautiful."

Amanda sucked in her breath as she tried to take in what Pearl was saying. "You're saying that Garrett never thought he was good enough? That's ridiculous. She married Garrett, not Roland."

"I don't know all that happened, only that it upset Roland. He came to Singapore to get away from Garrett and Eva, but they followed him here a few years later with the children. From what I've heard, there was a falling out, and the brothers barely spoke to each other until after the accident."

"Oh, dear."

"Yes." Pearl shook her head. "Jealousy is a terrible thing. Garrett feared his wife was still in love with his brother. At least that's what Roland thought and why he kept his distance as much as possible. But in a small town…" She sighed. "It's impossible not to cross paths. Accusations flew—all incorrect, but divisive nonetheless. Roland hates that it took Eva's death to bring the brothers together again."

Amanda squeezed her eyes shut. Garrett had been through so much. No wonder he insisted on such perfection in a wife. He'd been deeply hurt. "I understand."

Pearl hugged her. "Give Garrett time. It'll take him longer to trust someone than most men, but once he gets to know you, he'll see just how trustworthy you are."

Except that Amanda had a terrible secret, one that would never fit with Garrett's high ideals. Pearl had insisted she unburden her worries about Garrett. Her friend could be trusted. Pearl would never tell a soul what had happened with Hugh.

The words rose to her tongue, but Mrs. Calloway poked her head into the room at just that moment.

"Has anyone seen Fiona? She was supposed to help me with supper."

Both Pearl and Amanda told her that the last time they'd seen Fiona, she'd been working on the backdrop for the play.

"I'll help you," Amanda offered, but Pearl held her down.

"You finish Mary's costume. I'll help in the kitchen."

After Pearl and Mrs. Calloway were gone, the reality of the situation hit Amanda. Fiona was with Garrett. They'd been together for hours. The soprano with the beautiful silk gowns would make a far finer wife for Garrett Decker than a terribly imperfect orphan.

Fiona O'Keefe would drive a man to an early grave. Garrett couldn't shake the woman. She kept him working on the backdrop and stable until darkness began to fall. Only then could he break free from her with the flimsy excuse that he needed to tend to supper for the children. She knew they were at the store with Roland. Even if they were at home, Amanda would be with them.

Amanda. He had to speak with her. More than ever he needed her confirmation that he was doing the right thing. Yes, she'd seemed to approve of his decision to narrate the play, but he still wondered if Isaac and Sadie would be disappointed that they wouldn't have speaking roles. Though he'd gotten closer to his children the past two weeks, Amanda knew their likes and dislikes. The hours she spent with them gave her an advantage. As the bread-winner, he could never hope to spend that sort of time with his children.

Maybe Roland was right. Maybe they did need a new mother.

Amanda. The answer was obvious, but a new mother for his children also meant a new wife for him. That was the stumbling block. Could he wake up each day to those dark curls and violet eyes that so reminded him of Eva?

"What do you think?" Fiona stood back, surveying her artistry.

"It's good."

"Good? Only good?"

Apparently he'd given the wrong answer.

"It'll do," he amended.

The color rose in Fiona's cheeks, and her gaze narrowed. "You have no appreciation for the finer things in life."

Garrett was about to dispute that when it hit him. Fiona found that lack appalling, perhaps so appalling that she would finally let him be.

"Oh, I don't know," he drawled. "I do like a good chunk of fatback now and then."

Her horrified expression was priceless. He did feel a little bad for not issuing the compliment she clearly needed, but it was painfully clear that Fiona could never fill the role of wife and mother to his children. Dear Sadie had seen that long before he did. Her letter to Jesus begging for a mama by Christmas, Miss Mana in particular, went straight to the clear and only answer. Amanda was the one woman his children would accept.

"It's time to put an end to this for the night." He gathered his tools and put them in his wooden toolbox.

"But we can't leave the backdrop lying on the floor. We need the space for singing hymns and reading the sermon tomorrow morning."

"Roland and I will come in early and roll it up. Will it be dry by then?"

"I hope so."

"If not, we'll hang it." He tromped down the aisle in his heavy boots and grabbed her cloak from the peg. Its fur collar looked like a mink had clawed its way up there and was hanging on for dear life. "Here we go."

She breathed out an exaggerated sigh. "It might as well be a whitewashing as far as you're concerned."

He didn't bother to correct her. She'd done a fine job painting the stars, trees and woodland creatures. Everyone would know in an instant that the setting was here in

Michigan, not Bethlehem. But giving his approval would encourage what shouldn't be encouraged.

She let him help her into her cloak. "You will be at tonight's concert, won't you? Mrs. VanderLeuven promised mincemeat pie."

"Enjoy a slice for me. I'm going to spend the evening with my children." And Amanda. He couldn't help smiling at the thought of them seated around the big table sharing supper and the details of their day. Just like a family.

Though Fiona pouted, nothing could shake his anticipation. Perhaps that was the answer he sought.

Amanda Porter was the right mother for his children. After she settled the children into bed, he would talk with her. She'd answered that advertisement. Maybe she'd be willing to accept marriage in name alone, for Isaac and Sadie's sake.

Chapter Fifteen

Amanda looked out the boardinghouse windows at the winking lights above the store. Garrett and the children were there with Roland and Pearl, who had rejoined him after supper. Fiona was still at the hotel after her Saturday evening performance, and the male boarders went there after the early supper. That left Amanda alone with the Calloways.

Was this how life would be after Pearl wed?

"At least you got the bodice done on the wedding dress," Mrs. Calloway remarked while they scrubbed the dishes.

"I still need to finish off the buttons and fastenings and attach it to the skirt. Oh, and hem it. I do wish I had time to embroider, but the fabric is lovely on its own."

Mrs. Calloway bent close. "I did get a little lace for the neckline and cuffs. I know you said she wouldn't want anything fancy, but she can always take it off later. A woman has to look beautiful on her wedding day."

"Pearl will be beautiful."

Then why did Amanda keep envisioning herself in the gown? It wasn't fitted for her. It could never belong to her. She would not have a wedding gown, for the time Garrett needed was time she did not have. Each day that passed increased the likelihood that he would figure out that she wasn't the model of perfection that he desired.

It was hopeless.

She couldn't shake the gloom while finishing the dishes, or even later, when she stitched the bodice to the skirt of the wedding gown. She ran a hand over the shimmering fabric. Pearl would glow in this dress. She already glowed anytime she was near Roland. The dress could never match the pure joy that overflowed from her.

At the sound of the front door opening, Amanda hastily bundled up the gown into the large laundry sack that they used to hide it from Pearl. Mrs. Calloway usually kept a lookout whenever Amanda was working on the dress, hurrying back to snatch it from Amanda and bring it to safekeeping in the Calloways' rooms.

Not tonight.

Amanda looked for a hiding place, and ended up throwing the costumes on top of the sack just as footsteps approached down the hall.

"I thought I saw the light on." Fiona poked her head into the room. Her lavish hat sported holly and what looked like mistletoe. "Finishing up the costumes?"

Amanda heaved a sigh of relief. "I thought you were Pearl."

"Oh," Fiona said meaningfully as she slipped into the room. "You were working on *another* project. How is it coming along?"

"Almost done."

"Perfect." Inexplicably, Fiona settled down on the nearest chair.

Amanda went to the doorway and looked down the hall. "I wonder where Mrs. Calloway is. Pearl could return at any moment."

"When did you get back from fixing Garrett's supper?"

The question rankled. "His family ate with Roland and Pearl tonight."

"I see." Yet Fiona visibly brightened.

Amanda reentered the room and straightened the costumes so the bag didn't show, in case Pearl returned before Mrs. Calloway came to fetch the dress. What on earth did Fiona want? "How was the concert?"

"Fine," the redhead said with a wave of her hand. "As always. Sawyer did mention something you might find interesting."

The dramatic pause was no doubt for Amanda's benefit. Though she wanted to bite her tongue, curiosity made her ask what it was.

"Your Jake has taken a room in Allegan until the camps start up after Christmas."

Prickles danced up her spine. Her Jake. Her brother. Did she dare to hope that after fifteen years she might once again be united with her last living relation?

"Does Mr. Evans know where this man has taken a room?" she breathed.

Fiona stood. "A rooming house by the name of Aunt Ella's."

Her brother was within grasp, but for only a short time. Christmas was just a week away. After that, Jake would vanish again into the woods. She had to see him. She must.

"Thank you. You have no idea what this means to me."

"It's quite all right." Fiona waved off her gratitude. "I hope he turns out to be who you hope he is."

Her brother. Why wouldn't anyone say that he could be her brother?

Fiona swept from the room, and Amanda collapsed into a chair. For the first time, she knew exactly where to find the lumberjack Jake. From what she'd gathered, it was a difficult trip upriver some twenty miles or more. A boat would be required. Even then it could take all day, perhaps two or more if they ran into a logjam or ice, and had to resort to overland travel. And then another day or more to return. With Christmas a week away and Pearl's wedding the day after that, she must leave for Allegan as soon as possible. She had to find a proper escort.

She looked again out the window. The lights above the store still burned, but she could not disturb them at this hour.

In the morning she would speak to Garrett.

Dawn's light revealed the absurdity of the plan that had kept Amanda awake half the night, but she could not let this opportunity slip away. After Christmas, the lumberjack Jake would leave town. He might go into the forests nearby or decide to head north. If the latter, she would never find him.

She must act now.

Pearl bubbled on and on about the costumes and the play while they dressed for Sunday services. Since all Amanda's sewing was done except for the finishing touches on Pearl's gown, she would beg off assisting at school Monday afternoon and finish the gown. Hopefully by then she would have Garrett's promise to bring her upriver the following day.

She hadn't seen any steamboats on the river of late, but then she didn't make a habit of looking for them. Her life centered on the school, the boardinghouse and Garrett's house, none of which were on the river. Any number of boats might have come and gone. Someone must bring food and supplies and whatever was needed upriver.

"Have you seen any boats lately?" she interjected when Pearl paused to pin on her hat.

"Boats?"

"On the river. Surely they're still coming and going, at least upriver."

"I suppose. I don't pay a lot of attention to that."

"Oh." Amanda tried not to sound too disappointed. "I thought maybe you'd seen them from the store or that Roland mentioned something."

Pearl smiled. "We don't talk about business matters when we're together. We're too busy planning the future."

That only made Amanda's spirits dip lower. "With the snow gone, you can be assured Brother John will get here in time." A thought occurred to her. "Does he come by boat?"

Pearl laughed. "I think he walks, but perhaps he does take a boat part of the way. Why the sudden obsession with boats?"

"No particular reason." Amanda busied herself arranging her curls and pinning on her Sunday hat.

"Are you expecting someone or something?" Pearl clucked her tongue. "I told you I didn't want a gift. Your presence as my bridesmaid is quite enough. Do tell me you haven't done something foolish."

Amanda picked up her bag. "We need to hurry or we'll be late for services."

"Amanda," Pearl called out as she left the room on her heels. "I insist. No gifts. Understand? If you ordered something, send it back. In fact, I'll tell Roland to send it back."

Amanda had to stop this before Pearl caused an uproar and got the other women worried that she'd figured out their gift. She paused at the top of the stairs. Below, she could hear Fiona warming up her voice. They had privacy.

"There's nothing coming in by boat," she told Pearl. "I just…well, I heard Jake took a room in Allegan."

"Oh." Understanding dawned on Pearl's face. "Tell me you aren't considering going there by yourself."

Amanda touched a finger to her mouth to quiet her friend. She didn't want anyone spreading this all over town. "I'm going to ask Garrett."

A smile curved Pearl's lips. "I hope it works out for you. I'll give you the children's assignments before you leave."

Amanda felt her cheeks heat. Naturally, the children must go along. They would look like a family. This was a ridiculous idea. What if they had to stay overnight? Could she afford both passage and a night's lodging? And she really ought to pay for Garrett and the children. It wasn't right to ask him to pay the cost for her curiosity. The whole voyage might end in enormous disappointment right before Christmas. And before Pearl's wedding.

She caught her breath. Surely a week was more than enough time to travel twenty miles upriver and back again.

Garrett whistled as he readied the children for church. He'd gotten out the old harmonica last night but couldn't play it. It sat on the bureau in his room. Maybe someday he'd pick it up. Maybe he would teach Amanda how to play.

"Can we have a tree, Papa?" Sadie asked, her eyes wide with hope.

He hadn't put up one last year. Roland did, but Garrett refused to bring out of storage the little paper fans and ribbons that Eva had used her last Christmas. They'd ended up stringing popped corn and berries for decorations. It had been a sad tree without a single candle to light it at night.

"We will cut one down Friday after work. How does that sound?"

"Yippee!" Sadie hopped up and down so much that he couldn't tie the ribbon in her hair.

"Stand still a minute."

She settled just that long, and he managed a pitiful bow

that would make Mrs. Calloway shake her head. Amanda would do a much better job. She did everything beautifully and was good with the children, especially Sadie. It had taken him too long to recognize that.

"Woot-*woot*…" Isaac made the sound of a steam whistle as he pushed his toy tugboat along the tabletop. "Coming in to the wharf. All hands on deck."

Garrett marveled that his son had picked up some of the nautical jargon and was grateful he hadn't yet dared to repeat the more colorful language. If only Garrett could keep them at this age. He sighed. They would grow up and question everything. Sadie would need a mother's advice. He'd made the right decision.

Now, he had to trust that Amanda felt the same way, that she would put the children's welfare ahead of any fancy ideas of romance. Marrying for the sake of the children was one thing. Marrying for love was quite another. He wasn't ready for that yet.

"Let's get our coats on," Garrett prompted.

Through the frosty windows he could see the Calloways, Pearl and Amanda leaving the boardinghouse. They would wait for Roland to join them and then head to church. Garrett hoped to have a word with Amanda while his brother occupied the children. Roland had promised last night that he'd arrange that moment alone with Amanda.

Garrett finished buttoning Sadie's coat and straightened her hat. Isaac could put on his coat, hat and mittens without help, but Sadie still needed a little coaxing to get ready. He could envision Amanda buttoning Sadie's coat and kissing her before they all left for church. His heart swelled at the vision.

With the children waiting at the door, he threw on his coat, hat and gloves. Then he grabbed the Bible and ushered them out into the clear sunny morning. Not a breath of wind rustled the frosted grasses poking up from the remnants of snow that hadn't melted in the late day sun yesterday. The rest would melt today.

"Miss Mana! Miss Pearl!" Sadie called out, running to join the ladies.

The Calloways led the way, with Pearl and Amanda following. Roland brought up the rear. Isaac naturally joined his uncle, full of questions about tugboats, of all things. Garrett wondered why the sudden interest.

"Mr. Underwood said he saw a steamer headed this way from points south," Roland told his nephew. "Maybe it'll stop here."

Isaac danced along with his uncle. Underwood kept the light in the lighthouse atop the big dune. He'd see any approaching vessels, but Garrett was surprised that Roland had seen the keeper already this morning.

"Is there trouble up at the light?" Garrett asked his brother.

"Just needed something for his rheumatism." Roland grinned. "I haven't forgotten what you asked me to do." He then called Pearl and Sadie to his side on the pretense that they needed to discuss the family's Christmas dinner.

Amanda naturally dropped back, and soon Garrett found himself alone with her. Yet now that she walked beside him, he couldn't find the words. How did a man ask a woman to marry in name alone? A blunt question would not bring the hoped-for results, but he hadn't a gift for flowery language.

He cleared his throat. "Lovely morning."

"Especially after yesterday's snowfall." Her cheeks bloomed pink, and she did not look at him, as if fearing what he would say.

His heart sank. How could he get this out if she was afraid to listen or even look at him?

She pulled her coat tighter. It was probably the cold morning, but it felt like she was shielding herself against what he was about to ask. He fished around for something else to thaw the silence.

"I'm sorry about the misunderstanding yesterday."

She looked at him then. "What misunderstanding?"

Now it was his turn to be confused. "About supper."

"Roland said you and the children would eat with him. Was I supposed to fix supper for you?"

"No. No, but I hadn't intended to work so late. I should have come by to tell you."

"Oh. No, that's all right." Again she looked ahead, but her cheeks had that pretty pink glow to them. "I understand."

Garrett's mind raced for something else to say and came up empty. Surely she must realize what he wanted to ask. She had responded to that advertisement for a bride, after all. They both wanted more or less the same thing. Then why couldn't he find the words?

"I, uh…" He couldn't think of another word.

"Yes?" she asked hopefully.

Too hopefully. As if she expected romance.

His chest squeezed so tight that it felt like he'd suffocate. He tugged at the collar of his shirt. "I'm glad it stopped snowing before much accumulated on the ground."

"Oh." She sounded disappointed. "Me, too."

Garrett could kick himself. What was wrong with him? Last night he knew exactly what he needed to do. Now, he couldn't spit out one syllable. Silence stretched as they walked closer to the church. Other townsfolk joined their party, and the opportunity had passed. Another time, perhaps. Then Sadie turned back to look at them, and with a twinge of guilt he recalled her wish for a new mama.

He halted. "Miss Porter."

"Mr. Decker." She stopped also, her bag pressed against her midsection as if she feared someone would take it. Her gaze was riveted to the boardwalk.

The others trickled around them until they were again alone.

"I have something to ask you," they said at the same time.

Amanda blushed.

An embarrassed chuckle burst out of Garrett.

Her color deepened. He'd messed that up.

"I'm sorry," he said again.

"Me, too. You go first."

"No, you. Ladies first."

She fidgeted with her bag before heaving a big sigh and drawing up her shoulders. "I—I'm looking for a gentleman to escort me." Her voice trailed off into a whisper, so he had to lean close to hear.

"Escort you?" he echoed, not understanding.

"Upriver." Her face flamed red, and her eyes darted anywhere but at him. "You see, my brother—at least I hope he's my brother—has taken a room in Allegan, and I need to find out if he is who I think he is. Or hope he is." Only then did she lift her gaze to look at Garrett. Those long dark lashes swept nearly to her eyebrows and framed her violet eyes to perfection.

He didn't understand. "You don't know if this man is your brother?"

"I'm sorry. I didn't explain that very well. You see, when my parents were killed in a train accident, I was sent to live with my grandmother, while my older brother, Jacob, was sent to live with an uncle in Missouri." She bit her lip, the distress evident. "Grandmama died a little while later, and I was sent to the orphanage. They said my brother had run away, and no one knew where he was. I wrote my uncle, but the letters were returned, addressee unknown. Miss Hornswoggle—she ran the orphanage—said that meant he'd moved or died."

Amanda's story tugged at Garrett's heart. No wonder she understood Isaac and Sadie so well. She had suffered the loss of a parent, too, in fact both parents. To be sent to an orphanage… He shuddered. If something happened to him, Roland would take the children, but if anything happened to both of them, Sadie and Isaac would end up in an orphanage, too. Even more reason to marry.

"Earlier this fall, before the big logging rush," she said, "I'd heard there was a man about my age named Jake working up in the lumber camps. I expected him to come downriver with the logs, but he didn't. Some said he'd headed north. Just yesterday, Fiona told me that he's taken a room in Allegan. I need to go there soon, before the camps open after Christmas."

Garrett tried to take it all in. "Why do you think this man is your brother?"

"Because he has dark hair like me."

That seemed far-fetched at best. "And the same color of eyes?"

"I don't know." She bit her lip. "I don't remember if Jacob's eyes were blue or violet, but I have to find out for certain, don't you see? And Pearl says I need to have a reputable gentleman escort me. For my safety. The children can join us, make it an outing."

Garrett should be pleased that she considered him both reputable and a gentleman, but he could only think of the insanity of this proposal. "You have no idea if it's your brother. You said he was in Missouri. Why would he have come to Michigan?"

"For work?" Her voice wavered.

"That's a long distance to travel, especially for someone who would have had no experience logging. It would make more sense for him to have hired out on one of the farms between your uncle's farm and New York. You were from New York?"

She nodded. "I suppose you're right. But how can I rest, knowing that I had a chance to find him and gave it up? I've saved enough to pay for passage upriver. I could pay your passage also. And for the children."

Upriver. The single word hit with the force of a felled tree crashing to the forest floor. She intended to take a boat upriver. A boat. In the icy cold river. Visions of Eva struggling to cling to the capsized boat crowded his mind. The chunks of ice bumped into her. Frozen fingers could not hold on. She slipped beneath the surface while he raced frantically back and forth along the shore, looking for some conveyance, no matter how small, to take across to rescue her. Instead, Roland had grabbed the only boat and rowed furiously in her direction, but it was too late. By the time he retrieved her body and brought her to shore, she was gone.

And Garrett's anger had caused it all.

He closed his eyes against the memories, but such images never leave. They return again and again, each time just as raw and filled with pain.

"Please?" The whispered plea came with the clasp of a warm hand.

Eva's hand hadn't been warm. It had been cold when she clung to him. It had been cold when he pushed her away. But neither of those compared to the icy blue fingers that curled under, as if clutching for the last strands of life.

He had let Eva down.

"I will pay your fare, too," Amanda repeated.

He could not look at her, lest he still see Eva pleading for him to forgive her for betraying her vows. Adultery. Not with his brother, thankfully. Garrett now knew Roland would never have agreed to such a thing. Instead she'd succumbed to the charms of a stranger who'd come to town on one ship and disappeared on the next. She'd said she never intended the flirtation to go that far.

Garrett hadn't been able to listen. He'd shaken her off and turned away from her, to try to gather his emotions. She'd cried out, something unintelligible, and ran out of the house. He'd been relieved for a time, since he needed to simmer down. Then Roland burst into the house saying she was in trouble in the river.

The river.

Garrett shuddered.

"I'm sorry," she cried. Except that wasn't Eva talking, it was Amanda. "I didn't mean to upset you. If you'd rather the children not join us, I can ask Pearl to look after them. It might only take a day."

Garrett stared at her, trying to wash off the haze of memory to see the woman standing before him, but the dark hair and violet eyes only clouded every attempt to distinguish one from the other.

"I—I can try to find someone else," Amanda said.

Garrett shook off the past long enough to caution her. "Why don't you write instead? It would be less hazardous and not take you away at Christmastime."

Her gaze dropped. "I suppose you're right, but what if he can't read?"

"You were separated before you could read and write?"

She nodded, and then lifted her gaze in a desperate plea. "I must know. He's my only living relation."

Garrett glanced toward the river. Steam lifted sky-ward, for the water was still a bit warmer than the air. It wasn't icy like in early spring, but it was cold enough... cold enough to kill.

His heart turned to ice. "I'm sorry. I can't."

Chapter Sixteen

Amanda barely heard the sermon and couldn't recall a word of it afterward. She sang the familiar Christmas carols without one verse entering conscious thought. She prepared Sunday dinner for Garrett and his children, but what she'd envisioned as a joyous gathering was terribly quiet. The children sensed the tension between their father and her. Soon their chatter trailed off into careful silence.

Sadie picked at the chicken and dumplings, one of her favorite dishes. Amanda tasted it to make sure she hadn't added too much salt or pepper. It tasted the same as before.

During services, all she could think about was how to make the journey upriver on her own, but perhaps Garrett was right. Perhaps a letter of inquiry would do just as well. It might even bring the lumberjack Jake to Singapore. Tonight she would write.

"Do you expect someone to take mail upriver to Allegan this week?" she blurted out.

Garrett looked up from the plate of food he'd been shoveling into this mouth. He took a gulp of water and swallowed. "It's been a while. A tugboat should stop by before long.

"Good." She managed a weak smile. "I want to send a letter that way."

His gaze warmed. "A wise decision."

His approval meant more than it should, for it was strong enough to battle her desire to learn the truth. Deep down, she wanted to sprint to that boat and beg passage to Allegan at the earliest opportunity. A letter seemed a poor substitute for seeing the man face-to-face. She would know Jacob at once. Surely she would. Though they were just five and six years of age when parted, he was her only sibling. Even now she could recall the way he'd teased her about the curls in her hair. She thought of the broken locket. Perhaps he might have the other half. If he had changed as much as Pearl seemed to think, she would need some proof that he truly was her brother. The locket would be that proof.

"Amanda?" Garrett was looking at her in such a way that he must have asked a question that she'd failed to answer.

"I'm sorry. I was thinking." More like daydreaming.

"Are the costumes and animals ready for next Saturday?"

"Oh. Yes." Except for one item. When little Beth learned she must give up her doll for nearly a week, she'd refused. "Does Sadie have another doll besides Baby that we could use for the baby Jesus?"

Sadie solemnly shook her head, while her father answered in the negative. Yet he looked oddly uncomfortable. Younger men were sometimes embarrassed by any talk of babies or dolls, but Garrett had experienced both, with his children and with his daughter's dolls. Why would he react that way?

Sadie provided the answer. "Mama had a baby doll."

"No," Garrett snapped, "that one isn't a toy." He turned to Amanda. "It's porcelain."

That might have explained the reaction if he hadn't been so vehement.

"We will wrap it carefully so it doesn't break," Amanda offered.

"No."

"We will only use it Christmas morning," she pleaded.

He proved just as immovable as he had on escorting her to Allegan. Amanda was left empty-handed. She finished cleaning up and departed, the awkward silence again looming between them. If everything she requested was met with denial and this sullen silence, what sort of relationship could they ever hope to have? After the devastation of Hugh, Amanda hoped for a completely open and honest relationship in marriage. It didn't matter if Garrett did not love her as long as he was frank about it. He was completely honest about some matters and just as closed about others. Amanda could not tiptoe around those sensitive subjects for a lifetime, except perhaps for the sake of the children.

She pondered that as she returned to the boardinghouse. With Pearl still visiting Roland, Amanda had a little time to finish the buttons. Each one needed to be covered in the same fabric as the gown and then sewn in place. Small loops had to be attached to the opposite side of the back panels, directly opposite the buttons. It was detailed work that required a clear mind.

Mrs. Calloway brought her a pot of tea, but even two cupfuls didn't bring focus. After she made two mistakes, she gave up.

Mrs. Calloway bustled into the room. "She's almost here."

Amanda heard the front door open. Oh, dear, Pearl would head straight to the writing room. Amanda jumped to her feet and grabbed at the dress to shove it into the laundry bag that Mrs. Calloway was holding.

Hurry. Hurry.

She shoved and pushed. The gown could be pressed later.

Then something crashed to the floor. Her teacup!

Amanda looked down to see tea staining the beautiful silk fabric. No! Not Pearl's wedding dress!

She tried to blot it with her apron.

"Stop!" Mrs. Calloway wrested the gown from her and stuffed the rest of it into the bag.

"There you are," Pearl said, looking from Amanda to Mrs. Calloway and back again. "What happened? You look like the world is coming to an end."

Rather than answer, Amanda ducked under the sewing machine to pick up the teacup, which had suffered the loss of its handle.

Mrs. Calloway muttered something about laundry and bustled away.

"On a Sunday?" Pearl asked.

Amanda's hands shook as she gathered the pieces of the broken cup. Everything was going wrong. Her brother. Pearl's dress. Garrett's iciness toward her. The cup. A sob slipped out.

Pearl knelt beside her, took the pieces of china from her hands and set them on the nearby desk. "It's only a teacup."

The tears only increased. It was so much more. All her hopes were falling apart.

Garrett hated the wall that had risen between Amanda and him. Her request was outlandish—to travel upriver to Allegan this moment. The children and Pearl depended on her for the nativity play. Amanda was supposed to be Pearl's bridesmaid in just a week. Though it might take only a day, providing they could find a steam tug willing to make the run upriver and down, bad weather could strand them in Allegan. All because of a slim to impossible chance this man was her brother.

That's what Garrett told himself the rest of the day Sunday and all through work on Monday. But he'd have to face her and that disappointment the moment he returned home.

Instead he went to the store and explained to Roland what had happened.

"There's no chance that this lumberjack will be her brother," he summed up.

Roland shrugged. "There's a chance, though admittedly tiny."

"Too small to bother."

"What if it was your only living relation who went missing? To what lengths would you go to find him?"

Garrett hated that his brother had a good point. "But now? With Christmas coming? Who would go upriver?"

"Underwood sent word the mail boat's on its way in. The tug'll be by to pick up the mail and any cargo bound for stops upriver."

Once again Roland had a point, and it wasn't making Garrett feel any better about turning down Amanda's request. "I can't believe she'd risk missing her best friend's wedding."

"She shouldn't miss it. Here comes the *Donnie Belle* now."

The steam tug putted up and downriver, bringing supplies to the communities that had sprung up on the shores.

"Here to meet the mail boat," Roland added, "which is coming alongside the lower wharf as we speak."

That only roughened up Garrett's already irritated nerves. "I don't want Amanda on the *Donnie Belle*." There. He'd said it.

Roland grinned. "Afraid of losing her? You know how to remedy that."

"I'm not getting on a boat."

A laugh burst out of Roland. "I never thought I'd see the day when Garrett Decker was afraid to set foot on a boat."

"I'm not afraid."

"Then why are you here trying to explain yourself?" Roland rounded the counter. "Mail boat's landed. I need to go out back and get the mail. Watch the counter for me."

Garrett didn't mind watching the store on occasion, but he wasn't in the best mood to greet customers. Fortunately, there was only Louise Smythe, picking up a few things for the Elders. The tiny woman appeared from behind a display of heavy coats with a list in her hands.

"Some Epsom salts, camphor and sprain liniment. Put it on the Elders' account."

"Yes, ma'am." Garrett found the salts and liniment easily enough, but he couldn't locate the camphor.

"I couldn't help but overhear," the woman said while he was turned away from her. "I assume you were speaking of Amanda."

Garrett froze.

"She's a lovely woman," Louise said, almost dreamily.

"Yes." He wouldn't allow himself more.

"Kind and gentle and so good with children."

Was Louise involved with this matchmaking effort also? That seemed odd, considering she'd been one of the women who'd arrived in Singapore in answer to the advertisement for a wife.

At last he put his hands on the camphor. "Here we go." He swung around, but deliberately avoided her gaze. "Let me get out your account." He pulled the account book from under the counter and leafed through the pages until he found the one for the Elders. They always paid on time and in cash, unlike almost everyone else.

He quickly totaled the items. "That will be thirty-five cents." He jotted it down and then turned the ledger so she could sign for the items.

She began to put the jars in her basket, but he halted her. "Now, let me get this for you. You do know that you could have given us the order, and we would have delivered the items later today."

"I do, but I needed to get out. You know how it is sometimes."

Garrett didn't. Eva had liked to roam, saying she couldn't stand being inside the house all day every day with only the children for company. He didn't understand. He'd give anything to have entire days with them.

With a clatter and slam of a door, Roland entered the store carrying a canvas bag. "Here I am."

Louise couldn't hold back her eagerness. "Is that the mail?"

"Indeed it is, and if I'm not mistaken there is something for you to take back to the Elders." Roland hefted the bag onto a clean spot on the counter and opened it.

Garrett wondered how his brother knew that already, but then he spotted Captain Elder's name on the top envelope.

Roland spilled the mail onto the counter. One letter, badly trampled and torn, slid off the counter and onto the floor. Garrett bent down and retrieved it. The back flap had come unsealed. He flipped it over, and his gaze naturally drifted to the address. That's when his heart stopped.

That battered envelope was addressed to Amanda Porter. The sender appeared to go by the name Chatsworth, wrote in an elegant hand and hailed from New York City.

If Amanda was an orphan, who would write to her from New York? Someone from the orphanage?

He flipped the envelope over again, only to find that it had come completely unglued, exposing the contents. The single sheet of stationery revealed the same elegant hand and a letter dated more than a week ago. But that was not what made his heart stop.

The opening line exploded with anger.

How dare you ask anything of me after the way you seduced my daughter's fiancé.

He folded the flaps over the words to hide them. He would glue it shut again, but nothing could erase what he'd read and the doubts that wormed their way into his mind.

All Mrs. Calloway's efforts that day couldn't get the stain completely out of the wedding dress.

"I've ruined it," Amanda cried, trying desperately to hold back the tears.

All that work. All the love that had gone into each stitch. One careless moment ruined it all.

"What am I going to do?" she whispered. "There's not enough time to make a new dress, even if I could get the fabric, which I can't."

"Now, dear, don't you go fretting over this." Mrs. Calloway shook her head. "The way I see it, we got two choices. We can dye the dress to cover it up, or you can make a flounce to hide it. Do you got enough fabric for that?"

"I—I think so, but Pearl will hate that. She doesn't like frills of any kind."

"Then we'll have to dye it." Mrs. Calloway blew out her breath. "I got some blue dye in the laundry room."

"Blue?" Amanda wailed. "For a wedding?"

"Honey, a bride gets married in the best dress she has on hand, no matter the color. It's only those society types that can afford to fuss about wearing white. Besides, you know as well as I do that Pearl's going to dye it as soon as she can."

Amanda let the fabric slip through her fingers. A blue wedding dress. "What will Fiona and Louise think? They're part of this, too."

"You leave those girls to me. We'll get this whole thing settled good as you please."

Amanda wasn't so sure about that, but what choice did she have? One way or another she had to cover up the mistake. With a flounce, Pearl would always know it was there, whereas the blue dye might cover the error completely.

"How do we make certain the stain still doesn't show?"

"We give the whole thing a good dousing in tea first. Then the blue dye."

Oh, dear. This dress could end up looking worse than horrible. If the first attempt didn't work, they'd have to go darker and darker until it ended up good for only mourning.

Amanda gulped. "I suppose we have no choice. We'll make a strong pot of tea."

Mrs. Calloway shoved the dress back into her arms. "First you gotta finish it. We can't be having buttons and loops that don't match the rest of it. And that fabric'll fray if you don't finish off the open seams." She glanced at the clock. "But you'd better hurry off to Mr. Garrett's house or those children'll be getting anxious."

"Oh, dear." Amanda handed the dress back to Mrs. Calloway. "Can you put it away for me? I wish there was someplace you could hide it so I could work on it late at night. I have a feeling I won't be sleeping much this week."

Amanda did not mention the other trial that weighed on her mind. The days were ticking away for her to reach Jacob, and she was no closer to getting to Allegan than before.

"I could put it behind the sofa in the parlor," Mrs. Calloway suggested. "No one would think to look there, and you're the only other person here who cleans the room."

"Won't it get dirty?"

"Not in this." Mrs. Calloway patted the laundry bag with the dress safely inside. "You'll have to get down on your hands and knees to pull it out, though."

"That's no problem." Amanda had spent much time on her knees. Perhaps more of it ought to be in prayer these days. Could God straighten out this mess?

"Good. We'll do that, then. I'll tuck it there when the house is empty. For now I'd better put this in my room. I heard the front door. Could you check to see if it's a new guest and tell them I'll be right there?"

"Of course." Amanda took a few deep breaths to calm her scrambled nerves.

She then headed for the front hall, but got only a few steps outside the kitchen when Fiona rushed toward her.

"The mail boat is in," the redhead exclaimed.

It took a second for Amanda to pull her thoughts from the wedding dress to the importance of this statement.

"Then the boat from upriver will soon follow."

Fiona beamed. "It's already here. I hurried back from the hotel as soon as I got word. I know how important this is to you."

Amanda's heart raced. This was her chance to travel upriver to find Jacob, but she had no traveling companion and was expected at Garrett's house. The crushing desire to find her brother warred with the need to take care of the children. What should she do? There was just enough time to tell Garrett so he could arrange for the children to get supper elsewhere, perhaps with Roland or even here at the boardinghouse. Mrs. Calloway would never turn them down. Yes, that would work, if Amanda could find a traveling companion.

"Can you go with me?" she asked breathlessly.

Fiona stared. "Certainly not. I have both a concert to prepare for and my songs for the Christmas service."

"It will only be a day. You would have the rest of the week to practice."

Fiona hesitated just long enough that Amanda thought she might agree.

Instead, the redhead fixed her with a curious look. "Does Garrett know that you're abandoning him?"

After cringing at the bald terminology, Amanda immediately thought of the advantage Fiona would gain. She might use this against Amanda to win over Garrett. The image of Fiona bent close to him, consulting on the backdrop, flashed into her mind and would not leave. Stranding the children and Garrett at the last second would not endear her to him. Pearl insisted the likelihood that this Jake was Amanda's brother was very slight indeed. Garrett had suggested writing.

"Never mind. Do you know how long the boat will be here?"

Fiona shrugged. "Long enough to load any packages that came in on the mail boat."

That gave her just enough time to jot a quick note. "Excuse me, please." Amanda hurried away from the redhead.

"Safe passage," Fiona called out.

Amanda didn't have time to correct her. She clattered up the staircase and burst into the room that she shared with Pearl. She had a few sheets of stationery left and one envelope. Ordinarily she would have preferred to spend time crafting the perfect letter. There wasn't time. She could manage only the briefest of inquiries, asking if he had a sister named Amanda. If so, he might inquire for her at the boardinghouse in Singapore. Addressing the envelope was a bit more difficult, since she only had a first name, but she must trust that it would do.

After sealing the envelope, she rushed back downstairs and grabbed her coat. From the front window, she could see a dark column of smoke rising near the river, but could not tell if it belonged to the upriver boat or the mail boat. She had no time to waste. Eschewing a hat and mittens, she ran from the boardinghouse, her coat unbuttoned, and raced along the boardwalk to the docks.

Chapter Seventeen

Amanda reached the *Donnie Belle* before it left to steam upriver. Though her note was not in the bag of outgoing mail transported aboard, the mate accepted it and promised it would reach its destination in Allegan.

"Everyone knows Aunt Ella's Rooming House," he'd said. "I'll bring it there myself."

With that assurance, Amanda hurried off to Garrett's house, where Pearl was waiting anxiously for her arrival.

"Where were you?" her friend asked, even as she pulled on her cloak. "When we arrived and discovered you weren't here, I decided to wait with the children."

"I'm sorry. I had something to do at the last moment or I would have gotten here sooner. I hope I didn't disrupt your plans."

"This has nothing to do with my plans. You made a commitment."

The mild rebuke stung. Pearl was right. Amanda had gotten so caught up in troubles that she'd forgotten her duties and the pleasure those duties brought her.

"I'm sorry," she repeated. "Thank you for waiting. I needed to send a note upriver."

"To that lumberjack named Jake?"

Amanda nodded.

"You decided against going there?"

"For now. Garrett suggested I write."

"Very sensible solution."

It might be, but Amanda hated the wait and uncertainty that a letter brought. *Patience*, she told herself as she rooted through the cupboards, looking for an apron. In her haste, she'd forgotten to don hers.

"Did your mother have any aprons?" she asked Sadie.

The little girl slowly shook her head.

Isaac, however, said, "Papa put all her things away."

Pearl glanced at Amanda, who shook her head in turn.

"Where did he put them?" Amanda asked. The apartment above the store wasn't big enough for much storage, and the stockroom below couldn't be very large, either.

"In the warehouse," Isaac said.

"Hmm," Pearl murmured, as she fastened the last button.

Amanda knew the meaning behind that sound. Her friend thought Garrett hid everything that reminded him of his late wife so he wouldn't have to deal with the loss. Pearl might be right.

"Perhaps it's time to bring them out again," Amanda said to the children. "I will ask your papa."

"He won't listen," Isaac said.

Pearl took her leave and stepped out the front door.

That gave Amanda a moment to consider her reply to Isaac. She didn't want him going into that shell again. "I'm sure your papa was grieving the last time you asked, but perhaps enough time has passed. Perhaps this time he will listen."

"Listen to what?" Somehow Garrett had slipped into the house without her hearing him.

Amanda fixed a pleasant smile on her face and slowly

turned. "I thought it might be time to bring out a few of the children's mother's things. To remember her by." She thought of that little broken locket, her last remembrance of parents who had left this earth when she was very young. She could no longer envision them. That had been lost to the mists of time. "I don't want Isaac and Sadie to forget her, the way…well, the way I can no longer remember my parents. I don't even know what they looked like."

His expression froze. She'd not seen such a stony look since the evening that she, Fiona and Louise first appeared in the apartment above the store, each eager to become his bride. He'd not wanted them then. He didn't want this now.

"I'm sorry," Amanda whispered. "I was trying to think of the children."

"It's not the same," he said roughly, not looking her in the eye. "I have a daguerreotype of their mother, so they will never forget how she looks."

"That's not the only thing they need to remember. I wish I remembered the scent and feel of my mother's skin. Or the way she told me she loves me, or how she laughed and the way she sang. I wish with all my heart that I had those things."

Sadie tugged her skirt. "Don't you have a mama?"

Amanda crouched so she could look the little girl in the eyes. "No, I don't. My mama and papa died when I was very young, much younger than you."

Sadie's thumb popped into her mouth and tears began to form in her eyes.

Now Amanda had gone and done it. She hadn't meant to upset Sadie or Isaac, who was staring sullenly at the marbles that had enthralled him moments before. She wrapped her arms around Sadie and kissed the top of her head. Isaac was harder to comfort.

"Even though it hurts to remember, it can help," she said.

Isaac turned stormy eyes to her, and she realized in that moment how like his father he was. "I'm not an orphan!"

"Isaac," Garrett scolded. "Apologize to Miss Amanda."

She stood. "No, it's all right. Isaac is perfectly correct. He isn't an orphan, and I pray every night that he never will be."

Was that a shudder that ran through Garrett? Even so, his expression didn't soften. If anything, it had gotten stonier. What had she done?

She tried to catch his gaze, but he looked to the kitchen. "Supper isn't started?"

She felt even worse. A workingman needed one thing when he returned home, and in her hurry to appease her curiosity, she had neglected him and his children.

"I'll work on it right now." She hurried over to the stove, which was a good temperature thanks to Pearl stoking it when she brought the children home. Amanda surveyed the foodstuffs in the larder and settled on cabbage and potatoes with a bit of salt pork for flavor. Not fancy, but it would fill up a man.

Behind her, Garrett finally moved. She heard his heavy footsteps cross the room to where the children were playing. The scraping of a chair meant he was sitting at the table.

Her hands shook as she attempted to peel the potatoes. The knife slipped, and the sharp blade caught the edge of her thumb.

"Ouch!" She stuck the thumb in her mouth, even though it wasn't bleeding much.

She instinctively waited for Garrett to inquire, but it was Sadie who spoke up. "You hurt, Miss Mana?"

"Just a little nick." She turned to the child with a smile, hoping to calm any fears. Then her gaze landed on Garrett, who was staring at her as if he had never seen her before.

What was wrong with him? Maybe he'd seen her go to the *Donnie Belle* and was waiting for an explanation.

She wrapped a bit of rag around her thumb and cut the salt pork into chunks. "I needed to send a note, so Pearl watched Sadie and Isaac until I returned." Amanda looked out of the corner of her eye, but Garrett's expression had not changed. "I'm sorry I didn't tell you."

"Where were you writing? New York?"

"New York?" She almost asked why she would write there. Then she remembered the letter she'd written to Mrs. Chatsworth. By now, the entire family knew where she'd gone. Even Hugh. What if…? No. Impossible. Hugh and Lena would never come here. This was wilderness as far as they were concerned.

Amanda's head spun. *Don't faint.* She mustn't faint. She remembered Pearl's instructions and drew in deep breaths. It wasn't helping. She let go of the knife and leaned over, hands on her knees. Recently, that would have brought a cry of concern from Garrett, or his comforting presence. Instead, stony silence greeted each deep breath.

Gradually her head cleared, but not the dread. What was going on? Whatever it was, she must meet it head-on.

She drew yet another breath and stood. All three Deckers stared at her. "There. All better. I felt a little faint."

She mustered a smile, which drew nothing in return.

Something had happened. Something awful. Perhaps mentioning the children's mother had done it. Maybe it was something else. Whatever it was, this silence could not last.

"I'd better get back to work." The words came out shakily, and the knife wobbled in her hand.

"You need an apron." That was Garrett.

"I couldn't find one." She didn't want to get back to the reason the conversation had turned to the children's mother's belongings.

Garrett went into his bedroom and returned with a store apron. It wasn't the right size, but it would do. He handed it to her.

"Thank you." Again she attempted a smile.

Again he did not respond in kind. "You'll need to clean your gown."

She looked down to see greasy handprints on her skirt. Oh no. She'd grabbed on to her knees when she felt faint.

"It'll come out."

She suspected the stains on her skirt would vanish quicker than the frostiness that had arisen between her and Garrett.

Garrett didn't know quite how to broach the subject. The letter was in his coat pocket. He would give it to Amanda. The question was when. She would want to open it. If she did and read the first line, she would fall apart.

Not in front of the children.

He knew that much at least, but he couldn't stop watching for some sign of the degenerate qualities that this letter insisted she had.

It could be untrue. He knew that in his head, but every fiber of his being wanted to dismiss her at once. She was taking care of his children, his precious son and daughter. The thought of a woman of loose virtue having sole charge of his children made his temper soar. He was snapping at her. It was wrong. A person should have the benefit of the doubt, be innocent until proved guilty, but not when children were at stake. His responsibility was to guard Sadie and Isaac. Amanda could prove her innocence later—if she could.

He stripped off the vest he wore for added warmth. The room was getting terribly hot. "Can't you put a damper on that stove?"

Amanda's hands shook as she scooped cabbage into the skillet, and some fell to the floor. "I'm sorry." She ducked down to pick up the pieces.

Sadie made a choking noise. He looked across the table to see his daughter sucking her thumb.

"Stop that," he ordered. "Girls your age don't suck their thumbs."

The first tears slipped down her cheeks.

Isaac lowered his head over the schoolwork he was now focusing on, as if he did not want to meet Garrett's gaze.

Fine. This was between him and Amanda. Once she left, everything would get back to normal.

Naturally, she rushed to Sadie's side, gathering the girl in an embrace. "It's all right. I know you suck your thumb when you're scared, but nothing bad is going to happen. Can you help me by setting the table?"

Sadie slipped off her chair to fetch the plates, but the glare Amanda gave Garrett could freeze the sun. She returned to the stove without a word. He felt a bit guilty. He shouldn't have snapped at Sadie. It wasn't her fault.

It was Amanda's. To think he'd been about to ask for her hand in marriage. That letter had spared him a lifetime of regret. From this moment on, he was in control.

"Stop coddling the children," he demanded.

She ever so slowly turned her head. "You're speaking to me?"

"I am. My children need to learn discipline. Hardships inevitably come. If they're coddled, they will be too weak to withstand them."

She stirred the cabbage, potato and salt pork mixture in the skillet several times before speaking. "That's an admirable view. The question is when they must learn this harsh lesson."

"The answer is that it's my decision to make."

Isaac shifted, moving his schoolwork to the side, but still didn't look at Garrett. Sadie tiptoed around him, placing his plate within reach, but not coming close enough that he might wrap an arm around her. Did she fear him, too?

"I'm their father," he added.

"Yes, you are," Amanda agreed, still focused on cooking. "Perhaps Isaac can tell you what happened in school today."

Garrett narrowed his gaze. Something had gone on in school, too?

"Isaac?" he prompted.

His son looked to Amanda.

She smiled at him. "It's all right."

His children were turning to her first? Garrett clenched his hands.

Isaac glanced up. "Miss Lawson went over what we're supposed to do in the play. I don't know why I have to play Joseph. Why couldn't I be a king?"

Every drop of fear and temper fled in the face of Isaac's plea. Garrett had to admit that a king would be far more interesting to a young boy than playing the father of Christ.

Garrett motioned Isaac near. "You know that Joseph was a carpenter?"

His son nodded.

"I'm a carpenter, too."

Isaac wrinkled his nose. "You are? I thought you were a sawyer."

"That, too. But I'm also a shipwright. That's a type of carpenter, a very special sort of carpenter."

"Special?"

The question led to a discussion that lasted until supper was served. The food didn't look all that great, but it tasted good enough. Amanda would never make a fine cook, but she'd gotten past burning everything. She also ate like a bird.

Was she still upset? Garrett wanted to ask, to clear the air. His irritation had vanished with the full stomach. Amanda might have made a few mistakes, but she'd shown no sign of low morals. Every concern he'd had in the past had been unfounded. She had always been forthright with her answers as long as he asked the questions. This was one question he couldn't ask, though. He'd seen a private message—only one line, but an incriminating line that he'd best erase from his head.

When the dishes had been cleaned, and she was ready to leave, he would hand her the letter. Then he would watch her reaction. That would tell him all he needed to know.

Though Garrett's temper softened as the meal went on, Amanda stayed on edge the entire time. She couldn't get more than a few bites of food down. He focused on the children, completely ignoring her presence. She felt... unwelcome.

When the last bite had been eaten and the children excused, she rose to do the dishes. Garrett did not follow her. He did not comment at all, unlike the last few meals they'd spent together. Ever since their sledding tumble, he had taken to helping her by drying the dishes, or instructing Sadie on the finer points of wiping a dish dry. Tonight he moved to one of the stuffed chairs in the living area opposite the kitchen and began reading the Bible.

A frown furrowed his brow as he quickly flipped through the pages. He was looking for something. It probably had nothing to do with her, but Amanda could not shake the sense that he was searching for something with which to accuse her. Rather than inquire, she scoured the skillet with sand and then dumped that outside. Now a little soap and water would get the pan clean.

The children must have sensed something different in their father, for they kept their distance and played quietly at the table. More than once Sadie looked to her with an expression of such longing that Amanda's heart nearly broke. Sadie wanted to help. She loved to help, but Garrett was in such a mood tonight that she feared doing anything without his permission.

Amanda would take the brunt of any displeasure. "Sadie, would you put the plates away?"

Garrett looked up briefly but made no comment.

Whew. Whatever was bothering him, he wouldn't take it out on the children.

Amanda finished the dishes and then hung the damp towels above the stove.

"Will you play dolly with me?" Sadie whispered.

Amanda's heart ached for the little girl. Just when Garrett had begun to get involved with his children, he'd slipped back into the melancholy that had created the rift in the first place. Perhaps something had happened today to remind him of his late wife. That was the one thing that consistently sent Garrett's spirits plummeting. Until he accepted her death, the family could never heal. If only Amanda knew how to move him past that. The one thing that had made the most difference was their little sledding expedition. Perhaps she should plan another outing. Once she finished Pearl's wedding dress.

"Not tonight," she said to Sadie, searching for something they could do with no snow, "but perhaps your father would like to take a walk on the shore before the snow returns. I understand there are lots of stones to be found."

"The flat ones work best for skipping," Isaac piped up.

"Skipping?" She hadn't been aware the boy was listening to her and Sadie. "What is skipping? I know how to skip down a sidewalk." Though she had not done such a girlish thing in years.

Isaac laughed. "Not that kind. Skipping stones. On the water."

"Oh." She noticed Garrett's attention had shifted from the Bible to her, though his expression did not change.

Isaac didn't notice. "You don't know how to skip a stone?" He was incredulous.

This was where in the past Garrett would have stepped in to remind his son that she was a lady and didn't do the same things as little boys. He said nothing.

Amanda swallowed her embarrassment. "I'm afraid not. We never went to a lake or pond when I was young."

Both children found that impossible to believe. Amanda glanced at Garrett, expecting him to say something or even offer to teach her how to skip stones. He said nothing.

She managed a weak smile for Isaac. "Perhaps you'll teach me."

His chest swelled. "I'll show you, but nobody can skip a stone as many times as Pa."

"I'm sure not." Again her gaze drifted to Garrett.

This time he rose. "Let Miss Porter go, son. She has a lot to do this week, too much to spend time throwing stones."

Miss Porter. Not Amanda. Not even Miss Amanda.

His coldness chilled the warmth that she got from the children. He wanted her gone.

She went to the door to fetch her coat, and tried to think of something else. Perhaps she could get the buttons done on Pearl's wedding dress tonight. Perhaps the lumberjack Jake had received her letter by now. Perhaps he would come downriver tomorrow, or the next day or the next. Soon she might find her long-lost brother.

That thought should have lifted her spirits, but Garrett's displeasure had wound its way deep into her heart. She took one last stab at making peace.

"Good night, children. Good night, Garrett." She wrapped a scarf around her throat and pinned her hat on.

"That reminds me," Garrett said. "I have something for you."

"For me?"

Perhaps his silence had been nerves. Garrett had never given her anything. Her mind leaped to the impossible. Would he ask for her hand? No, that was not his way. He would have broached the topic before saying anything in front of the children. Yet the near kiss lingered in her mind.

He drew close, and the scent of him, woodsy and very masculine, made her skin prickle in the most wonderful way. He reached around her. After all this coolness, was he going to embrace her? Her knees threatened to give out.

But he simply slipped an envelope from the pocket of his coat.

"This came in on the mail boat. I figured since I was going to see you tonight, I would bring it here." He handed over the envelope.

Disappointment shattered her hopes. A letter. He only wanted to give her a letter. Granted, it was the first she'd received since arriving in Singapore, but it couldn't be from Jake. Her note had gone out earlier today and could not have brought a response so quickly.

She looked down at the envelope in her hand. It was so battered that the corners were bent and ripped. The flap had come unglued, yet the contents were still there. She flipped it over, and her gaze drifted to the return address. She gasped and lifted a hand to her lips.

"Unwelcome news?" He hovered near, painfully near.

"No." She shoved it in the pocket of her coat. "Until today, I forgot I'd written to them." In the excitement over this position as Garrett's housekeeper, she had neglected to follow up her request for a position with the Chatsworths with a second note retracting that request. "I'm sure it's nothing."

She attempted a smile, but Garrett's close proximity made her feel that she had to explain further. "The Chatsworths claimed me from the orphanage."

"Are they your papa and mama?" Isaac asked.

"No." They should have been, but they were not. Parents loved and nurtured. She'd received neither from the Chatsworths. Her discomfort grew. She backed to the door and turned the knob. "I should get going. Good night."

"Good night!" the children said in chorus.

Garrett remained silent, his brow drawn low in thought. That was what made her stomach churn long after she closed the door behind her.

Chapter Eighteen

Only after Amanda was alone in her bedroom did she dare to look at Mrs. Chatsworth's letter. She turned it over. Even in the low light of the oil lamp, the envelope looked like it had been pasted back together rather clumsily. The edges didn't align, and the paste was a darker color. A large fingerprint marred the last seam.

Someone had taken the envelope apart and glued it back together. Or, more charitably, it had fallen apart before the poor attempt at piecing it together again had taken place. She held her fingertip alongside the print, which was much larger. A man's.

Though she hoped a postmaster had attempted the repair somewhere along the line, she feared it might have arrived damaged in Singapore. That meant either Roland or Garrett had repaired the envelope.

Except for the flap. She fingered it.

The glue looked smeared and darker here, too. It had simply failed a second time.

Had someone read the letter?

She glanced at the opening line and her heart stopped.

How dare you ask anything of me after the way you
seduced my daughter's fiancé.

Amanda's hand trembled, and the letter dropped onto
the bureau.

Why would Mrs. Chatsworth say such a thing? She
never knew the extent of Hugh's attentions to Amanda.
She had no idea Hugh had promised marriage before attempting to take what she was not willing to give. No one
knew—except Mrs. Brighton. Oh, dear. Mrs. Brighton. But
she wouldn't have said anything. She'd promised never to
speak of that night.

Amanda pressed a hand to her midsection. Yet that was
the only explanation. For some reason, Mrs. Brighton must
have revealed what Hugh had done. Once the secret was
out, Hugh must have twisted things to make it sound like
Amanda's fault.

Though that had turned Mrs. Chatsworth's opinion
against her forever, Amanda could not mourn her loss,
nor indeed any of that family. None of them had welcomed
her like the people of Singapore had.

She fingered the loose flap.

Oh, dear. Anyone and everyone might have seen the accusation. Postmasters. Roland. Garrett. Especially Garrett.
He'd brought the letter to her.

That would explain his behavior tonight.

He'd seen the accusation and believed it. He didn't know
how wrong it was. A complete lie. Garrett must think her
the worst sort of woman, certainly not someone capable of
caring for his children. A pious man like him would never
marry a woman with that sort of reputation.

All was ruined.

A sob formed in her throat before anger swept it away.
How could Hugh do such a thing? What a foolish ques-

tion. The viper had lied to her. Of course he would lie to his mother-in-law.

Amanda leaped to her feet. She must explain, must tell Garrett that she had done no such thing, that the fault lay with Hugh. Garrett would understand.

No, he wouldn't.

Her righteous anger evaporated. He'd pointed out the virtues of the perfect wife. A perfect woman would never have fallen for Hugh's lies. She would never have allowed herself to get into a position where a man could take advantage of her. Amanda couldn't live up to Garrett's expectations before this letter. Now? Impossible.

Though she had not committed the sin Mrs. Chatsworth hurled at her, she had failed. She had been deceived by Hugh, misled into danger from which she could not escape. Singapore and a mail-order marriage had looked like a glimmer of light in the darkness. The past could be blotted out with a new future. But the groom demanded perfection that could never be reached.

After seeing this letter, he would dismiss her. He wouldn't let her near his children again. Isaac. Sadie. Garrett. Amanda's heart ached from the loss. The moments of joy she'd shared with them would never be repeated.

She sank to the bed. What would she do? Come morning, Garrett would expect an explanation. He hadn't dismissed her tonight. He was waiting for her to read the letter. The questions would fly tomorrow. Her already upset stomach knotted even more.

What could she say?

Nothing, for the truth would not lift her in his esteem. He would still consider her imperfect and unfit, her reputation irreparably stained. There was no way to save either her housekeeper position or any chance at a lifetime with Garrett and the children. He would dismiss her. When people asked why, he would be forced to reveal what he'd read. Then Mrs. Chatsworth's accusation would circulate around town. Amanda would be shunned. They might not even let her into church. Pearl would certainly be forced to keep her distance. School? Someone of Amanda's reputation couldn't be trusted around children.

A sob threatened.

She pushed it down even as her head spun. News, especially speculation, ran through town like wildfire. Soon everyone would know some version of the falsehood. The reprisals she'd feared in New York would come to pass here.

She hunched over, unable to draw a full breath.

What should she do?

Her first instinct was to run to safety. She could not stay here, could not face the stares, the snide comments and the blatant disrespect. Mrs. Calloway might even tell her she must leave the boardinghouse. Amanda would have nowhere to turn except the saloons, but she could never fall into those pits of despair.

No, she must find another safe haven. That had once been the Chatsworth household, cold though it was. Was it possible that in spite of the opening sentence, she would find forgiveness in this letter?

With trembling hands she unfolded the single page.

Mrs. Chatsworth was brief. The remainder of the letter stated in no uncertain terms that Amanda was to have no contact of any sort with the family. Five months ago, that would have been a blessing, but now she had nowhere to turn.

The people of Singapore had become dear to her, dearer than anywhere she'd ever lived, almost like what she imagined a family ought to be. Mrs. Calloway taught and consoled her like a mother. Pearl was her dearest friend.

Everyone listened to what Amanda had to say. Even Louise and Fiona, rivals for Garrett's attention, granted her a measure of respect. All that would disappear.

She could not stay.

Amanda stood. She began to crumple the letter, but could not toss it in a bin hoping no one would read it. She must burn it thoroughly, and the only fires were downstairs. Soon Pearl would return from whatever she and Roland were doing tonight. Their wedding quickly approached. Between ruining the dress and withholding secrets, Amanda was not worthy to be Pearl's bridesmaid. Fiona, Louise or even Mrs. Calloway would fill that role much more ably.

Amanda swiped at a tear.

She didn't want to hurt Pearl, but the stain of this horrible letter could taint her happiness. By claiming Amanda as a friend, Pearl would be viewed differently. Amanda couldn't let that happen.

Her hand drifted over the letter again. Mere hours ago she'd written to the man she hoped was her brother. Jacob was her last hope, and she knew exactly where to find him in Allegan. She'd promised Pearl not to travel there alone, but Garrett would never accompany her now.

Surely this Jacob wouldn't have gotten her letter yet. Even if he had, he wouldn't have set off downriver at night. He would wait until morning. Or send a note by return mail. She could not wait for him to arrive in Singapore. The moment he set foot ashore, he would hear the rumors about her and turn back.

No, she must go to him. Now. Tonight.

She shoved her few belongings into her carpetbag. It took mere minutes, but by the time she finished, she'd gained the sense to know she couldn't just walk out of the boardinghouse in the middle of the evening without

raising a lot of questions. Even now she could hear Fiona
return. The front door slammed as Mrs. Calloway asked
how the rehearsal went.

Amanda could never slip away unseen now. She must
wait until everyone retired and fell asleep. She shoved the
carpetbag under the bed. In the meantime, she could finish
sewing Pearl's wedding dress. Mrs. Calloway could dye the
gown. When everyone had fallen asleep, Amanda would
slip out and make the journey upriver on foot, guided by
the light of the crescent moon.

Amanda had to wait until well after the clock struck
midnight, because Fiona picked that night to stay up late.
Pearl drifted into a deep sleep more than an hour before,
and Amanda slipped from bed so she would not wake her
friend. Every few minutes she tiptoed to the door in stock-
ing feet, but the glow of Fiona's lamp didn't dim until sleep
began to press on Amanda's eyelids. At last the lamp went
out. She then waited another length of time until she could
be certain Fiona was asleep.

Then she crept out of the room and down the creaking
stairs, fearful that each movement would awaken someone.
Be with me, Lord, she silently prayed. Though she struggled to believe He would involve Himself in the tiny details of everyday life, tonight was a crisis. Not like that
evening with Hugh. Tonight Amanda feared her last hope
would disappear, leaving her nothing. Even after Hugh's
betrayal, when silent tears had dampened her cheeks during the long night, she'd had Pearl. She'd always had Pearl
to rely upon.

No more.

After donning shoes and coat, Amanda slipped outside. The porch creaked underfoot, and she froze. She'd

forgotten something. Her carpetbag! But she couldn't return now and risk being discovered. She'd send for it once she reached Allegan.

The crisp night air bit into her cheeks and made her shiver inside her woolen coat as she hurried through town onto the rutted, narrow road that wound its way upriver. No snow dusted the ground, thanks to the unusually warm days, but the night air was cold enough to turn her breath white.

On and on she walked, the sliver of moon revealing each exhale.

The children loved the way their breath turned to clouds of white in the cold air. They would say "ha" over and over just to see it take shape in front of them.

Oh, the joy of childhood!

Amanda had known so little of it. The years before her mama and papa died were too short to recall. Grandmama was strict and feeble. She would not play with her or make any concessions for a girl's imagination. Dolls were for viewing, not playing with. The orphanage had been just as dreary. Toys were few and highly contested. Since Miss Hornswoggle showed her preference by giving Amanda the prettiest dresses, the other children made sure she received none of the toys or was soon divested of any she was given.

The Chatsworths? An exercise in obedience and learning a skill that would bring her a decent position in service. A lady's maid, if she paid attention.

Yet her imagination had run wild, dancing briefly upon each beau that visited Lena, until it landed firmly on the young man who noticed Amanda first. Hugh would catch her when she least suspected it, popping from a doorway or a hidden nook in order to bestow a compliment on her hair or her gown or her smile. Soon compliments gave way to declarations of his affection, followed by the briefest of kisses that left her longing for more. When he promised marriage and an escape from a future in service, she believed him.

Oh, how wicked that man's deceit! He had drawn her in slowly until she was caught in the net. Singapore was supposed to erase that. Marriage, even in name alone, would give her what she most craved—a real family.

Now Hugh had shattered even that.

Her foot sank into the ground, and she stumbled forward, landing on her knees. The cold, damp earth soaked through her mittens and gown. She gingerly rose to her feet. Nothing broken. Her ankles were still solid, but where was she?

She must be past the burned area. The dim light revealed nothing but saplings and scrub, tall enough to block her view. She ought to hear the river, but the night was soundless except for a snapped twig here and a rustle there.

Again she shivered.

There might be wild animals out here. Wolves. Coyotes. Pearl had mentioned bears, though no one had actually seen one in town.

Amanda was no longer in town. She wasn't anywhere familiar at all, but the road continued on. So she would plod forward and hope that by dawn she would find herself in Saugatuck.

Crash!

The sound of something falling sent her heart into her throat. What was that? A bear? A man?

She ran as fast as her legs would carry her. It didn't matter where, as long as she got away from whatever had made that terrible sound.

* * *

"I saw something I shouldn't have," Garrett admitted to his brother.

He'd stared out his bedroom window and gnawed on the letter's damaging words all night. The sliver of a moon lit the snowless landscape just enough to remind him of the nights after Eva's death. Nights when guilt had tormented him, when he'd revisited every word and gesture until he could list every chance he'd missed to avoid the tragedy. He'd dragged through the days and weeks, barely conscious, until the men told him to go home from the mill before he got someone hurt.

Too late. He'd already hurt Eva. He'd driven her to her death.

In those dark days, only Roland would listen. He'd seemed to understand, and from bitter enemies they became allies. Their sole cause was to spare Isaac and Sadie as much pain as possible. To do so meant swallowing their own guilt and pressing forward.

Garrett had done it, and in time he'd found a new life. It wasn't as exciting, but of late it had become more appealing than a single day of that combative marriage. He looked forward to seeing Amanda each day. He longed for her smile, the shy glances and flush of her cheeks. She'd been perfect in every way that Eva had been imperfect.

Then he'd seen the letter.

If only he could undo that moment. If only he hadn't bent over to retrieve the envelope. If only the front had landed up instead of the back. If only the glue hadn't failed. But none of that was true.

He had read the evidence against her.

"What did you see?" Roland leaned against the store counter, a gleam in his eye. "I hope it was worthwhile."

Garrett frowned. His brother was so happy these days that he turned everything into a joke. "This isn't a game. It's a letter."

"A letter?" Roland's grin vanished. "Since you haven't received one in years, I'm guessing you mean someone else's letter."

"I didn't mean to look. The envelope was falling apart, and the flap was open. The sentence was right there in front of me."

"So, you saw one line of a letter by accident. No one knows, so forget it." Roland scribbled something in his ledger.

"I can't."

"What do you mean? You just forget and go on."

"The letter was to Amanda."

That drew Roland's attention. "Oh?"

Even now, Garrett couldn't repeat the scurrilous words that he'd read. "What if it isn't true? It can't be." He raked a hand through his thick hair. "I've thought about it all night. After all, she's been the model of modesty and Christian kindness ever since she arrived. Sadie and Isaac certainly think so." The idea that she might have deceived his children made Garrett sick.

"Wait a minute. What are you talking about?"

"Amanda," he said miserably.

"Maybe you'd better tell me what, exactly, you read."

Garrett blew out his breath. This was the tough part. Seeing what wasn't meant for his eyes was bad enough, but repeating it turned what he'd seen into gossip. Unless it was true. Then he would be warning everyone against the worst sort of deceiver, someone exactly like his late wife.

"She might be more like Eva than we thought."

Roland stared at him. Then he laughed. "I never thought

I'd see the day when Garrett Decker was scared. Did you ask her to marry you yet?"

"No." Garrett regretted mentioning to Roland his intent to ask Amanda for her hand in marriage, but he'd needed advice after his first attempt to ask her had failed. Roland had naturally leaped to assuming Garrett loved Amanda, and nothing Garrett said could convince his brother that this marriage would be in name only. Maybe it was a good thing that he'd never asked for Amanda's hand. Maybe God was sparing him another disaster. "How could I after I saw that letter?"

"What did you see?"

Garrett rubbed his stinging, sleepless eyes. "Promise me you won't say a word to anyone. There's always a chance it isn't true. After all, I saw only one line."

"This sounds serious."

"It could be. The writer accused her of…of improper behavior toward her daughter's fiancé." Even now Garrett couldn't say the word. *Seduced.* It carried horrible thoughts with it, things he didn't want to ever consider again, not after dealing with Eva's infidelity. He'd vowed never again to take such a chance. "I almost walked right back into it again."

"Into what?"

Garrett didn't realize he'd spoken the last bit aloud. "A bad marriage."

"Look." Roland grabbed his arm. "Stop thinking about what one line from a letter might mean and pay attention to what you know. You've had four months to get to know Amanda. Is this 'improper behavior' that she's accused of something that you think she could do?"

"Not the Amanda I know," Garrett admitted. "It seems far-fetched at best."

"Then ignore it. For all you know, the letter came from someone who has a grudge against her."

Except it hadn't. Garrett had put that much together overnight. The letter had come from the Chatsworths. Amanda had said they were the family that claimed her from the orphanage. This wasn't a vengeful rival. This accusation had come from Amanda's new mother.

The front door of the store flew open with a rush of cold air.

"Garrett! I'm glad you're here." Pearl, her green cloak unbuttoned, flew into the store. "Please tell me Amanda is at your house this morning."

Garrett stared at her, not comprehending. Slowly he shook his head. "Why would she be at my house? She doesn't start work until after school."

Pearl's hopeful expression vanished. "Oh, no. Then where is she?"

Chapter Nineteen

Cold. So cold.

That's the only thought that went through Amanda's head when she opened her eyes to daylight. Inside her wool coat, she was shaking and could barely quiet the trembling.

Every part of her body ached, and she had no idea where she was. She'd run last night until she collapsed. Using her last bit of strength, she'd crawled beneath a thick spruce whose boughs offered a bit of shelter against the cold and any rain or snow that might fall. But it gave no warmth.

The morning's feeble sunlight could not warm her, either. She had survived the night somehow, perhaps by the grace of God, but the new day brought no relief. Her body ached. She was lost. Her dress was torn and muddied. She'd lost her hat somewhere. Nothing but scrub trees surrounded her. She could not hear the river.

"I asked for Your help," she whispered with thick tongue and chapped lips. "Why did You abandon me again?"

I will not fail thee, nor forsake thee. The Bible verse echoed through her mind. That's what God promised, but He felt so very far away.

Alas, she knew why. Sin separated people from God. No matter how many times she'd cried out to Him to forgive her, the stain of shame remained. He could never accept her, just as the Chatsworths could not accept her. Or Garrett. Or anyone.

A bitter sob wrenched from Amanda's chest even as another shiver seized control of her body. This time she could not stop the trembling.

If she stayed here, she would surely die.

Yesterday that had sounded preferable to facing Garrett's scorn. But what of the children? Isaac and Sadie had suffered a terrible loss less than two years ago. If Amanda died, they would suffer yet again.

What a selfish woman she was! She saw it so clearly, and the dagger of shame drove even deeper into her heart.

"Forgive me, Lord," she sobbed. "Spare them. Whatever happens to me, spare them any more pain."

She laid her cheek against the tree trunk. Sharp needles bit into her skin like thorns, but no pain could remove the guilt of her actions.

Then she thought of Pearl, who would also worry.

"Oh, Pearl. I'm so sorry."

If only Amanda hadn't acted so rashly. If only she'd stood by her friend and taken the backlash that Garrett would level at her. Deserved punishment, to be sure. She deserved to stand alone.

I will not fail thee, nor forsake thee.

Pearl had stuck by Amanda no matter what happened. She lived out what God promised. In spite of Amanda's neglect during those months that Hugh secretly courted her, Pearl had stayed true. She'd always stayed true. Why hadn't Amanda confided in her? Pearl would know what to do.

If only Amanda was still in Singapore. Even being shunned was better than dying alone in the wilderness. Alas, she had no idea how to return there. In the darkness she'd gotten horribly mixed up and lost. Singapore might lie in any direction.

A gull squawked overhead.

Often she'd watched the gulls soar and loop over the dunes. They lived near water.

The river. If she could find the river, she could find her way home.

Slowly she moved each weary limb, forcing herself to her feet. The way would be hard, and success was not assured, but she must try. Somehow she must right the wrong she'd done last night.

The storm would pass. Storms always passed.

A whisper of wind wrapped around her, but it was warm, not cold. It comforted, as if to reaffirm that truth. She was not alone. She'd never been alone.

"We'll need every man from the mill," Garrett stated, each muscle straining with the combination of fear and the desperate need to hurry. "We will fan out across the area looking for her. Do you have any idea where she might have gone?"

Pearl looked pale, as if the life was draining from her. "I can only think of one possibility. She wanted to see that lumberjack named Jake, who is in Allegan, but she told me she would wait until the New Year. Why would she suddenly leave? And in the middle of the night, no less."

It was Garrett's turn to feel remorse. "I refused to take her there." But that wasn't all. "She got a letter. From someone named Chatsworth."

Pearl nodded. "Her foster parents. They never had a good relationship. Amanda was more of a servant than a daughter."

That explained Amanda's statement that they weren't her mama and papa.

Pearl continued, "Relationships got very strained this past June. Amanda was engaged to marry, but her beau jilted her for her foster sister."

"He did?" That didn't fit one bit with the line Garrett had read from the letter.

"Rascal. Good for nothing," Roland murmured. "A man like that isn't good enough for Amanda."

A few days ago, that would have been Garrett's sentiment, too, but he couldn't sort this all out now, while Amanda was alone and cold in the wilderness. Hopefully, she'd found shelter, but if she hadn't…well, he'd known men who'd succumbed to warmer temperatures than they'd experienced last night.

"Roland, get every man you know and split into teams of two. Send some up Goshorn Lake way. The rest should spread out between the farmland and the ridge above the dugout road. My men and I will take from that ridge to the river." He choked as the memory of Eva's body flashed through his mind.

"I can help," Pearl stated.

"You're teaching school," Roland pointed out.

"I can't teach when Amanda's missing."

Since this was turning into a fight that only cost them time, Garrett put a stop to it. "Why don't you walk the Saugatuck children back home and try to summon help from that quarter?"

Pearl brightened at the suggestion. "I'll send Isaac and Sadie to Mrs. Calloway."

"Sensible." He stopped a moment. "Don't tell them why."

Pearl's expression told him that she understood. His son and daughter couldn't take another loss.

"We'll find her," Pearl whispered. "We have to."

* * *

The sound came upon her gradually. Perhaps it had always been there, and Amanda had been too overwrought to hear the gurgle and rush of water.

The river.

Excitement energized her aching limbs. The scratching branches no longer mattered. She pushed through them as if they weren't there. Soon she would know which direction to travel.

Sand worked its way into her shoes. Bits of frost and ice glued the grains of sand to the hem of her tattered gown. None of it mattered.

The river was near. She would not die alone in the wilderness.

The brush grew more dense with each step. The rush of water had become a roar. She must be very near it.

Rather than get tangled in the impenetrable brush, she skirted along the growth until she found a place where she could peer through the prickly branches and see the river. It flowed from her left to her right. Now she knew which way to travel. Downstream to home.

Home. Until yesterday she'd not quite thought of Singapore that way, but the town and the people had become dear to her. The Calloways, the Elders, Louise... And even Fiona, though she made no secret of her almost desperate attempts to secure Garrett's affection. Amanda understood, for she felt the same way. Her life seemed to begin and end with Garrett Decker.

After the letter, her chances had most decidedly ended. Garrett's coldness toward her yesterday made that perfectly clear.

She found a clear spot along the river and watched the water flow. It rushed down from Allegan, where the man who might be her brother was staying. Downriver lay the familiar, with all its aches and triumphs. Love and despair battled each other there, whereas upriver dwelt only hope.

For an instant she considered resuming her walk along the river. How far was Allegan? Everyone seemed to think she would need to take a boat there. That meant travel on foot was either too long or too dangerous for anyone to attempt.

Her stomach rumbled.

She hadn't had the good sense to bring one bit of food or water with her. If Allegan was very far, she could never make it on foot. But perhaps she might find someone in Saugatuck willing to take her upriver.

All she had to do was find the town.

It could be upriver or down. She had no idea.

Yet it must be fairly close, for students and even some parents walked the distance regularly. She'd wandered long hours last night. Most likely the town was downriver.

Having made that decision, Amanda set off to her right. Before long the thickets cleared at a bend in the stream. She scrambled down to the bit of mucky shore to get a glimpse downriver. Over the top of a cedar, smoke rose in a single column. A house!

Never before had smoke brought such joy.

It couldn't be more than an hour's walk. Soon she would be lost no more.

Chapter Twenty

The single column of smoke came from a house on the edge of a town. This must be Saugatuck. It wasn't Singapore, and no other town lay that close. From all appearances, Saugatuck was at least as big as Singapore, if not larger.

As Amanda drew closer, she grew more concerned about her appearance. Even if she'd had a comb, it could not undo the many snarls that the night's adventure had created. Bits of twigs and cedar were caught in her hair. Something sticky—sap, perhaps—glued an entire lock into a rope-like strand. Her mittens were coated in dirt, as was her dress and coat. Her skirt was torn in a dozen spots. She looked atrocious.

Who would let in such a woman? They would think her a hermit or crazy woman. Yet she must try. She could not spend another night in the wilderness. Last night was cold but without snow. Terrible winter might make its appearance at any moment.

She shivered.

There was no choice. She must go to town.

Since the riverbank was overgrown in most places, she needed to skirt around the brush and climb a small slope before descending into town. From that vantage point, she could see down the main street. Many people were out and about at this early hour, but one in particular made her catch her breath.

Pearl was here.

Angela and Beth Wardman skipped ahead of her, stopping before a tidy little house. Their mother stepped outside, wiping her hands on her apron. Though Amanda was a good distance away, she could see the woman's surprise in the way she stood straighter and gathered her daughters near.

What on earth was Pearl doing? The children should be in school. Pearl should be teaching, not wandering the streets of Saugatuck.

Amanda stumbled forward, slipping down the small slope until her feet met the rutted roadway.

"Amanda?" Pearl left the Wardmans and ran toward her. "Amanda! Oh, my. Look at you. What happened?" She stopped before her, pausing only an instant before wrapping her arms around her. "We were so worried."

A lump formed in Amanda's throat. Pearl cared, truly cared, but would she still after she heard the truth of what had happened with Hugh?

Amanda began to tremble.

"My dear friend," Pearl exclaimed, drawing her toward the Wardman house, "why are we standing here when you must be half-frozen? Debra, will you make sure the fire is hot?"

Debra Wardman squeezed Amanda's arm very gently. "Come to the kitchen. It's the warmest room in the house, and I have the fire stoked for baking. Girls, bring that quilt from my bed and make sure the kettle is boiling. We'll make you a nice cup of tea to warm you through and through."

Amanda barely heard anything else. The cold and the anguish and the fear had turned to numbness. She let Pearl lead her into the house, knowing all the time that her welcome would be brief. Once they learned the truth, they would throw her out. Even if she said nothing, Garrett would soon spread the word, and all of Singapore and Saugatuck would know she was a fallen woman.

A sob must have escaped her lips. She heard it, though she did not feel it.

Pearl hugged her more tightly. "You'll feel better once you warm up and have a cup of tea."

The little house was just as neat on the inside as it was on the outside. Like Garrett's house, a table dominated the main room. Even now, at midmorning, it was already set for lunch with two place settings, for Mrs. Wardman and her husband. Ruffled white curtains floated at the windows, lending cheer to the room. The walls had been papered in a delicate floral pattern, lending an elegance to the small house. Every lamp and corner was spotless. The lovely smell of bread rising made Amanda's stomach growl again.

"You must be starved," Debra Wardman said as she bustled ahead of them to the rear, where the kitchen was located.

The main bedroom must be on the other side, with the children sleeping in the loft, Amanda thought dimly.

The kitchen was just as cheery as the main room. Here the walls were whitewashed and spotless, with children's drawings tacked to them. Pretty china gleamed from shelves lining the wall opposite the stove. Beneath those shelves sat the worktable and two wooden chairs.

Pearl drew a chair near the stove and led Amanda there.

"I can't," she protested.

As usual, Pearl didn't take any nonsense. "You can and you will."

Fearing her friend would begin to chastise her, Amanda sank onto the chair. Its hardness bit into her sore limbs, but the heat of the stove began to thaw the numbness in her fingers and mind.

Pearl drew the other chair near as Debra handed Amanda a cup of tea. The girls hovered at the table, staring at her. She must look dreadful. Amanda lifted a hand to her knotted hair.

"I'm sorry," she said thickly.

Debra turned to her daughters. "Girls, just because you don't have school today doesn't mean you don't have assignments to complete. Why don't we go to the big table to work through those arithmetic problems." She bent low to whisper something in Pearl's ear before leading her daughters out of the room.

Soon Amanda was alone with Pearl. She bowed her head, waiting for the rebuke.

None came. In fact, Pearl said nothing at all.

Amanda looked up. "I'm sorry." She couldn't think of anything else to say. The wedding dress was sewn, but that was a surprise gift from all of them, and Mrs. Calloway still had to dye it. She'd left her friend without a helper at school, but Pearl could manage the classroom without her now. If Amanda had managed to get to Allegan and discovered the lumberjack was her brother, she wouldn't have returned for Pearl's wedding. She couldn't bear to stand up with Garrett. No doubt he would have refused to stand beside her too. "Louise or Fiona would do."

"For what?" Pearl's green eyes bored into her.

"For a bridesmaid." The words squeaked out.

"You planned to abandon your responsibilities?"

Ouch! Stated like that, her actions sounded petty and selfish. Amanda bowed her head. "I'm sorry."

"Sorry isn't good enough. Perhaps you ought to explain what really happened back in New York."

Amanda sucked in her breath. Pearl knew. Somehow she knew. "N-N-New York? Did Garrett tell you? He must have. How could he?"

"Garrett didn't tell me anything." Pearl reached into her bag and produced a crumpled piece of paper, which she handed to her. "I found this next to the bed this morning."

Oh, dear. It was Mrs. Chatsworth's terrible letter. It must have fallen off the bed when Amanda was packing her carpetbag. In all the turmoil, she'd forgotten about it. And the carpetbag.

Amanda closed her trembling hand around the wad of paper. Pearl must have read it. "It's not true. Not entirely." She stopped, unable to say more.

"What's not true?"

Oh, dear. Pearl was not going to let her off. Amanda worked the words over in her head, but they still stung. Nothing could take that away.

"I didn't seduce Hugh." How the word made her cheeks flame. "At least I didn't intend to. I—I was in love with him. He promised marriage, but then—" She buried her face in her hands, ashamed that anyone, even her dearest friend in the world, should know how far she'd fallen.

"He jilted you at the altar," Pearl finished.

Amanda shook her head, unable to look her friend in the eye. "It never got that far. I'm sorry I led you to believe it had."

Instead of chastising her, Pearl wrapped an arm around her shoulders. "Perhaps we'd better start at the beginning."

Tears rose to the surface and could not be stopped.

Pearl had not abandoned her yet, but once she heard the full story, she would.

Amanda looked to the kitchen doorway. Mrs. Wardman had not returned. Still, the thought of revealing all that had happened, even to her dearest friend, burned a mark of shame on her soul.

"Must we?" Amanda whispered.

"I'm afraid so. The only way to move forward is to release the burdens of the past."

Was that what she'd done? Held on to burdens? No, this wasn't a burden. It was guilt that she deserved to bear. "I don't think I can. I did sin."

"No one is innocent." Pearl brushed a tangled lock from Amanda's brow. "Not me. Not Roland. Not even Garrett. No one."

Amanda looked at her friend. "But some sins are worse than others."

"Even the smallest separates us from God. Without Jesus, we would be lost."

"I know all that, but…"

"But?"

"But I am at fault. I did not turn him away when I should have." The words tumbled out now that the dam had begun to crack. "Hugh was so handsome, and he paid attention to me. He said I was beautiful, that I would make a fine lady one day. He promised to marry me, but asked me to keep it secret until he could convince his parents. You know how it is being an orphan. We have nothing to offer a gentleman."

"We have our love, which is far greater than the largest fortune or finest bloodline."

"Hugh didn't think so."

"I know, my darling." Pearl hugged her close. "But that is a mark against his character, not yours."

"But—" this was where the shame burned deep "—but I wanted to believe him, so I let him get too close. Much too close."

Pearl stiffened.

It was all over. Now Amanda's dearest friend had guessed her deepest secret, and all affection between them would come to an end.

Instead, Pearl grasped her shoulders and looked her in the eye. "A gentleman will stop whenever the lady tells him to do so. Did you ask him to stop?"

"Y-y-yes." The tears flowed again. "I begged him. I pleaded. I even tried to get away, but he would not stop." Memories of that terrible night, the horrible betrayal and the wrenching pain crashed in on her. "He wouldn't. Oh, Pearl, he wouldn't. He—he said I didn't matter, that I was only an orphan and a servant, that I didn't count, that he could take whatever he wanted."

Pearl held her tightly as the sobs wrenched out of her while Amanda relived every moment of that terrible night.

"He pinned me. I couldn't move. He tried… Oh, Pearl." The sobs squeezed her throat shut. "He wouldn't listen. If Mrs. Brighton hadn't pounded on the door, demanding I come out, he might have…" She shuddered at the thought of what might have happened if the housekeeper hadn't unwittingly put an end to Hugh's actions.

Pearl held her even tighter, though Amanda felt her sigh of relief. "It's all right," her friend murmured.

No, it wasn't. "Everything changed after that. Hugh treated me with contempt, denying he'd ever felt anything for me, saying he would never marry someone like me. I thought he loved me," Amanda sobbed. "He promised. He promised."

"I know, dearest," Pearl whispered into her hair. "I know."

Yet the memories would not stop tumbling over and over, reminding her of all she'd lost—innocence and trust, even hope. Hugh had told her that it was all her fault, that she'd seduced him, that she was wicked and could never amount to anything. Life had changed that night, and she would gladly have taken a loveless marriage just to keep up the appearance that she was worth something. Now, she realized just how hollow that was.

She loved Garrett. Loved Isaac and Sadie. They might leave her, but she could not stop loving them.

The sobs returned, worse than ever. "What will I do?"

Pearl just rubbed her back and let her cry.

For a long time they sat quietly by the stove, until Amanda's tears stopped flowing and the sobs quit shaking the life out of her. Then Pearl handed her a handkerchief. Amanda wiped her eyes and nose, but nothing could wipe away the shame.

"I'm ruined," she choked out. "Garrett will never forgive me."

"You are not ruined. This is not your fault, and Garrett will understand that. If he doesn't, it's his loss. You are a child of God, cleansed white as snow by the blood of our Savior."

"But Garrett looks at me like I'm wicked."

"That is his problem." Pearl squeezed her hand. "God loves you. He always has and always will."

"How is that possible?"

"Grace."

"But—"

"No 'but.' He loves you. Just as you are."

Amanda bowed her head. "How can He after what happened?"

"He loved the woman at the well, who was living with

a man who wasn't her husband," Pearl continued, "and the woman caught in adultery. What did He tell them?"

"Go and sin no more."

"He also said they were forgiven, the past wiped clean. So are you. So are all of us, the moment we give our lives to Christ."

Amanda shook her head, struggling to believe. "Then why didn't He answer my prayers?" Or had He? Was Mrs. Brighton's knock the answer she needed? But then why not rescue her sooner? "Why would He let such a thing happen?"

"I don't know." Pearl hugged her tighter. "But I do know that you did nothing wrong."

But she had. She had. This was the part that hurt most to admit. "I wanted him to love me. Deep down I knew that I couldn't trust his promises, but I wouldn't listen to that warning. I let him get too close. I didn't tell Mrs. Chatsworth. I didn't tell anyone, because I wanted to believe someone might love me."

"Oh, Amanda. You are loved." Pearl tipped up her face. "You must believe that. By me. By those who truly know you, and by God, who knows every secret of your heart. You need to stop taking on this guilt."

"Then why won't the pain go away? I try, but I can't stop thinking about what happened."

"Have you forgiven this man?"

The question seared to her soul, and the tears brimmed again. "How can I?"

"With God's help. Sometimes that's the only way." Pearl hugged her again. "Oh, dearest. I should have been there for you. If only I hadn't gotten so caught up studying to become a teacher."

"No! It's not your fault." Amanda would not let Pearl

accept the blame. "You are not my protector. You were called to teach."

"I should have kept in touch. These last months I should have noticed how much you were hurting."

"I didn't want to talk."

"Then I should have tried harder. I could tell something was terribly wrong, and I thought I could fix it by matching you with Garrett Decker."

Oh, how that reminder hurt. Amanda turned her face away.

"I'm sorry," Pearl continued. "It was wrong of me to interfere and try to push you two together."

"You weren't wrong. That's what makes this so terrible." She struggled to maintain her composure so Pearl wouldn't feel guilty. "I love him. I truly hoped he would want to marry me, but now that's gone. He knows."

That was the worst part of all.

"What do you mean, 'he knows'?"

"Garrett gave me the letter."

"That letter?"

Amanda uncurled her fingers from around the wadded sheet of paper. "Yes."

"Mrs. Chatsworth hinted at what happened?"

Amanda stared. Pearl truly didn't know what Mrs. Chatsworth had written. "How did you know it came from her?"

"The envelope."

Then she truly hadn't read it. The very first line was all anyone needed to read. Garrett must have. Amanda smoothed out the sheet of paper and handed it to her friend.

"It's your private letter," Pearl protested.

Amanda pushed it into her hands. "It's a lie, but who would believe me over Mrs. Chatsworth?"

Pearl glanced at the page. Color dotted her cheeks.

"What gall! She's no mother to you. And why would she say all that about not hiring you as a servant?"

"Before I got the job taking care of Garrett's house, I wrote asking for a position as a maid."

"Oh, Amanda. Why would you do such a thing?"

"You were getting married and moving on, and I can't afford a room on my own. How could I stay here?"

"You could have asked. Mrs. Calloway told me she has every intention of keeping you on to help out around the boardinghouse in exchange for room and board."

A ray of sun streamed through the window. "She did? She's going to let me stay?" Even after losing the housekeeping job at Garrett's, which would surely happen, Amanda could afford to remain in Singapore.

"Of course she is. They expect a booming year at the mill, and that means a lot more workers at the boardinghouse."

"I can stay."

"I certainly hope you will." Pearl squeezed her hand. "I'd be lost without you. A lot of people would."

Not Garrett. The thought stabbed with the pain of a sharp knife.

Pearl guided her to her feet. "Now let's get you cleaned up. You'll feel much better."

Perhaps she would. Until she faced Garrett.

Each step brought a flash of pain, but Garrett no longer saw Eva's body floating in the water. In this nightmare, when he looked across the river, it was Amanda's purple dress and curly dark hair spread out there. Her lifeless violet eyes stared up at the winter sky.

Why did she go running off like that? Eva would disappear whenever she didn't get her way, but Garrett had never figured Amanda for that type of woman. It had to be the letter. Roland was wrong. That accusation must be true, for Amanda to take off like that in the middle of the night.

Still, Garrett couldn't bear the thought of her ending up like Eva. Amanda had been good to his children. Better than their own mother had.

He shook off the past and plodded a few more feet along the riverbank.

"Amanda!" He cupped his hands around his mouth, and her name echoed across the river until it died beneath the sound of rushing water.

He waited a full ten seconds, ears pricked for a reply, however weak.

"Didn't find nothing, boss."

Garrett had been listening so intently that the sudden words made him jump. He whipped around to see Sawyer standing some ten feet away on the path that wound down to this part of the shore.

"Get my attention first," he growled.

"Sorry, boss."

Garrett tugged at his hat and gloves. "Well, then, head up past the burned out school. Have Raiford walk a little upslope from you. She might be unconscious."

"Yes, sir." Sawyer took off at a brisk clip.

Once again Garrett was alone with his thoughts and memories. This river had claimed his wife. That had been terrible. Surely God wouldn't make him relive that day with another woman. Not just any woman, but the one he'd planned to ask to marry him. True, it would have been in name only, but in time...

He puffed out a breath. It no longer turned into a cloud of white. The sun was warming up the earth. Maybe she had managed to survive the night.

He must cling to that hope.

His anger had sent Eva to her death. Last night he'd

been upset—even angry—over the letter that he shouldn't have read. Then he'd accused Amanda, not in words, but with his silence and actions. But what if Roland was right? What if Mrs. Chatsworth was mistaken or lying? What if Amanda was innocent?

What if she wasn't? Garrett must protect his children. At all costs. He closed his eyes and listened again.

Nothing.

Perhaps that letter had been a warning. Perhaps it had spared all of them from more misery. If that was true, then why did his gut churn? Lack of breakfast. That must be it.

He strode forward, eyes glued to the ground. Any shrub could hide her from sight. He kicked at them and pulled aside prickly juniper and scrub pine branches. No Amanda.

Time and distance ticked by. He walked in a zigzag pattern, but found nothing to indicate she'd come this way. No footsteps or torn bits of cloth. Nothing.

"Amanda!" he called out again.

Again, only the water answered. Far off, he could hear the men calling her name. No one had found her yet. If Pearl was right, she might be anywhere between Singapore and Allegan. No, not that far. Even a hardy man couldn't make that hike overnight. The swamps and rough terrain would slow her down, not to mention the cold.

He shivered.

Amanda was delicate. She might not have survived the night. It had been cold enough for frost to coat every blade of grass and fallen leaf. The pines had looked white in the early morning light. Now all that frost had melted away. The air warmed, but the rescue team might be too late.

He pushed onward.

The river curved up ahead, at the settlement of Saugatuck. Some thought that town would surpass Singapore and even wipe it off the map, but Garrett held to the same thinking as his brother. Singapore was situated by the river mouth. It would grow, and Saugatuck would fade away. Roland would find a way to get that glass factory back under way. Then Singapore could move forward if the timber ever gave out.

"How long are we searching, boss?" Sawyer again stood above him.

"Until we find her." Garrett thought he'd been clear enough, but Sawyer didn't resume the search. "Well? Get on with it."

Sawyer shuffled his feet. "Well, you see, boss, it's not bothering me, but the men are wondering about work. They don't get paid to search."

"We're talking about a human being here, a woman." His temper exploded. "They'll get paid." If he had to pay them himself.

"Thank you, boss. I'll let 'em know." Sawyer hurried back to rejoin the rest of the search party.

Angry and frustrated, Garrett stomped through the brush, shouting Amanda's name. He didn't wait for a response. He'd see her first.

The river began its slow turn, and he picked his way to the bank. From here he'd get a good view of the water, good enough to tell if a body was floating downstream.

He squinted into the rising sun, which reflected off the river's surface. A long dark lump caught his eye, and he tensed until he realized it was a snag. Nothing else resembled a boat or a body. He let out his breath.

At least she hadn't drowned. Not in this stretch, anyway.

He moved forward, and the first buildings of Saugatuck came into view. The town looked much the same as Singapore, except that the streets weren't made of sand. Saugatuck had dirt and grass. It was bigger than when he'd first arrived a half dozen years ago.

The river path widened as it joined up with the road. This was the route the students from Saugatuck took to school each day. It was a long one, and would be difficult in winter. They really needed to rebuild the schoolhouse, which had been situated between the two villages before the fire.

The growth thinned out here, and he could see his men scattered across the timbered land. They were spaced the correct distance apart. He pushed his shoulders back with pride. They were a good group who took instruction well.

Unlike Amanda. What was it with women that made them so resistant to following instructions? She seemed to understand what he was telling her, and then went and did exactly the opposite. He couldn't count how many times her sympathy had undermined his authority with the children. Then again, she did love them.

Since the road now wound near the shore, he made better time. There wasn't a lot of brush here. His calls still brought no response. In time he reached the foot of Saugatuck's main street. People were out, hurrying here and there in the crisp morning air. He knew most of them and stopped to tell each one to look out for Amanda.

"She's got dark, curly hair and violet eyes."

"Violet?" they invariably asked, with that pitying look. Everyone knew his late wife had violet eyes.

Then Al Farmingham gave a very different answer. "Saw someone by that description at the Wardman house."

"What? When?"

"This morning."

Relief eased the tension from Garrett's shoulders. "Are you certain?"

The man looked affronted. "Of course I'm certain. Now, I can't go telling you that it was her for sure. I can only say it looked like her. The light was poor."

"Of course." Desperate to know the truth, Garrett bade the man farewell and hurried across town to the Wardmans' place. A year ago, he'd come here to try to talk the man of the house into working at the Singapore sawmill rather than the Saugatuck mill. Unsuccessfully. David Wardman wanted to work close to home. No amount of money would sway him. Now Garrett understood that desire. He, too, had to be near his children.

And Amanda. That realization sent a jolt up his spine. Regardless of the accusing letter, he wanted to believe she was innocent. She had to be. Soon he'd know.

Excitement drove each step. Amanda was here. And safe. Soon he would see her. She might be frostbitten or suffering other ill effects from the cold. She might be feverish and need a doctor. Whatever she needed, he would get it for her.

When he was just two houses away, the door of the Wardman place opened. Three women stepped out. Mrs. Wardman lingered on the stoop while the other two conversed with her. Pearl's height hid the third woman. Then she moved aside.

Garrett halted in his tracks.

Before him stood Amanda Porter, and her gray skirts looked as neat and clean as if she'd just left the boardinghouse this morning.

She'd deceived him. Just like Eva. Amanda hadn't been lost at all. While the whole town had gone out searching for her, she'd been having tea with a friend.

He fisted his hands, but there was nothing to punch. Only his foolish trust.

Never again. He was done with Amanda Porter.

Chapter Twenty-One

Pearl had been right. Amanda felt much better after a bowl of porridge and a general tidying up. Her coat was brushed clean. Debra Wardman loaned her a dress. It was plain, dull gray and made of coarse muslin, but it fit reasonably well. Her plum dress would require laundering and repair. Pearl graciously carried it for her.

By the time Amanda and Pearl said goodbye to their generous hostess, Amanda was ready to face Garrett. She would hold her head high, like Pearl instructed, and tell him the truth. He needed to know, and she would accept his decision regarding her employment without dispute. In his place, she would be concerned, too.

"I'll send your dress back tomorrow," she promised.

Debra waved her hand. "No hurry. It's an old one I use in the garden. It'll be a long time before I'm digging in the dirt again."

Amanda liked Debra's cheerfulness. Like Pearl, she could find the positive side to any calamity.

"Thank you again," she said, as she and Pearl bade Debra farewell. "I'm sorry that my foolish behavior closed down the school."

Amanda had never imagined her actions would affect

the children. She'd figured life would go on as usual in Singapore, just without her. But along with losing the letter, she'd forgotten to write a note to Pearl. That showed she hadn't been thinking straight. Of course Pearl came looking for her.

"Don't fret about it," Debra said, with another wave of her hand. "It'll be a pleasure having the girls home to help out with the baking."

After another round of farewells, Pearl turned to walk away, but halted at once. Amanda looked to her friend, who was staring down the street. She shifted her gaze and saw what had made Pearl freeze.

Not twenty feet away stood Garrett. His hat was drawn low against the rising sun, but she couldn't mistake his figure. His shoulders were squared, and his gloved hands were fisted at his sides. Tension radiated from him.

"I found her," Pearl said.

He responded by wheeling about and stomping away from them.

"Garrett!" His name caught in Amanda's throat, coming out garbled. She started toward him. "I can explain."

But he didn't stop. He didn't turn around. He didn't answer.

She ran a few steps, but her head began to spin. She had to stop.

Pearl took her arm. "Let him go."

"Why won't he listen?"

"He was worried," Pearl suggested. "Maybe he feared you were dead."

Amanda shivered in spite of the thick woolen coat. Dead like his late wife. That was what Pearl had left out.

"I'm sorry," she breathed. "I've made a mess of things."

"Nothing that can't be fixed."

Amanda wasn't so sure.

* * *

Garrett couldn't talk to her. He couldn't stand to see her looking so pretty and cheerful, as if nothing had happened. The whole town was searching for her. He'd stopped work at the mill and the building berth to search for her, and she'd just gone to visit a friend.

He stewed about it while bringing back the searchers with a blast of the mill's steam whistle. He grumbled when Roland mentioned how everything had turned out for the best. But Garrett could not let her back in his household.

"Have Pearl tell Miss Porter that her services are no longer needed," he told his brother.

Roland's eyebrows rose. "You hired someone else?"

"We'll get by. Maybe you can find something for the children to do here at the store after school."

"Whoa, there. Those children need someone to cook their meals and spend time with them. I won't be able to do either. I'm getting married next Monday. Remember?"

Garrett shook that protest off with some mumbled excuse about it being temporary, but Roland was right. He needed to hire someone else.

"I'll start looking for a new housekeeper right away. But you get word to Miss Porter that she's not to show up tonight."

"Oh, no. If you intend to dismiss Amanda, then you'll have to do it yourself."

No amount of scowling and demanding would change Roland's mind. Fortunately, Mrs. Calloway was more amenable. He met her at the boardinghouse door and handed her a note for Miss Porter. It detailed her dismissal.

"Don't you want to see her yourself?" the woman chattered, doubtless thinking that he and Amanda were still on friendly terms.

"I have to get back to work. Lost a lot of time this morning."

"Oh. I see." Mrs. Calloway's smile faded. "I'll give this to her."

"Thank you." Before she could offer a sweet or a cup of coffee, he retreated, his boots clattering down the wooden steps.

He had to do it. Not just for his sake but for the sake of his children. He couldn't trust the most precious people in his life to a woman who lied.

That's what he told himself, but it didn't loosen the knot in his stomach.

"I've been dismissed." Amanda closed the simple note, scrawled in Garrett's untidy hand.

"Dismissed?" Pearl stopped removing the pins from her hair and sat down beside her on the bed. "Why would he dismiss you?"

"Because of the letter."

"The one from Mrs. Chatsworth?"

Amanda nodded.

"But how would he know what she said?"

Amanda then told Pearl how the letter had arrived, with the envelope recently glued back together and the flap open. "Anyone could read the opening line. Since he gave me the letter, I'm sure he read it."

"That doesn't sound like something Garrett would do. He's very particular about doing what's right. He wouldn't violate anyone's privacy by reading a personal letter."

"It might have been inadvertent," Amanda admitted. "Like I said, anyone and everyone could see it."

"But not everyone would read it."

"Regardless, I have been dismissed." She heaved a sigh

to push back the tears that threatened. "I'll miss Sadie and Isaac so."

"We'll straighten this out." Pearl stood. "I have a mind to go over there right now and tell him just how wrong he is."

"No!" Amanda leaped to her feet to stop her friend. "Please don't. This is between Garrett and me."

Pearl gazed at her a long while before conceding. "Very well, but don't think for a minute that you can get out of being my bridesmaid."

Amanda had forgotten about that. She would have to stand beside Garrett during and after the ceremony. Somehow they needed to be civil to each other. Surely Garrett would do that much, for his brother's sake if for no other reason.

Pearl hugged her. "This will pass. In time Garrett will see you for who you really are."

Amanda wasn't so sure. "He is terribly stubborn."

"But he's up against three equally stubborn people. In the end he'll see reason." Pearl smiled. "In the meantime you can see Sadie and Isaac every day at school."

"Except when Mrs. Calloway needs me at the boardinghouse," Amanda pointed out. It was, after all, the only way that she could stay in Singapore.

"I'm sure she'll give you a little time off each day to stop by the school. And you must help out with the nativity play."

Amanda's nerves flared, and she sank to the bed. Garrett would be there. He was narrating the play. "I can't."

"You need to face him."

Though deep down she knew that, facing Garrett would not be easy. Earlier today, she'd been ready, but the more time passed, the harder it would be to reveal the full truth.

She couldn't upset Garrett in the midst of the nativity play or at Pearl's wedding.

"Later," she promised. "After the holidays."

Chapter Twenty-Two

Garrett put out the word that he needed a housekeeper. For good measure he tacked the posting to the counter at the store. There, everyone would see the advertisement, and all those interested could apply in person during the evening hours, after seven o'clock.

He didn't have time to hunt around in person, like he'd done the last time. Work on the shipbuilding berth and launching ways was in full swing so they could finish before the ground froze. They were fortunate the weather had stayed warm this December, and the men could still drive the pilings into the ground at the riverbank.

At the end of the day he returned home, gathering Sadie and Isaac from the store on the way.

"Where's Miss Amanda?" Sadie asked each day. "I miss her."

If Garrett was honest with himself, he did, too, but the Amanda he'd known wasn't the real Amanda. That had been a figment of his imagination.

"Is she sick?" Isaac asked.

"She had some bad news and needs to rest." That was probably true. Neither he nor Roland had seen her around town. But he still felt a twinge of guilt. He wasn't telling his children the full story. Maybe someday. They were too young to understand now.

He opened the door and ushered his children into the cold house.

"I'm hungry," Sadie complained. "Miss Amanda would have supper ready by now."

Garrett bit back his frustration and knelt so he could address his children at eye level. "Miss Amanda can't be here anymore, but we'll get another lady to help out around here. How does that sound?"

Sadie's face crumpled, and tears filled her eyes. "Why did she leave us? Doesn't she love me anymore?"

Garrett wrapped his arms around his daughter, his heart breaking. Wasn't that why he'd vowed not to take a second wife? His children couldn't handle another loss.

"I'm sure she still loves you." The words stuck in his throat even though they were doubtless true. Amanda did love his children. He saw it in the tender care she extended toward them, in the way she listened intently to everything they said, and the way she guided them toward doing the right thing. A pang shot through him. That's what a true mother did. By that measure, Eva had never been a true mother. She would play with the children on occasion, but mostly she complained about the work or left them with Mrs. Calloway so she could go visit friends.

He gripped his son and daughter tight. "I promise everything will work out." It had to. His family depended on it. "And I'm not leaving you. Not anytime soon."

Isaac and Sadie buried their heads in his shoulders, nuzzling as close as possible.

"Don't ever leave us, Papa," Sadie murmured.

His mind flitted to the construction at the launching ways. The steam tractor had nearly run over Sawyer's leg when the man slipped in the muck. How could Garrett promise to always be with his children when at any moment he could be struck dead in an accident?

"And you'll always have Uncle Roland and Aunt Pearl."

Sadie lifted her head to look him in the eye. "She's not Aunt Pearl yet."

That little girl was perceptive.

"You're right." He tousled her hair. "Now what do you say we light a couple lamps and make some supper?"

Sadie liked to help out. Amanda must have taught her a lot about working in the kitchen, because she did things without being asked or instructed. Even Isaac knew how to set the table and keep the fire going. His children were growing up.

After supper, the children played in front of the stove while Garrett settled in a chair to read the Bible. It fell open to the thirty-first chapter of Proverbs. The good wife. He began to turn the page when his eye caught the verse about making clothing for all in the family. And then the one that described her looking after all the needs of the household.

Amanda. She fitted the description perfectly.

Then what about that letter?

He shut the Bible.

A knock sounded on the door, and his heart beat harder. Someone had come in answer to his posting for a housekeeper. Two days had passed since he'd tacked it up in the store, and this was the first person to respond.

A bit shaky, he rose to answer the door.

"Maybe it's Miss Amanda," Sadie said excitedly.

Before Garrett could get to the door, his daughter opened it.

On the stoop stood Fiona O'Keefe in all her finery, the tall feather in her hat dancing in the breeze.

Sadie stared, openmouthed. Garrett's heart leaped into his throat. Fiona? She'd outright refused the position at the beginning of the month. Perhaps her situation had changed. He hadn't paid any attention to the concerts lately. Maybe she wasn't doing too well with them now that the town was quieter.

"Are you going to invite me in?" she asked.

"Uh. Yes. Come in, Miss O'Keefe." He opened the door wide and stepped aside, while Sadie returned to play with her brother. Neither made a move to do so, though. They watched every move carefully.

Fiona entered the house and surveyed the small main room with its little kitchen, dining table and seating area all in one. "I trust I'm not here too early."

"No." Garrett shut the door. "That is, yes, you're not too early. We've finished supper."

"I put the dishes away," Sadie stated.

Fiona nodded and turned to Garrett. "Could we have a moment alone?"

Fingers of ice slid through his heart. Not only had Fiona failed to recognize Sadie's need for recognition, but she'd asked to speak with him away from the children.

"Isaac and Sadie will have a say in who I hire," he pointed out.

She gave him a funny look. "I'm not here for the position."

She wasn't?

"Then why are you here?"

She lifted her chin. "It's a rather personal matter."

Personal? With Fiona? But they'd had no relationship beyond sitting together in church and a couple outings, including one ill-advised evening walking her to her concert. And that was at Sawyer's request.

"Uh…" Garrett swallowed. "Oh, all right. I hope it won't take long."

"That depends on you, Mr. Decker."

Mr. Decker? The formality struck an additional chill in his bones. Nevertheless, he would not be rid of her until he got through this "personal" conversation, whatever that was.

"All right. Sadie, Isaac, please go to your room. You may take a lamp with you."

The children gave the two of them a suspicious look. They would probably try to listen. He would have, in their situation. Fiona's behavior was too perplexing to ignore.

Once the children had retreated, and he ensured they'd closed the door, he turned back to the main room. Fiona stood in front of the small wood stove in the sitting area. No doubt she'd chosen this part of the room because it was farthest from where the children were located.

He pushed a chair closer to the stove. "Would you care to sit, Miss O'Keefe?"

"Thank you." She settled in the chair without unbuttoning her coat.

Good. She didn't intend to stay a long time.

He took the other chair and sat within easy hearing range, yet far enough away to not suggest he wanted to be close to her. "If you're not here for the housekeeper position, then what is your purpose?"

She settled back in her chair. "Direct and to the point. I always liked that about you, Garrett. Too bad you're not that way in every matter."

He took the blow without comment. If she was here to insult him, best to let her have her say and get it over.

She tilted her head. "You might be surprised by why I've come tonight."

Again he waited.

"Not on my behalf," she continued, "but on the behalf of another. Since you've been direct, so will I. You don't need another housekeeper."

He couldn't hold his tongue this time. "That's not your decision."

"No, it's not, but I can't bear to see a friend suffer unnecessarily."

"If you're talking about Miss Porter, I didn't realize you were friends. You always seemed more like competitors."

Fiona smiled. "Perhaps we once were, but she has a kind heart and helped me when I needed it. That is the mark of a friend." She thrummed her fingers on the arm of the chair. "Moreover, I hate injustice, and this is injustice."

Garrett steeled himself for whatever she had to say.

She sat tall. "You have no cause to dismiss her."

"That is not your concern," he said icily.

"Perhaps not, but I must speak up for a friend." Her fingers stilled. "I understand she has been accused of some sort of moral failing."

The words of Mrs. Chatsworth's letter came back to him clearly. *Seduced.* An ugly word, but one that left no doubt of its intent.

"Let me tell you a story," Fiona said.

"I didn't realize you knew Miss Porter before coming here."

"This story isn't about her. It's about a young girl from the tenements who sneaked into the back of a theater and saw the beautiful actresses. She longed to rise above the filth and hopelessness until she had the beautiful clothes and fame of those actresses. She would do a great deal to reach her dream, but she never suspected the price was her soul."

Garrett shivered. Fiona was talking about herself. He held his tongue and let her continue.

"She wouldn't give in to the demands that assaulted her daily. She still believed talent and hard work could get her to the top."

Garrett breathed out heavily. Fiona wasn't the sort of woman he'd imagined.

"Humph. I see you have the same thoughts as most everyone else. Few would believe anyone could survive the theater world without compromising her morals, but I did." She leaned forward. "It meant giving up the biggest venues and the most lucrative shows. It meant settling for less. Even so, the rumors still flew." Her jaw set. "Few would believe I prefer hymns to popular tunes, that I would rather glorify God with the talent He gave me than waste it on the louts who frequent the cheap seats."

Garrett examined his hands. He'd been just as guilty of assuming the worst.

"Do you believe me?" she asked.

He recognized the sincerity in her voice. "Yes."

"In spite of what other people say?"

"It doesn't matter what people say. I can tell you're speaking the truth."

"Good." She rose. "Then you won't judge anyone else by what others write about her."

The bullet found its mark. She meant Amanda. But that was different. Or was it?

"I'll let myself out," she said. "Thank you for your time, Mr. Decker."

Amanda didn't leave the boardinghouse all week. She avoided most people by cleaning whichever room happened to be empty. By Friday night, Pearl confronted her in the kitchen.

"I need your help at rehearsal tomorrow."

Amanda continued scrubbing the stove. Garrett would be there, and that was reason enough not to attend.

"I'm not ready," she hedged, "and Mrs. Calloway might need me." The first dye wash of the wedding dress hadn't come out right. They needed to do another and planned to do it while Pearl was at rehearsal. With Christmas on Sunday and the wedding Monday, this was their last chance.

"She can let you go for an hour or so. Besides, don't you want to see Sadie and Isaac?"

Pearl knew how to tug on her heartstrings. Amanda had missed those two terribly. But their father would be there, since he was narrating the play.

"I'll see them Sunday at Christmas service." At least Garrett couldn't accuse her at church. She hoped.

But she also wouldn't be able to spend any time with the children then. They would be busy with the play and then leave with their father.

"You can't hide forever," Pearl stated bluntly. "Eventually you'll have to speak with Garrett." Her mouth slowly curved into a grin. "You could ask him for your old position. I understand no one has applied."

"Pearl! I couldn't! Don't even suggest such a thing. He dismissed me."

"A big mistake that he's too bullheaded to admit. He did concede that you're the best housekeeper in Singapore."

"He did? Oh, no. You must be making that up. I'm not the best. That's Mrs. Calloway."

"The best at what?" The boardinghouse proprietress breezed into the kitchen with empty cookie plates from the parlor. No doubt the men had monopolized every single buttery shortbread wafer she'd set out for them.

Amanda worked the brush into the grooves of the stovetop to get out the cooked-on food and grease.

Pearl answered. "I was just saying how sorry Garrett Decker must be that he let Amanda go. There isn't a better housekeeper for those children."

"Indeed not," Mrs. Calloway confirmed. "Miss Amanda loves those two like her own. Why, Sadie is practically in tears that she doesn't see her every day." She turned to Amanda. "You should spend time with them when they're visiting."

Amanda didn't need to point out that Garrett's children hadn't visited the boardinghouse since the letter arrived. Though she'd thrown the offensive missive into the fire at Debra Wardman's house and watched the flames consume it, people treated her differently now. A sideways glance or whisper meant speculation was running rampant. Sunday service was going to be torture.

"...so I told her she should apply for the job," Pearl was saying. "That'll force Garrett to swallow his foolish pride."

Mrs. Calloway burst into laughter and clapped her hands. "Well, I do say that's about the most audacious thing I've ever heard."

"Too audacious," Amanda pointed out, in case Pearl decided that was good reason to pursue the ridiculous idea. Knowing her, she would act if Amanda didn't. "Moreover, I don't want you or anyone else applying for me."

"I wouldn't," Pearl protested.

Amanda stared down that statement.

"Well, I might," her friend admitted. "One of you has to see reason. If Garrett won't budge, then you'll have to nudge him."

Amanda didn't like the sound of that one bit. "Please don't." She clutched Pearl's arm. "You said to give Garrett time."

"He's had enough. Sometimes a person just needs a little push." Pearl turned to Mrs. Calloway. "You don't need Amanda tomorrow morning, do you? Say from nine o'clock to noon? I could use her help on the nativity play."

"Of course not. Go! Go!" Mrs. Calloway urged.

"But..." Amanda jerked her head toward where the

wedding dress was stored. "I thought we had a special project to do."

"Never you mind about that. I can take care of it myself." Mrs. Calloway breezed out of the kitchen, doubtless in search of stray teacups or misplaced napkins.

The kitchen quieted considerably.

Pearl could now direct all her attention to Amanda. "See? You've been given permission to take the morning off. We'll leave at nine o'clock sharp."

Without giving her a chance to protest, Pearl rushed off, leaving Amanda with a dirty scrub brush and the niggling worry that her arrival would bring play practice to a screeching halt.

At nine o'clock the following morning, Pearl made Amanda step outside for the first time since her ill-advised adventure.

Amanda let a wry laugh escape as she closed the door. Instead of freeing her from the pain, that escapade had imprisoned her. She dreaded any encounter with people in the community. Mrs. Calloway had been kind, but what of the rest? Speculation must be running wild. Had Garrett spilled the contents of Mrs. Calloway's letter? Pearl said Roland didn't appear to know, but the men staying at the boardinghouse seemed to look at her differently.

Even if the community had no idea why she'd run off, Garrett knew, and he would be at the rehearsal this morning. Her heart pounded in her rib cage. Her breath grew short, and her head began to spin.

"I can't," she whispered, turning around.

Pearl guided her back in the direction of the school. "You can and you must."

"But Garrett—"

"That man needs a good comeuppance, if you ask me."

"Pearl! He's a pillar of the church."

"He's behaving like a self-righteous fool."

"He has children to consider."

"Children who adore you and whom you adore."

Amanda blinked back a tear. "That's not enough."

"It is in my estimation." Pearl threaded her arm around Amanda's.

The gesture surprised Amanda until she noticed the curious looks of the parents walking their children to rehearsal.

"Miss Lawson." A tall, gruff man tipped a finger to his hat. He ignored Amanda.

"Mr. Bailey. *We* are glad to see you here," Pearl said emphatically. "Amanda put so much work into the costumes. Your boys will look wonderful in the kings' robes."

"I'm sure they will," he said stiffly, hurrying ahead. "Better catch up with my boys."

Amanda kept her gaze fixed on the boardwalk. This was exactly what she'd feared. Mrs. Chatsworth's accusation had somehow gotten out into the community. Only two others knew the contents of that letter. Pearl wouldn't have spread it. Garrett must have.

Now Amanda must face him.

The trembling intensified when they reached the building that served as temporary school and church. Garrett would be inside. What would he say when he saw her? Would he demand she leave? Would he turn away and refuse to even greet her? Whatever happened, it couldn't be the happy resolution that Pearl envisioned. Even if he did treat Amanda with civility, she would have great difficulty forgetting that he'd read her private letter and spread Mrs. Chatsworth's accusation to the whole of Singapore.

"You can't stand out here all day," Pearl said to her with a touch of laughter.

Amanda dreaded this moment, but there was no escaping it. She stomped the light snow off her shoes and entered the building. It took a moment for her eyes to adjust to the lower light. When they did, she saw that a great many children had already arrived.

"Miss Mana!" Sadie hit her with the force of an affectionate dog. "Where were you? Were you sick, like Miss Pearl was? Are you better now? When are you going to come home?"

The questions tumbled out too rapidly for Amanda to answer, but slowly enough for her heart to ache. Last month, Sadie had worried about Pearl, who had suffered burns in the fire. Garrett had told his daughter that Pearl was sick. Amanda's disappearance the last few days must have drawn the same explanation.

"I am better," she said simply, when Sadie finally paused.

"Then you'll come back?"

The little girl looked up at her with such innocent trust that the tears rose to Amanda's eyes.

She knelt. "Not just yet."

Sadie looked puzzled. "Why? Don't you like us?"

"I like you and your brother very much." She had to stop before telling the children she loved them. With the rift between Garrett and her, that revelation would only bring sorrow. She hugged the girl a brief moment. "Now, go with Miss Lawson so you can practice your part."

"I know my part. I practiced, but Isaac won't."

Amanda spotted the boy at a distance, arms crossed and shoulders hunched just like his father. He even had the same scowl.

"Sadie. Do what Miss Porter told you to do." Garrett had come close while she was distracted by the children. "Go along with Miss Lawson now."

Sadie obeyed, and that left Amanda alone with Garrett. He extended a hand to help her to her feet. At least he wasn't afraid to touch her. His hand was strong, warm, and sent the same shivers down her spine that it had the very first time she'd met him. Oh, dear. This could not be. Not now when all bonds between them were surely broken.

"You are well?" His voice was raw, rough.

She nodded, unable to look him in the eye.

"You had everyone worried."

That's the part that had stuck in her throat since the morning she'd awoken and realized she was still alive. "I'm sorry. I wasn't thinking clearly."

"Understandable."

Was he trying to make amends or at least treat her with cordiality? She hazarded a glance, only to find his brow furrowed and his lips pressed together.

No, he had not forgiven her.

"I'm sorry," she whispered again. She couldn't think of another thing to say, except… "It's not true."

Startled, he jerked his head back. "What's not true?"

This time she was puzzled. Hadn't he read the opening of Mrs. Chatsworth's letter? Had Amanda misread the situation entirely?

"What Mrs. Chatsworth wrote," she whispered, hoping beyond all hope that he would say he hadn't seen one word of the woman's letter.

"I see."

Her hopes crashed. He did know, and that meant he must be the one who'd spread the rumors about her.

She licked her suddenly parched lips. "It's not what everyone thinks."

"Everyone?" He shook his head, brow even more furrowed.

Oh, dear. What *had* he read or not read? Pearl would

say she ought to ask bluntly and get it all out in the open. That had never been Amanda's way, but she was tired of running and hiding and keeping everything secret. She hadn't lost the love of God or of friends by telling them the truth. Silence had driven Garrett away.

She took a deep breath. "Did you read the letter?"

His neck flushed, and he looked down at the floor while shuffling his feet uncomfortably. "The envelope fell apart in my hands." He paused. "I happened to see the beginning of the note."

The incriminating sentence.

"I should have looked away," he continued, "but I didn't read any further. I pasted the envelope back together and gave it to you."

He must be speaking the truth, but it didn't make her feel one bit better. That sentence had changed his attitude toward her, had caused him to dismiss her from her position and seek someone else to look after his children. He didn't trust her.

"I see," she said. "It's too late then."

"I, uh…" His voice trailed off. "Maybe it is."

She thought of the way Mr. Bailey had treated her, all because Garrett had told people about that letter. Because Garrett believed someone else rather than her. That wasn't love. It wasn't even friendship.

She lifted her chin. "Yes, it is."

Without a second glance, she left to help Pearl. Though Amanda held her head high, her heart was breaking.

Chapter Twenty-Three

What had just happened? After two long days of prayer and thinking and repentance, Garrett had decided to make amends with Amanda. He would tell her the truth and grant her the benefit of the doubt. It was the right thing to do.

He hadn't expected her to grill him or to stand tall and secure in the face of his admission of guilt. He wasn't sure what he'd expected. Anger. Tears. Certainly a full confession of her role. He'd been prepared to forgive and begin anew. He had even dared to hope that she would let bygones be bygones and return to her position as his housekeeper.

That had definitely not happened.

The Amanda who walked away from him did not cower under the weight of guilt and shame. She looked…well, blameless, as light on her feet as a young girl. She greeted each of the children, laughed and embraced them. They surrounded her, oblivious to the accusations in the letter.

"Best be done with that one," a man murmured at his elbow.

Garrett glanced over to see Ben Bailey standing near. The merchant from Saugatuck liked to create social distinction where there wasn't any.

"What one?"

"Miss Porter. I heard some mighty raw stuff about her."

Garrett clenched his fists. That man deserved a blow to the jaw. "Falsehoods and lies."

"You don't say." Ben shrugged. "Never can tell, though."

Garrett narrowed his gaze. "Where'd you hear those rumors?"

"From Lloyd Stevens on the mail boat. Apparently he happened to run across some proof that Miss Porter isn't what she seems to be."

The envelope. It hadn't been poorly made, but had been taken apart by someone intent on spreading gossip.

"Personal mail is private," Garrett snapped. "Reading something not addressed to you is wrong and ought to be against the law, if it isn't already." Even as he said the words he was aware of his own guilt in that matter.

Ben held up his hands. "I didn't read it."

"Then you got this secondhand. I wouldn't put any stock in malicious gossip. Amanda Porter is a loving, kind and giving woman. I'd trust her any day with my children."

"You don't say. I thought you'd dismissed her."

"I was wrong." Garrett glared at the man, daring him to fight it out, with his fists if necessary. "Something I intend to correct at the first opportunity."

Ben backed down. "Didn't mean any harm. Well now, I'd best be heading back to the store."

He practically flew out of the church, leaving Garrett steaming mad. Amanda had been wronged, but deep down Garrett knew it wasn't all Ben Bailey's fault. Garrett had been the worst offender. He'd readily believed the word of someone he didn't know over a woman he did. Roland was right. He'd acted as judge and jury when he had no right to do either.

Righting this wrong would take more than words. It would take action. He eyed Amanda as she worked with the children, and the last of the bitterness slipped away. She was so beautiful, so strong, so caring. She'd asked him for just one thing, and he'd denied her because he'd been afraid. He'd gripped onto the past so tightly that there was no room for the future.

"What was that all about?" His brother drew near.

Garrett would not repeat Ben Bailey's words. He had work to do and little time to do it. "Was the *Donnie Belle* still at the dock when you came here?"

"Yes. Why?"

"I need to go upriver. Today."

Roland stared. "On Christmas Eve?"

"Yes." Garrett tromped across the room and flung open the door. "Come with me. I have a favor to ask." He needed his brother to watch Sadie and Isaac—and to keep this secret from Amanda.

Roland followed. "Where are you going?"

"To do something I should have done long ago." Garrett ushered his brother out, and the wind slammed the door shut behind them.

Amanda didn't tremble at the slam of the door. She'd found joy among the children, who didn't question her every motive. They accepted her for who she was. Unlike Garrett. Let him stew. Let him stomp around and slam doors.

"I think he's coming around," Pearl whispered to her while they watched the children take their places.

"I can't imagine who you mean." Or what. The Garrett she'd seen was just as angry as the day she'd come face-to-face with him in Saugatuck.

Amanda straightened Sadie's veil. She would need to pin it more securely tomorrow morning, or Sadie would lose it halfway to the inn at Bethlehem. Amanda made a mental note to bring more pins.

For the next few hours, all the details of getting ready for the play occupied her thoughts. Roland had to narrate for his brother, who didn't return. It annoyed her that Garrett would shirk his responsibilities, and Roland refused to offer any explanation. Soon she was too busy to dwell on it. She and Pearl ran around, making adjustments when children went the wrong way or entered at the wrong time or gave up entirely and began playing under the benches. By the time rehearsal ended, the adults were exhausted.

Later that day, when the excitement had died and Amanda was alone in the kitchen scrubbing away the day's grease and grime, Garrett returned to her thoughts. Why had he left and not come back? Was it because she'd suggested that it was too late to forget what he'd read in Mrs. Chatsworth's letter? Before that, he'd seemed to want to talk. Garrett didn't speak with flowery phrases or bold declarations of love. He didn't issue copious compliments or shower a woman with gifts. Instead, he let down his guard and showed his vulnerable side. He'd opened himself to her this afternoon, but she'd been too preoccupied with her own doubts and fears to recognize it.

On the other hand, he must have been the one to spread Mrs. Chatsworth's accusation around town. That was reason enough to break off further contact. Then why did Amanda feel so terrible about it, as if she'd lost her last chance?

Add to that difficult situation the disastrous second dying of the wedding dress, which Mrs. Calloway had revealed when Amanda returned, and the day had gone from bad to worse. At least Fiona and Louise hadn't been upset.

"I'm sure you can do something with it," Mrs. Calloway had added hopefully when she showed Amanda the gown.

If anything, the stain had gotten more obvious.

"I can add an overskirt," Amanda had said with a sigh, "but not in time for the wedding."

"That'll be perfect, dear. We can give it to her later. She'll love it."

Amanda couldn't escape the knowledge that it was all her fault. She'd spilled the tea on the gown in the first place. Stained. Just like her.

She attacked the grimy oven with a vengeance. Perhaps something in her life could be clean.

"Try to leave some of the cast iron intact," said a familiar voice.

Amanda lifted her head out of the oven to greet Pearl. "You're home early."

"I'm exhausted." She sank into the chair that Mrs. Calloway kept in the kitchen. "The play and the wedding preparations, it's all too much. I wish we'd kept it simpler."

"It seems pretty simple to me."

"Is it? Christmas is about remembering Jesus's birth and why He came to earth. It's not about decorations or remembering lines or costumes or backdrops. They're all fine, but I fear they're taking too much attention away from the real meaning of Christmas."

"Perhaps we should pray about that."

A faint smile creased Pearl's tired face. "I think you're right."

Amanda wiped her filthy hands on her apron. Together they knelt on the floor and prayed for the focus tomorrow to fall entirely on Jesus.

"Let it be about You, Lord," Pearl finished.

"Amen." Amanda squeezed Pearl's hands. "All will go well. You'll see."

Except the dress. Oh, well. What was the gift of a dress compared to the gift of a Savior?

Pearl smiled. "I certainly feel better, and it appears Garrett is coming around."

Amanda stiffened. "I don't know how you can say that when he stomped out of rehearsal and didn't return."

"What did he say to you?"

Amanda had expected her friend to ask what she'd said to him to send him off angry, not the other way around. "He seemed to imply he wanted me back as housekeeper," she admitted.

"A first step?"

"I'm not sure I should. Not now."

Pearl's brow furrowed. "What happened? I could tell you weren't happy with what he told you."

"That's not it. It's the way Mr. Bailey acted toward me. Didn't you notice?"

"Um, yes," Pearl said. "But what does that have to do with Garrett?"

"Garrett is the only other person who knew what was in that letter. He admitted he read the first line. He's the only one who could be spreading rumors about me."

"I don't believe that for a minute! Garrett would never do such a thing."

"Are you sure? He was angry with me. Something might have slipped out to one of the men. Even one stray comment. From there, well…" She didn't need to explain further. Pearl would know.

But her friend shook her head. "Not Garrett. Never."

"Then who?"

Pearl heaved a sigh. "I don't know."

That was the problem.

Garrett stood at the front of the church the following morning, exhausted from his trip upriver and back. His brother should be here by now, and with him the man Garrett had fetched. Soon Amanda would have her answer. He drummed his fingers on the podium that served as a pulpit. What was keeping them?

Today was Christmas morning. One of the most important days of the year. He didn't look forward to reading— narrating, Pearl called it—the nativity play. He could read just fine at home or even in front of Roland and Pearl, but standing up in front of a congregation was different.

His mouth was dry as sawdust, and his heart pounded away like a sledgehammer. To distract himself, he recalled Sadie and Isaac's excitement when they'd tugged him awake before dawn. In the glow of a candle, he'd told them the Christmas story. They'd hung on every word. The congregation wouldn't be so attentive. Already the buzz of conversation had increased to a roar.

"Decker." Ben Bailey passed on his way to a bench on the opposite side of the room that served as the community's church.

"Ben." The man's condemnation of Amanda still stuck in Garrett's craw. It was one thing to confront her in private and quite another to spread rumors in public. No doubt the truth had been so badly distorted that it bore no resemblance to fact. Still, this was no day to hold a grudge. "Merry Christmas."

The man nodded. "To you and yours, too."

"Mrs. Bailey here?" Garrett spotted her conversing with some of the other mothers. From the severe looks they gave Amanda, none of it was good.

"Holding a meeting, it appears." Bailey shook his head. "Better go break it up."

As Ben headed across the room, Garrett's gaze drifted to Amanda. She was helping ensure the children's costumes were all in place. Sadie clutched Eva's porcelain doll, wrapped in rabbit fur to play the role of baby Jesus.

The youngest shepherds had taken to chasing each other, and Pearl was having a time corralling them.

Garrett stepped toward them, eager to help, but Pearl shook her head and pointed to the door. Roland entered. Alone. Garrett tried to catch his brother's attention, but Roland wasn't looking his way. Garrett's heart sank. What had happened? Last night, after talking to the lumberman Jake, Garrett had been certain he'd found Amanda's brother. Had the man slipped from his hands? Or rather from Roland's hands, since that's where Garrett had left Jake last night.

Sawyer Evans brushed past Roland with Fiona on his arm. Apparently that friendship had rekindled. Garrett couldn't say he was sorry. Sawyer escorted Fiona toward the front of the room. She would sing, but there was no space for her that Garrett could see.

"Miss O'Keefe," Garrett said as she passed.

"Don't forget your cues, Mr. Decker." She breezed to the pulpit and plunked her songbook on it.

Garrett cringed. Where would he stand to narrate the play? For that matter, where would the minister put his notes and Bible?

"Brother John hasn't shown up yet," Sawyer whispered in his ear. "We might have to go it alone."

That made Garrett's stomach churn. He'd counted on the itinerant pastor directing the flow of the service. Garrett was too tired to remember everything. "Maybe Mr. Calloway will do it."

Sawyer gave him a cynical smirk. "And talk for hours? By the time he finishes, the children will have lost all interest. Best get started."

Garrett's heart pounded again. Thinking of his role being in the future was one thing. Knowing he'd have to begin right away made the palms of his hands sweat in spite of the chill in the air.

Next thing he knew, Amanda was at his elbow. He knew that even before he looked. Whenever she was near, he felt this peculiar heightened awareness, similar to when he made a breakthrough on a problem at the mill. Except Amanda had nothing to do with work. Neither did those feelings.

He gazed into her violet eyes. For the first time he realized just how different they were from Eva's. Amanda's eyes were lighter, with a dark rim. Eva's had been the same deep color throughout.

Amanda leaned a bit closer. "Pearl says we need to start now before the children get too impatient."

That was a kind way to put it. The children were bored and about to cause trouble.

"Tell her we'll start right away." He guided Amanda past the folks gathered in the front row, and that jolt hit again. There was something about her that brought his emotions to the surface. He couldn't deny it any longer. He loved her. But to have any future together, he had to win back her affection. That could be in jeopardy if Jake didn't show.

Garrett stepped to the pulpit.

No one paid the slightest attention.

He cleared his throat.

A few looked his way and stopped chattering. To the rest, he might have been invisible.

"Good morning," he said loudly, "and may the grace of the Lord be with you." He hoped it was all right to repeat the opening that Brother John always used.

More people turned to him, but a few insisted on chatting. Did that drive Brother John crazy? Garrett wasn't going to muddle through the noise. He whistled.

A few more looked his way. Fiona gave him a pitying look.

He patted his suit coat. On a whim, he'd tucked his old harmonica in the inner pocket, thinking perhaps he'd show Isaac how to play it after the service. He brought it out now and blew a quick verse of "Hark! The Herald Angels Sing."

Everyone stopped talking and stared at him. Amanda, though, smiled softly, as if she knew how difficult it was for him to pick up that harmonica this morning.

"Thank you," he managed to say. The quiet, with every eye on him, was unnerving. He cleared his throat. "Turn to Luke, the first chapter, beginning with verse twenty-six."

The story would be familiar to everyone there, yet perhaps this Christmas Day it would reveal a new truth to some. That's what he'd prayed this morning.

His hand trembled as he leafed through the pages to find that chapter. Out of the corner of his eye, he saw Pearl readying the children. His Sadie was dressed in robes of blue, like so many portrayals of Mary, the mother of Christ.

A mother.

They hadn't attempted to make her appear with child. For that he was grateful, but as he read the verses about the angel Gabriel bringing the news to Mary, he couldn't help thinking about that Jewish girl so many years ago. So young. Had she known what she would face? With child before she'd wed. People could be vicious. Rumors would spread.

Yet each one was false.

Nowhere in the Word did it say that she explained or retaliated. Had she simply borne the snide comments and innuendo, treasuring the truth deep in her heart?

He moved on to the second chapter and read about Joseph taking Mary to Bethlehem to register. Sadie and Isaac walked toward the front now.

A lump formed in his throat. How could he protect his children? He couldn't. Not entirely. The realization hit hard.

He looked up at Amanda. She watched his children with such love, following each step with the kind of attention that only a parent could give. He had misjudged her terribly, had leaped on a single sentence without considering there might be another explanation. Then he'd demanded she explain. No, not in so many words, but in his heart. He wanted her to tell him not only that those words were wrong, but to reveal every detail of what had happened.

Had Mary told Joseph everything, even about the angel's visit? Would he have believed her if she had?

The lump in Garrett's throat made it impossible to speak.

Pearl was waving frantically. He opened his mouth, but nothing came out.

Then, before he quite realized it, Amanda was at his side. Mrs. Bailey stiffened, her lips pressed tightly together in disapproval.

Garrett's temper flared. No one had a right to condemn Amanda, and no one would if right now he stood up for her.

She appeared oblivious to the whispers as she read, "'And there were in the same country shepherds abiding in the field, keeping watch over their flock by night.'"

Garrett stepped closer and, to show his approval, joined her in the reading.

"'Glory to God in the highest, and on earth peace, good will toward men,'" they said together.

"Toward *all* men and women," Garrett added. "Each of us has failed Him, yet He came to earth to extend forgiveness. We do not deserve it, but He granted us mercy, anyway."

The comments hit the mark with the Baileys, who

ducked their heads. Garrett looked every man and woman in the eye. The whispers stopped, and he felt Amanda stand taller. He looked at her then.

She smiled at him, and his heart soared higher than it ever had with Eva. This beautiful woman was giving him a second chance. He would not let it slip away. Not this time. God had answered his prayers all along, but he'd been too blinded by his own guilt to see it. The advertisement for a mail-order wife, Amanda's arrival, her love for his children, their joy while sledding, even the mishaps in the kitchen. It all blended together into the perfect family.

As Fiona led the congregation in the hymn "Joy to the World," he gazed at the woman he loved and sang with all his heart.

God had brought them together. Even Sadie and Isaac watched him and Amanda rather than the congregation. As the hymn wound toward a conclusion, he placed his hand over hers, resting on the Bible.

"Thank you," he said.

Her eyes lifted to him in silent acknowledgment.

Then the church door opened.

Something had changed. Amanda felt it the moment she joined Garrett. Pearl hadn't needed to prod her. She saw him floundering, saw the emotions written on his face, and went to him. She didn't think about it. She just went.

She had never spoken in front of a crowd before, yet with Garrett at her side, all fear was gone. When his voice joined hers, joy filled her heart.

Yes, something had changed in him. Tears filled the corners of his eyes. He swallowed frequently. His hand trembled. But as they read together, his voice steadied.

When he placed his hand over hers at the end of the closing hymn, she felt like her heart would burst.

His gratitude was genuine, and he held back nothing. She could see on his face the hurt of the past get swept away by a rush of hope and wonderment.

"Merry Christmas," she said, after Mr. Calloway gave the benediction.

Garrett continued to hold her hand. "Thanks to you, it will be the best Christmas ever."

"It will?"

He nodded. "We have a tree."

"And presents," Sadie chimed from her father's side. "Papa gave me a real baby doll."

Amanda gave him a questioning look. "The baby Jesus?"

He shook his head. "A new and less breakable one."

"And I got a steamboat," Isaac announced. "My papa made it himself."

"Of course he did."

Happiness welled at the sight of their joy. Her handmade gifts for them—a bonnet for Sadie and a new cap for Isaac—could wait for another day. This day belonged to family.

The children rushed off to get out of their costumes.

"I should help," Amanda said, gently moving away.

He didn't release her hand. "Can you spare one moment?"

Her heart raced. What would he say to her? Harsh words? Demands she explain? It must happen. He deserved the whole truth, but she'd hoped to wait until after Christmas and Pearl's wedding. "I'm needed."

He did not release her. "There's someone you need to meet."

Only then did she realize a stranger had wandered to the front of the little church. Though he was roughly clothed, the man's dark hair and bright blue eyes made her catch her breath. "Jacob."

He wrung a cap between his hands. "I got your letter, but I missed the tug downriver. Then Mr. Decker showed up yesterday on the *Donnie Belle*."

Tears flooded her eyes. "Garrett? You did this?"

He'd stepped back to give her some privacy. "You needed to know."

Gratitude swelled until she thought she couldn't bear it. "Thank you." The words were so inadequate in the face of what Garrett had done. He'd set aside everything, even his fear of the river, to bring her brother to her on Christmas Day.

If this man was her brother. She'd long thought she would recognize Jacob at first sight. That wasn't the case. Too many years had passed. This man was about the right age and had the right colored hair and eyes, but she couldn't be certain he was her brother.

The man dug into his coat pocket and held out his hand. Slowly he uncurled his fingers, revealing the other half of the locket.

"Jacob!" She flung her arms around him. "It really is you."

"And it's you, little sis."

In a flash she recalled that he used to call her that all those years ago. She held him at arm's length. "We have so much to talk about."

He nodded. "We will this afternoon at Christmas dinner. Roland and Garrett invited me to stay."

"That's wonderful." Her heart swelled toward Garrett and his brother. "And then tomorrow is Roland and Pearl's wedding, if Brother John arrives. Do stay."

He shook his head. "I have to head back upriver to get to the camps. They're expecting me. If I don't go, they'll replace me on the crew. I wouldn't have come at all if this man hadn't insisted." He grinned at Garrett, an expression that made him look young again and so much like the brother she remembered. "He can be stubborn."

Amanda laughed. "Bullheaded." Still, the tears rose to her eyes. "I hate to say farewell so soon."

"We have the day, and I'll be back as soon as I can."

That would have to do. At least she knew Jacob was alive and well.

He winked at Garrett. "I'd better get myself a room at the boardinghouse. See you later, sis." He grinned at her before ducking out the door.

Amanda wobbled, overcome by emotion, and Garrett was instantly at her side, an arm around her waist to support her. "Take a deep breath."

She did as he suggested and was struck again by all that he'd done. "You found Jacob." Tears welled anew.

"It was the least I could do." He took her hand. "Amanda, I have treated you poorly, and you have every right to spurn me." He held her hand now between both of us, oh so close to his heart.

"I could never spurn—"

"Please," he interrupted. "Allow me to finish. This must be said. I listened to gossip when I should have paid more attention to all I know about you. Your actions and love for my children speak louder than anything another person could say. I should never have listened. It was wrong. Very wrong."

"It's all right," she whispered, thrilling at the gentle way he held her hand and the even gentler way he gazed into her eyes. Direct. Unencumbered by the grief that had weighed him down since they first met. Had the trip upriver done all that?

"No, it's not all right. You see, I love you."

The declaration hit with the impact of a tree crashing to the ground. "You do?" Her head spun. It was more than she could have imagined just minutes earlier, and more than she could take in after the reunion with her brother.

"I'm sorry it took me so long. I was clinging to the hurts of the past. Then I saw that letter."

Her heart sank. Had Mrs. Chatsworth's words irrevocably ruined her future? Yet protests meant nothing. Only truth could bridge the chasm between them. "I'm sorry. You deserve the full truth."

She took a deep breath, prepared to confess every painful detail.

He put a finger to her lips. "I don't deserve it, and I don't need to hear it, not after the way I treated you. When I heard people repeating the falsehoods in that letter, I got angry at them, but didn't think to forgive you. That was doubly wrong."

Then rumors had spread. She didn't need to know how. They had, and now she had to live with that. At least Garrett had called them falsehoods.

"I don't deserve your love, yet you have still given it," he continued.

Her heart began to pound.

"You've shown nothing but love to my children and me."

She flushed. Hadn't she believed Garrett guilty of spreading the rumors around town? Clearly, he was not. "I bear some of the guilt, too."

"No. Don't explain. Mary didn't explain to Joseph. It took God's messenger to change his mind about her. I hope it doesn't take that much for me. I love you, Amanda, and I promise to always love you." Garrett halted and swallowed.

Her head began to spin again, but in the most delightful way. Dare she ask? She must. "Will you let me work as your housekeeper?"

"No."

The blunt reply tore a hole in her heart. She pulled her hand away and turned her head to hide the gathering tears. That he might ask the unimaginably marvelous one moment and the next roundly dismiss her hurt more than she could bear.

She stumbled two steps forward.

His hand cupped her shoulder. "Stop, Amanda. Look at me. Please?"

She dared a glance and saw not the usual scowl and furrowed brow but an openness and hope that buoyed her spirits.

He took her hand again. "I don't want a housekeeper. I want a wife."

She stared, not believing what she was hearing.

"You, Amanda."

"Me?" It came out in a breathless squeak.

"Yes, you. There's never been another woman."

"There was Eva."

He cringed, and Amanda regretted her foolish words.

"No, there wasn't," he said. "Not really. I loved her, but in a different way. Possessive. Competitive. Wrong. Not the way a husband should love his wife. No wonder she turned from me. No wonder our marriage turned out the way it did. No wonder Eva—" His voice broke.

Amanda cradled his chin in her other hand. "I'm so sorry for your loss."

He shook his head. "That's in the past, and I'm resolved to leave it there."

"It must be dealt with."

"It will. Eva was Isaac and Sadie's mother, after all. She will always be with us. But my son and daughter need a new mother, one who loves them. You."

Amanda's mouth went dry. For the second time she questioned if she'd heard correctly.

Garrett confirmed it. "And I need a wife. Desperately. I can't promise not to make mistakes, but I do promise to love you until the day I die."

"Forever," she whispered, through a constricted throat. Tears welled. She let them fall.

"Yes, forever."

The tears streamed down her cheek uncontrolled.

He looked aghast. "Did I say something wrong?"

"Nothing wrong. Everything right."

"Then you agree?"

She nodded through the tears. "Yes, yes. Oh, yes."

"Yes?" He looked like he didn't believe her.

"How many times do I have to say it? I will be your wife and mother to your children. It's everything I've hoped for from the moment I first met you."

"You will." He seemed unable to digest that.

She feared he would change his mind, but then he let out an uncharacteristic whoop and kissed her. Right there in church. With everyone watching. Not a brief brush of the lips but a kiss so deep and filled with commitment that it warmed her clear to her toes. He did love her. Truly. He would love her always. No question. She felt it deep in her bones.

Every bit of heartache melted away. Amanda Porter was going to marry a good man and have a family at last.

Epilogue

"Are you sure?" Amanda repinned Pearl's wedding bonnet. "I don't want to intrude on your special day."

Pearl laughed. "Our special day. If you ask me, Brother John's delay in Allegan gave us the perfect solution." She squeezed Amanda's hand. "I wouldn't want it any other way."

The moment Garrett announced his engagement to her, Pearl had insisted they marry at the very same time.

"I can wait." Amanda had repeated that halfheartedly the past week. "Perhaps when Jacob returns from logging."

"That will be months and months away. The children need a mother now. After all, that's what Sadie asked for in her Christmas letter."

"But she didn't receive her wish by Christmas."

"Close enough." Pearl straightened the ribbons on Amanda's bridal bonnet. "God's timing is always perfect."

Amanda touched the locket at her throat. Garrett had reattached Jacob's half so it was now whole. At least she would carry this tie to her brother with her into the ceremony. "God keeps His promises. He was always with me, even in the dark times."

That knowledge had helped her forgive Hugh and even

to thank God for guiding her away from that mistake to a wonderful future with Garrett and the children she loved.

"It's almost more joy than I can bear," she exclaimed.

Pearl hugged her as the sound of a harmonica filtered out of the church building into the brilliant winter air. Garrett was playing again, filling his house with joy, but today Sawyer Evans manned the instrument. Fiona would later sing, while Mrs. Calloway and Louise stood by as bridesmaids.

Pearl took her hand. "Are you ready?"

Amanda straightened her skirts, which the breeze and the walk from the boardinghouse had gotten a bit askew. She wore her periwinkle-blue Sunday gown, while Pearl wore the dress that Amanda made for her. The delay had given Amanda just enough time to add the overskirt to hide the stain. To her surprise, Pearl hadn't raised one objection, but had blinked back a tear when the ladies presented the gift. Still, it wasn't the wedding gown it was supposed to be.

"I'm sorry about your dress," Amanda said for the umpteenth time. "It was supposed to be a beautiful white."

"Blue is much better."

"Even with the stain?"

Pearl lifted the overskirt. "Especially with the stain. It's the perfect reminder that life has its messes, but love covers all offenses."

"Thank you." Amanda squeezed her friend's hands yet again. "Let's go then. The men must be getting anxious."

Pearl laughed again. "Nervous as choirboys, I expect." Her eyes gleamed. "Perhaps we should make them wait."

"Not on your life!" Amanda tugged her friend toward the church door. "I'm not going to let Garrett Decker slip away."

The moment she entered the church and saw Garrett's

face, she knew he would never leave. Neither would she walk away from him again. He beamed, his gaze only on her. The two Decker men were flanked by the children, all with the widest smiles imaginable. Amanda linked arms with Pearl, and they walked up the aisle together, to the approval of their friends gathered in the pews.

Together they would step toward the future.

* * * * *

If you enjoyed MAIL ORDER MOMMY,
look for the first book in the BOOM TOWN BRIDES
series from Love Inspired Historical:

MAIL ORDER MIX-UP

And keep an eye out for Fiona's and Louise's stories
coming soon.

Dear Reader,

What fun it has been to follow Amanda and Garrett's story! I'm so glad you joined me for their fitful journey toward a long-lasting relationship.

During childhood, I loved winter. My siblings and I would dig in the snow, ice-skate and go sledding. I even attempted cross-country skiing, but after one spectacular face-first fall into deep powder, I've taken steep hills on my backside. I can certainly understand Amanda's trepidation when facing the slope on a sled. While researching for the story, I learned that the Flexible Flyer sled with the metal runners and steering bar wasn't patented until 1889. That means Garrett and Amanda probably had to steer their sled by shifting their body weight. In my childhood I bailed off a lot of sleds that wouldn't steer. Anyone remember the flying saucers?

Of course the best part of winter is Christmas. In 1870, Americans didn't celebrate Christmas the way we do now. It was more of a solemn holiday, focused on the birth of Christ. Small, inexpensive gifts might be exchanged. Christmas trees were a German tradition, but weren't found in every home. Ornaments were mainly handmade and were often food, like gingerbread, fruit and nuts. It must have been great fun for the family to decorate the tree.

I wish you a blessed Christmas with family and friends.

Christine

REQUEST YOUR FREE BOOKS!

2 FREE INSPIRATIONAL NOVELS
PLUS 2 FREE MYSTERY GIFTS

Love Inspired HISTORICAL

YES! Please send me 2 FREE Love Inspired® Historical novels and my 2 FREE mystery gifts (gifts are worth about $10). After receiving them, if I don't wish to receive any more books, I can return the shipping statement marked "cancel." If I don't cancel, I will receive 4 brand-new novels every month and be billed just $4.99 per book in the U.S. or $5.49 per book in Canada. That's a saving of at least 17% off the cover price. It's quite a bargain! Shipping and handling is just 50¢ per book in the U.S. and 75¢ per book in Canada.* I understand that accepting the 2 free books and gifts places me under no obligation to buy anything. I can always return a shipment and cancel at any time. Even if I never buy another book, the two free books and gifts are mine to keep forever.

102/302 IDN GH6Z

Name	(PLEASE PRINT)	
Address		Apt. #
City	State/Prov.	Zip/Postal Code

Signature (if under 18, a parent or guardian must sign)

Mail to the **Reader Service**:
IN U.S.A.: P.O. Box 1867, Buffalo, NY 14240-1867
IN CANADA: P.O. Box 609, Fort Erie, Ontario L2A 5X3

Want to try two free books from another series?
Call 1-800-873-8635 or visit www.ReaderService.com.

* Terms and prices subject to change without notice. Prices do not include applicable taxes. Sales tax applicable in N.Y. Canadian residents will be charged applicable taxes. Offer not valid in Quebec. This offer is limited to one order per household. Not valid for current subscribers to Love Inspired Historical books. All orders subject to credit approval. Credit or debit balances in a customer's account(s) may be offset by any other outstanding balance owed by or to the customer. Please allow 4 to 6 weeks for delivery. Offer available while quantities last.

Your Privacy—The Reader Service is committed to protecting your privacy. Our Privacy Policy is available online at www.ReaderService.com or upon request from the Reader Service.

We make a portion of our mailing list available to reputable third parties that offer products we believe may interest you. If you prefer that we not exchange your name with third parties, or if you wish to clarify or modify your communication preferences, please visit us at www.ReaderService.com/consumerschoice or write to us at Reader Service Preference Service, P.O. Box 9062, Buffalo, NY 14240-9062. Include your complete name and address.

LIH15

"You have spunk, Josephine Dooly. I've never heard of a woman riding the Pony Express. And now here I find you outside when you know it could be dangerous."

Josephine turned her gaze back on him. Had she misheard him a few moments ago? The warmth in his laugh drew her like a kitten to fresh milk. Was she so used to her uncle treating her like a child that she expected Thomas to treat her the same way? She searched his face. "You aren't angry with me."

"No, I'm not. I am concerned that you take risks but I am not your keeper. You can come and go as you wish." He pushed away from the well. "I came by to tell you that tomorrow we'll go into town and get married, if you still wish to do so."

Josephine exhaled. "I do."

He nodded. "Can I walk you back inside?"

A longing to stay out in the fresh air battled with wanting to please him and go inside. The cold air nipped at her cheeks, helping her to make the decision. Josephine nodded and led the short distance back to the house.

His boots crunched through the snow as he followed her to the kitchen door. She stepped up on the porch but then turned to face him. He deserved an apology. "I'm sorry. I should have done as you asked and stayed inside."

He reached up and brushed a wayward curl from her face. "I understand your need to come outside. I'm not sure I could stay inside for three whole days, either."

The light touch of his fingers against her cheek surprised Josephine. Her gaze met his. She felt the urge to lean her face into his warm palm. He smiled and pulled his hand away. "I best be heading back to the house. I'll see you tomorrow."

As he turned to leave Josephine called out, "Thomas."

He stopped and searched her face.

"I'm glad you are home." She smiled as her mind went blank. She could think of no more words to retain him.

His lips twitched into a grin. "Good night, Josephine." And he walked into the shadows.

She stepped into the kitchen but turned to watch Thomas climb onto his horse and head into the darkness that now enveloped the world. It seemed she was forever watching him leave.

Tomorrow they'd be married. Would they be compatible? Or would he soon tire of her and want to go on with his life, without her? She didn't know why, but the last thought troubled her.

Don't miss
PONY EXPRESS CHRISTMAS BRIDE
by Rhonda Gibson, available December 2016 wherever Love Inspired® Historical books and ebooks are sold.

www.LoveInspired.com